After Dark

Family Secrets

Book Seven

Rebekah McClew

Dedication

To my childhood friend Missy — thank you for helping me believe in myself. Your support got me through the hard times and kept my passion for writing alive. I'll always be grateful.

Chapter One

Where Am I

The last thing I remembered had been standing on top of a ladder while Jacob was holding it steady. Not that it would have mattered if I had fallen. After all, how often can I die? I had just asked Jacob to pass up another stack of tiles when he hadn't responded. Looking down there was a woman I hadn't seen before standing where Jacob had been, she started passing up a block of tiles for the roof. Taking them, I set them on the roof and then worked my way down the ladder.

"I do hope those were what you wanted." She watched me rather intently.

I wasn't sure what to make of her, after all, we all thought she was dead. What was she doing here and where was Jacob? Before I had a second to look around for him the last thing I had seen was Katherine towering over me with a smirk on her face as the world around me had gone pitch black. When I came to, I knew that familiar ache. Except for the last time I had been in the old asylum and the ones hiding there had only used it to protect themselves, not intending on harming me. I couldn't say the same thing for Katherine, knowing her I'm sure she would take pleasure in destroying me. Looking up. I couldn't figure out where I was, however, I could see in the darkness. Katherine always preferred the dark over any possible light. She felt if vampires could see in the dark then what purpose did we have with lights at all? I knew Jacob couldn't see as well as I could except, he wasn't in the same room with me. I could barely hear the hum of his mind working. He was either out cold or when he did wake up, not wanting someone to know what he was thinking or doing, he would concentrate the thoughts in his mind to hum, a useful trick especially in our family when we knew what the other was thinking. At times I wished we were like others outside of the family who could not read each other's thoughts. There were things I wished I never knew Jacob's thoughts about my sister, but then it was hard not to hear his thoughts when her husband was my best friend.

Jacob started waking up as he found himself in an especially enforced room with no lights. He woke up lying in a soft fluffy bed in a room that had red velvet on the walls with black accents all over the room. For a second it seemed like a dream. Jacob remembered bending over to grab something for Lucian and the next thing, he was in this room. How could this be and where did Lucian go? His head throbbed so much he wouldn't have been able to contact Lucian if he wanted to. The pain hurt so much that he could hear the buzz in his head confusing him. Looking straight up. I was positive I had hit my head harder than I thought as I looked Katherine directly in the face until the blur had finally gone, except, she still stood there.

"I would offer you an icepack, but I prefer to see you in pain. It's much more enjoyable for me that way. Besides, I should keep you both separated. That way I can have fun with both of you, a bit of individual attention if you will, so don't ever say I didn't give you something." Walking away from me she had a rather strange smirk on her face.

"Seriously how many lives do you have, you're like a cat! How is it that you're still alive? And why the hell am I tied to a bed or is it something I don't want to know about?" Moving around trying to get loose from the ties.

Looking at them rather closely they were rather unusual. It was not regular rope and not metal material, so what could it be? Leaning slightly, I could bite it except it had been extremely tough.

"Is your flaw keeping you from getting loose? I could help you with that. I could finish the change for you. I could change the way you look at the world and give you everything you want. Sound tempting enough?" She almost purred while speaking.

What was she trying to offer me? How could she possibly change my outlook on the world?

"Having a permanent bond with you isn't exactly what I would want to be cursed with. It's bad enough most of my family already does." I watched her expression which showed she was rather proud of herself.

Katherine hadn't seemed upset by this at all. She simply sat in the chair opposite me watching me be stuck here. I had stopped trying to get loose.

"Just think, it can only get better. Besides, as a vampire living so many centuries, you've dabbled in theater, art, music, and even simple architecture. Monogamy is for silly humans that only have so many years. Who would want to be stuck with the same person for centuries? I can offer you great power or anything you want. I need a new partner, apparently, I've worn out my last few." She seemed rather relaxed for saying all of this.

"I'm happily married; the only thing you could offer would be a step-down. You couldn't possibly offer me something better than what I already have. I don't need power to live the life I want. You can have anything you want, there are so many men out there that do want power, or they want to be around you because of your reputation or other reasons, why me?" I was curious why she was trying to offer me something unless it was to get me to hurt my family or get something out of me that I haven't figured out yet.

"I know I can get anyone, but I want what I can't have. Besides, marriage is only a business arrangement. There's no point to it unless both partners are getting something out of it. Monogamy is far overrated. We have variety in food, drink, clothing, housing, toys, and how we travel, why not a variety of partners? Then there is the bonus of disrupting my old family. Not to worry, eventually, you will come to your senses. You've only lived so long. Eventually, the same old routine is going to tire you out, and then you will be crawling to me or in this case, calling out for me. After all, you're not going anywhere. I have Lucian to be checking on." Standing up, she walked out of the room leaving me there stuck for now.

After leaving me there Katherine had gone down the long dark corridor, what would be a cold, dark cave was quite comfortable and home to her. At least this way there was no chance of humans living near her and certainly, no one venturing in, if they had risked it, they never left. Smiling to herself she knew what to expect from Lucian. He was so much like Charlie which meant it was going to take a lot to break him. Their worst weakness had been they cared too much for others, which is what she enjoyed using against Charlie, and now with Lucian. She would hurt the ones they cared about just to watch them be in misery. Feeling justified, what was the purpose of showing emotion or having something or being too close to it if it can only be taken away or used against you? Two guards stood outside of the charmed cell not that they were needed. Peering through the two-way mirror she could see Lucian lying on his side still not moving.

"Did you find anything on him?" Handing over the brown bag on the floor it held the contents he had been carrying on him at the time.

A basic wallet with a few pictures of his family. Taking those out, she tore them to pieces dropping them back into the bag. Next, she pulled out a set of keys she had guessed went to their house or a vehicle. Partly laughing to herself at the idea of using a vehicle to get around and blending in with the humans. She wasn't worried if she attracted attention, she simply took care of it before they had the chance to talk to anyone else. She had known the Augustus family rather well but then it was hard to live as long as she had and not know them more than most. She had at one time been intimate with Kristopher Vondrak while he was married to Ruby. Rifling through the rest of the contents there wasn't much as she broke a small charm that he had carried with him. It wasn't the one she was looking for, opening the door as she walked in throwing the bag down next to him.

"I know you're not sleeping. You can get up, nothing is holding you to the floor, unlike your brother-in-law who is strapped to my bed." Lucian grabbed the bag seeing that she had torn the few pictures he carried with him.

It was all ruined, so he dropped it to the ground not needing it now.

"You will never get him to sleep with you. He's not into sleeping with filthy animals." Standing up now looking directly at her showing no fear or emotion to protect himself.

"You give him far too much credit, after all, he married a filthy animal. I offered him something he won't refuse. A chance to be a full vampire versus being stuck partially as a lame human. Now don't forget to smile, we're sending pictures back to your family to show how great you're doing." Even before she finished what she was saying, two of the guards stepped in closing the door behind them.

Stepping back, she simply watched as both men went after Lucian. One of the men launched a punch just barely grazing Lucian as he stepped back to avoid contact with his fist. He hadn't been so lucky when the other had come in with a round house kick to the back knocking him forward now into the other guy, slamming a fist into his chest. Feeling bored with the fighting Katherine had left them for a while to handle other matters. Taking a few pictures of Jacob tied to the bed, she worked her way back to see what damage they were able to do. Lucian managed to break one of their arms even though he had no chance of escaping. The door had been sealed shut. Opening the door to let the two guards out Lucian sat on the floor bruised with a broken leg that one of the guards had managed to kick at just below the knee. Looking at her guards she gave them a rather distasteful look.

"He doesn't look damaged enough." As she said this, a very evil grin came across her face.

"Want us to beat him up more?" The guard seemed rather eager to get even for his broken arm.

"No, I have this one." Pulling on the lever in the hallway.

It affected the small little circles in the room allowing the fire to come shooting upward leaving no space to move to get out of their way. Engulfing in flames she took a few more photos before turning the lever back to its original resting place.

"That's much better, he'll eventually smolder the flames. Get these pictures printed out and find a courier not affiliated with us to deliver these. I want them to get them as regular mail. They should love their little gifts, perhaps it will show them how serious I am this time. I was far too lenient last time." Walking away she left them to do their jobs.

Feeling pleased with herself knowing how angry Charlie would be as soon as he was to see the pictures. Not taking too much time Katherine left to search a few places owned by the families. She had seen a vision of the piece she wanted, except she hadn't been able to distinguish who had it. She hated the fact it always came down to her family who owned or possessed these items. But then they had been around long enough that many were left to them to keep safe. Originally it had been a large medallion with directions to a secret location except it had been separated in two and each placed on a chain. Alana had one of the pieces she acquired from a traveling merchant centuries ago except when she killed her, it wasn't on her or in her home. She had searched many of the places she had gone except it wasn't there. It had been picked up by Sydney except she now lay in a nursing home and certainly didn't have it on her, she pretended to be cleaning up in the room, but she couldn't find anything.

The second piece was a little trickier; it had been lost

while voyaging across the ocean on a ship that was sunk. It was never found among the wreckage that eventually washed up on land. However, looking for it, she had not seen it in her crystal ball surrounded by water which led her to believe it never made the journey in the first place. As she searched, she found the person who was selling it and sent a fake in its place. The piece had been resold several times without the buyer knowing what they had until eventually, Elijah, a close friend of Lucian's bought it and has been the last keeper of it. When the family had parted. Elijah had given Lucian what was an invaluable gift which she could only hope had been the other piece of the medallion.

Charlie's family had two other summer spots they liked to go to; before they showed up, she wanted to make sure they were thoroughly searched. Leaving both places in shambles, anyone looking at the place would know they had been vandalized. Heading back to the town she had started her group. There were only pure vampires living, no half breeds, and certainly no humans. There had been a rumor of a vampire carrying around a human child, while the child wore a necklace that resembled the piece she was looking for. Each time she heard a description of the vampire it sounded like Lucian except he didn't have any children while Rose's child was already older than the description. Taking all the family pictures from the cabins. She sat down in her private quarters flipping through the pictures, the ones that held no interest to her went into a trash can filled with a strange liquid. Each picture once it had the liquid on them, the color would start to blend many times making the picture un-viewable.

The majority of the pictures went into the trash can. There were only a few that caught her attention, and it had been Lucian standing on the outside of a certain castle. She wasn't aware that it had belonged to anyone in the family. One photo had shown Lucian holding a little girl with blonde hair and blue eyes as she looked to be around the age of four to six years old. She hadn't looked like the rest of the family and right there on her neck was the piece she wanted.

Judging from the style of clothing and material used in the photo, it must have been at least twenty-some-odd years ago this was taken. She needed to look for an older woman and no longer a child. Changing into clothing she preferred for the evening, she wore her black and purple strapless gown made of satin, she had liked it so much that it reminded her of what a bruise should look like. Unlike many of the newer vampires who preferred softer beds, she still liked her old-fashioned silk-lined and goose-down-filled coffin to a modern bed. Walking in like the shadow she resembled, she left her room to enter the attached room where Jacob was still being held captive. Standing in the doorway she stared at him feeling amused.

"I could get used to this sight; you look rather delicious strapped to the bed. I have to say it's the first time I've liked one." Flashing her evil grin, it had felt good to make him uncomfortable.

"What do you want?' Jacob was getting tired of the games.

"You know what I want. I found something interesting today." Holding out the picture of Lucian holding onto the little smiling girl, Katherine watched his expression to give away anything.

Instantly she could tell he recognized the little girl except he was trying to hide it.

"Too bad she's human, she might have had a fighting chance if she was even a half-breed. But I'm sure my guards will have fun with her; sort of the way I'm having fun with you." Speaking slowly and deliberately she went and sat back down in her chair looking at the picture over again.

"What are you hoping to get from us or are you just having fun torturing us?" Not wanting to discuss the picture he wondered what it had to do with them being here and how she found it.

"Can't I want both? I enjoy torturing both of you, besides, you have the sweeter end of the deal. Your poor brother-in-law looks like something the cat puked up. Now did the family have a new addition that I'm not aware of. If so, shame on them for not telling me if Lucian is a father, not exactly something he's capable of." She was fishing for reactions to see if this little girl might have been his and if so, she might be fun changing if she still hasn't been yet.

"Lucian doesn't have a child. I have no idea who that is in the picture with him." Sounding rather sure of himself.

"I'm sure you do know who she is. You just don't want to say and that's alright. I understand you like to consider yourself loyal. I know you have a daughter. It would be a shame if anything bad happened to her or rather would be a shame if something bad didn't stop happening to her." Standing up and walking over near the bed, she knew this would get him riled up.

Attempting weak threats and telling her to keep her wicked hands off her was rather thrilling.

"You don't waste your time unless there's something you want, tell me what it is." Sounding not too sure if Katherine already had his daughter or not.

"Well, now you're being too supportive of the idea of helping me find what I want. I think it's too easy just to tell you. However, if you insist. I want this piece this girl is wearing around her neck. Get it for me and I'll give you and your brother-in-law your freedom. Are you curious to see Lucian, I think he looks rather well for what he's been through. Just remember if I choose to let you go. If you even attempt anything sneaky. I won't just torture him. I'll kill him." Maybe if they were to finally have a death in the family, they would start taking things much more seriously.

"I must speak with Lucian first to find out if he knows where it is, all I would know is to check the cabin and it might not be there. I don't even know if it's something we have anymore?" Choosing his words carefully not to include the fact the little girl was wearing it or if he might know where she could be found.

"I suggest you find it, or Lucian dies, can you live with

that guilt? I know I can. As long as you work for me, I can call you to me at any time, I will be checking on you, don't waste your time with anything else. Don't even attempt to get out of this or share with anyone what I am looking for. I don't need anyone else getting a hold of it, unlike others, I learn from my mistakes." As she was saying her last words, she slapped something on my wrist rather quickly.

A black magnetic-looking band wrapped itself around almost like a liquid once it was covering my wrist, it seeped into my skin disappearing only leaving a slight hint there was something there.

I wasn't sure if the girl would have the necklace or not, the last time we had seen her she wasn't wearing it and for a child, as I had last seen her, could have lost it easily. Even my daughter had lost things we gave her rather easily; it was part of being a kid and absent-minded. Not having a chance to look for or speak with Lucian before I left, she simply had smoke form around me as I now found myself outside of the dark forest. At least I knew where I was. Not that I was close by anything. Lucian was usually the one who figured these things out. Besides, the little girl would be more likely to trust him than me, she had only seen me a few times. Lucian had kept so much of her secret, somehow, she had found or been involved with his secret hiding place when he wanted to get lost or be left alone from everything he knew. None of us knew why she was allowed to know about this place other than the fact he trusted her from the start. Might have been because she was an innocent kid that expected or wanted nothing from him other than kindness. Who knows other than Lucian and her?

At first, the family had wondered if he changed her, he had formed a rather unusual bond with her but then after missing out on his niece, it might have made him curious about wanting to raise a child. I didn't even have a name to go on, I certainly didn't want to involve the rest of the family, or they might be used against me also, but then they are already being stressed out not knowing what happened with Lucian and me.

The only thing I could think to do had been to head out to the old cabin. Maybe there would be a clue. On the way there I decided at least to leave a message on the family company phone, I knew no one would be around it right now, I didn't want to talk to anyone. I just wanted to let them know I was safe. I tried to be as vague as I could, I didn't want to tell them what Lucian was going through, and even though I was sure Charlie could guess, I didn't have to say anything at all about him.

After traveling for several hours, I was already worn out except I hadn't wanted to waste any possible time since I wasn't sure if this would bring me any leads, Lucian was always careful about covering his tracks in case he was found out or observed by a mortal, even if I had felt like slowing down images of Lucian crept into my memory as I kept moving. It had taken a couple of days to get to my destination. I wasn't sure if the lady would bring me back to her or not. I wanted to find whatever this piece was and get back to save Lucian, except it did make me wonder if it was safe to give her whatever it had been. After all, she originally wanted the life stone, now she wanted this. Ever since Harmony had come along with the life stone Lucian had yet to be the same. Before he never held back anything, after that he became much more silent almost as if he's lost in deep thought, he keeps much more to himself than he used to.

As I was getting closer to where I was going, I could see a clearing in the distance where a small town had started working its way closer to his cottage. It was a cabin that he had built as a kid with his sister, my wife Rose.

Getting to the front door it had been locked, however, oddly enough the window was still unlocked. Pushing up on the window frame I was able to let myself in, stepping in. I looked around the room, not much had changed not that I expected it, other than the fact everything looked as though it was covered in several inches of thick dust. I couldn't stop sneezing as I moved item after item searching for either the necklace the lady had wanted or some sign of where the girl was. I knew if I had found her, Lucian would want me to keep her safe, I just hope I would find her and get it before the lady called me to her. There was absolutely nothing around, any papers or anything that would have given a clue to the person that owned this place or had even been living here. Lucian was extremely careful to cover his tracks, no dishes or anything decorative in any way. Lucian liked decorating with genuine Indian dream catchers, dance belts, and hand-woven belts from the basin of Ecuador, the Shuar tribe, or the Navajo tribes of the states. Standing around feeling extremely frustrated. I wasn't finding anything and at this point, I wasn't sure how I was going to save Lucian.

I always felt funny calling this place a cabin; it felt more like a glorified castle on the edge of the water far out in the woods. Lucian had bought up much of the land out here knowing eventually the town would grow up around it, except there were few paths that led out here and he let the woods fill in as much as possible around it. He was always fascinated with secret rooms and tunnels that Rose and Lucian incorporated into the cabin. Keeping the appearance of a cabin out front, other than the general lookout tower you could view the vast ocean with, however, much of the cabin had been built into the side of a large rock. Standing near the sink. I had turned it on hoping to rinse the bit of blood off my arm. At least the water still came out except it had not been used for so long that it was a rusty red color. Sad to say, I had momentarily forgotten the brace that was on my skin until the water had hit it causing it to glow. Running my other hand over it I could feel sharp pin pricks all over my wrist as it surfaced. Apparently, water made it separate from my skin.

Not sure why I felt I had to do this. I grabbed a plug for the sink and filled it with as much water as I could. I wanted to make sure I would be able to douse my wrist under the water if the option was there. I hadn't cared what the color of the water was or if it would help me so that I could take off the brace. I would except I couldn't risk doing it yet.

I had tried my best to avoid the inevitable, except I had no idea where else to look and I had serious doubts whether I should even give the necklace to the lady or not. Pulling out my cell phone and holding it in my hand for a moment. I finally dialed Charlie's number hoping no one else would answer the call. I hadn't wanted Rose to worry about me except I wanted to keep her as far away from me as possible in case the lady was able to draw anyone else back with me.

"Jacob, where are you? We've been trying to call you. Is Lucian with you?" Charlie had asked all the questions I assumed he might.

Not taking long I had wanted to get to the point.

"Do you remember the little girl that Lucian used to bring around? The one we haven't seen in a long time; I think she might even be a teenager or in her twenties by now. I need to find her or rather. I need to find a necklace that Lucian gave her," I could hear Charlie sigh.

He was no doubt wondering why I needed to find her, and what the necklace had to do with all of this unless he did know why.

"What is the necklace needed for?" Charlie asked.

Hesitating on my end for a second, I knew I couldn't keep it from him, if Lucian had called him, he could have asked him the right way without letting out too much information, "the lady in black wants it and as a condition, if I find it, she said she would release Lucian, the only reason I am allowed temporarily free is to look for it, even though she has some sort of bracelet that melted into my skin that she can call me to her which is why I haven't stopped by to see the family. I don't want to risk her taking anyone else with me. We were ambushed by her when we were replacing the roof tiles." Not answering right away I knew Charlie was doing his best to think over the situation.

"I wish I could say I knew where to find the girl except Lucian never shared that with any of us, it's one of the many things he kept to himself. At times I doubted he wanted the girl around except somehow, she attached herself to him and he just grew fond of her. I know what necklace you're talking about; I just don't understand why Katherine would want it? It was a necklace Lucian had made by an Indian tribe." More silence on Charlie's end as he was trying to figure out how to solve this.

"Charlie, I think something is happening, not sure but I'm starting to feel dizzy, she might be calling me to her. I'm going to hang up. I don't want her to know I was talking to you; I'll try to call you again later." Flipping the phone shut, I placed it in my jean pocket just in time to find myself phasing out.

I was right she was already checking on me no doubt making sure I wasn't trying to escape her. As before, I was standing right in front of her, I wasn't sure how she was able to send me away or what kind of magic she was using to do it, however, she was just as physical in front of me as she had been before I left the first time. The only difference had been Lucian crumpled up in the corner looking even worse than the last time I had seen him.

"Do you have it yet?" Katherine seemed rather impatient and from the tone of her voice I could tell Lucian had probably angered her somehow; even in pain, he had a rather evil grin on his face.

A look I don't see too often unless he had something planned. Especially for his sake. I could only hope he had something planned.

"I've almost found it; I was getting close and then I was called here." I was hoping to be vague not that I had found it, but I needed to stall somehow.

"Are you blaming me for you not finding it?" Her tone of voice had deepened.

"No, I'm not blaming you at all; I was simply searching and found a clue to where it was. Before you send me back out to find it, please let me talk with my brother first." I was hoping if I were over next to Lucian, he would at least let me know what he was thinking.

The family may have shared a special gift of reading each other's thoughts and feelings except I had yet to develop that skill and I was beginning to wonder if I ever would. At least I wasn't the only one limited in this way; Lewis was the same way even though he was rather gifted at reading expressions. He always explained anyone could do this if they had simply practiced.

"You can't do or say anything and keep it from us, anything he says to you we all hear it." I was aware of the others standing in the room with her keeping an eye on Lucian, no doubt they were the ones who had been attacking him.

Walking over to Lucian I had wished I could read his mind; at least it would have given me some kind of idea of what was happening to him. Kneeling next to him I couldn't get over the way he looked. How could I possibly face Rose if I didn't return with Lucian, but then who's to say I will end up walking away from this whole thing? Taking a deep breath there was only one thing I could do and that was to search more for the girl, and hopefully, Charlie had come up with something.

"Lucian, do you know where she is? Possibly somewhere you and I have been? Some sign you can tell me?" Shaking his head no, I should have known he would rather protect her instead of saving himself.

"Don't worry about me. If I die it will only be a relief and not pain, just take care of Rose." Not moving too far from Lucian I glanced over at Katherine.

"I'm ready to head back out and I will be back with the necklace." Trying to sound more determined not just to convince Katherine but also myself.

"Remember if you fail to bring it back to me, I'll kill your brother here. Until you bring it back, we'll have a little fun with him." I could see a strange shiny glint flash across her eyes as she said that which is why I was worried to leave Lucian here any longer than necessary.

She had that strange look on her face, the same expression she had before I had disappeared, and I could only hope I wasn't making the worst mistake for both of us, except I couldn't risk leaving him here any longer. Making sure I had a hold of him. I knew she could call me to her at any second as soon as she realized what I had done. When she moved me back to the cabin. I was standing directly in front of the sink where I had been standing using the phone before she had called me to her. Letting go of Lucian. I dipped my arm back in the water forcing the brace to submerge itself as I pulled at it as quickly as I could scraping off the top layer of skin as I peeled it away taking it off. The second I had it off and it had fallen to the bottom of the sink, not only the brace had disappeared but also the water that surrounded it. I'm sure Katherine wasn't expecting that surprise when it comes to her. Looking down at Lucian. I had only hoped she wouldn't be able to find us here. I doubted I would be able to move Lucian very far without doing serious harm to him.

"Jacob, take me to the second-floor library." I wasn't sure what he wanted there I just knew to do what he had asked.

Lucian insisted on walking not that he could barely walk on his own. Putting his arm over my shoulder and my other arm around his waist, lifting him as carefully as I could, we left the large room we were in, half of the house was built into the side of the rock. Taking the stairs on the left side up to the library. Lucian was incredibly stubborn but determined to climb the stairs, it was awkward going up the stairs with him this way. I stopped in the main room surrounded by books. The only room that had anything left inside of it. Pointing over to the corner he wanted me to bring him to. I walked over there with him, and as I did, he reached out for a few books simply pulling at the spines of three. As he pulled the last one out the bookcase at the far end opened showing one of his hidden tunnels. Assuming this is where he wanted me to take him, I had brought him inside. Following the steps down. We went well below the first floor going down to the ground area into a small narrow passageway that simply ended. There were emergency supplies and a cot. Laying him down on the cot. I used the supplies to clean up the blood he lost as well as covered many of his wounds with bandages to protect it. At least here we could hide hopefully until he healed. After tending to Lucian, I noticed how much of my own blood I was covered in. I used a few bandages to cover my bloody sore arm.

"Lucian, do you know where to find the girl? Eventually, if we don't find her, Katherine will find her, and she needs to be protected." As he grimaced, trying to get the strength to answer me.

"I know I need to protect her; it's why I had left here for so long. I was hoping she would forget me and move on with her life. I thought if I left her, she would be safer away from me. She's human and far too easily destroyed. I can't risk Katherine finding her. She doesn't live here, she only comes here to vacation with her family, and I'm sure by now she's no longer coming here." Taking a deep breath Lucian tried to relax a little.

"I understand if you don't want to tell me, but do you know if there was anything special about the necklace?" Looking directly at me Lucian simply nodded showing he knew what was special about it.

"I knew it would be safe with a human. Who would assume something that powerful would be with someone who couldn't safeguard it? You're the only one that hasn't asked me why I bothered spending time around another human, especially one so young." Eyeing me with curiosity he wasn't the only one that had asked me that question.

Even Rose had wondered hoping if I asked, he would have at least said something to me about it.

"If it was something you wanted me to know you would have said it." Which is true, I didn't want to bother him with something if he wished to keep it silent.

I had respected his personal space, not that the rest of the family hadn't. I just didn't like to pry.

"I don't mind telling you, besides, if I don't make it you might need to protect her for me." I didn't like the way Lucian was thinking.

"You're going to make it; unfortunately, it's going to take longer for you to heal. If I could safely make it back to one of the new guardians maybe, they could heal you?" I had to be extremely careful not to be caught especially coming back here in case the lady had her men out looking for us and I was sure she would by now.

    "I found her when she was around the age of five years old, she was lost and if I left her, she would have been killed. Another vampire was watching her, so I saved her. She never knew she was being watched. She had a habit of being in the wrong place at the wrong time and getting herself in trouble. Her parents didn't watch her, if I hadn't, there were plenty of reasons she would have died. As she grew older, I just felt attached to her. I never saw her as more than a very sweet little girl, she reminded me of Rose when she was little. Things didn't start to get uncomfortable until she was in her teens, and I stopped bringing her around the family. She was discovering the difference between men and women, and I didn't want to confuse her or make her feel I was confining her, in truth. I didn't want to risk her falling for me for any reason. It was never my intention. I've accepted that I may never have what you and Rose have together. I was worried people would think I was trying to influence her. I encouraged her to date. I would avoid mortals if I could, but they are everywhere now. I could never tell her she wasn't loved but I couldn't risk condemning her to this life. She should be in her late twenties by now. I gave her the necklace as protection; it was a specially crafted necklace that at one time belonged to Harmony and was given to her by another guardian. After she died in the nursing home, "I gathered the few precious things that carried meaning for us. Objects too sacred to be misused, too powerful to be left in hands that might twist them or be broken by them." I knew it was still difficult for him to speak about Harmony, and I was sure even he didn't believe he could ever fall in love again, especially the way he had with her.

    However, when he spoke of this young woman. I could tell even he couldn't hide his feelings for her, the slightest curve to his lips as he spoke about her. The same look I had when I spoke of Rose and how much I loved her.

    "I'm going to take off and bring back one of the guardians to see if we can heal you. I'll look for the girl to make sure she is safe, not to worry. I'm positive you will be around to see her again." Giving a light nod, he knew I had already understood without having it all explained to me.

Making sure he was comfortable. I hadn't planned on being gone for very long. Being careful not to be noticed I had called Charlie on the cell phone setting up a safe place to meet, I hadn't explained much other than simply to say, 'have one of the guardians meet me at the crystal lake,' after I had said this, I put away the cell and ran towards the lake. I knew it would take a while before they were able to arrive there, except it had been a family meeting place for years so at least they would know how to get there. I had only arrived two days before they joined me.

Chapter Two

Unexpected

I knew it wasn't going to be easy heading back, by now there would be so many looking for us. I had to be careful and make sure no one saw me leaving the cabin. I can't believe the place that was so secretive had been the place he shared with Rose, if we had known, there were so many times before we had looked for him, we could have found him much quicker. As for the information he had given to me about the girl. I decided to keep that private until Lucian shared it with the rest of the family. For now, my main goal was to get one of the guardians to heal him. In one area I had to take off from as quickly as I could, I was spotted, I knew it wouldn't take long for the lady to show up once it was reported to her that I was in the area. I had to deceive them making sure they had no idea where I was heading, leading them off the path quite a bit.

One clearing had been a closer incident than I cared for. Trying to pass through at night that way I would hopefully avoid people, at least no one should have been out here this late at night. Moving through as quickly as I could I hadn't seen or heard anyone. There was a town on either side of me as I tried to avoid both except before I was ready for it, I was already lying flat on my back hitting the ground with a rather strong thud. I could feel pain shoot through my chest to my head as I finally saw what had hit me. Another vampire had moved out in front of me slamming his fist into my chest and knocking me to the ground. Having my breath knocked out of me momentarily had given him enough time to make another move on me. Grabbing me by the leg and chest he threw me into the air into a tree causing the tree to break in half, as soon I hit it causing the upper half of the tree to land halfway on me. I had only been a hybrid vampire still with humanity, so I injured much easier than a typical vampire. The second I looked up he was already charging me again. Moving out of the way he had taken out the second tree himself this time.

Barely needing any time to turn around he was already after me again as I moved aside avoiding the collision with him. Turning, he shot his fist out attempting to hit me in the side, as he did, I was able to block the punch by twisting his arm. Moving into the twisting motion to control his actions he struck out at me again. Before he could get his second blow, something else happened that I hadn't expected. A hand from behind me came forward grabbing a hold of his fist, feeling air rush around me. I had almost expected to see Charlie standing there except it wasn't. There was a man I had never seen before let alone the fact I had no idea why he was helping me, other than being grateful. Pulling the vampire in closer to himself he quickly put him into a lock hold twisting his neck, not permanently killing him, only slowing him down for now. It took much more than simply snapping the neck of a vampire to kill one.

Whoever it was that was assisting me I was thankful he seemed to be on my side as three more vampires had come out of the darkness. I knew I could have handled one with no problems, but now looking at the other three they were all dressed the same so I could only assume they were here for the same reason. While I fought the one, I could see out of the corner of my eye, that he was taking out the other two as if they had been no match for him, then I started to wonder how he had learned to fight the way he was. It almost looked like mixed martial arts and with the strength and speed of a vampire behind it, he was rather impressive. I had still been dealing with the one when he had come over and lent a hand to me again taking care of him. If this guy turned out to be a good demon, I would have loved learning from him, even Lucian would have had his curiosity peeked by him.

"I highly doubt you will want to be here once he is healed. Where are you heading to?" I know this stranger just helped me except I wasn't exactly sure I wanted to tell him just in case this was some new way of catching me off guard.

I certainly wouldn't expect one demon to help me only to catch me himself afterward. Somehow, I had the feeling this person didn't have that plan. He sort of reminded me of Charlie in a way.

"I was meeting up with family and this vampire sidetracked me." I had hoped I wouldn't have to explain more than that.

"Do you know who this person works for? Katherine Hawthorne rarely bothers with nobody's; this happens to be one of her upper guards she sends out when she wants to make sure there are no mistakes made. He's a straight-up hunter and killer, he wastes his time with nothing else, no life, breathing, and eating, nothing else but death, so I wonder what he wants with you? You don't look like her usual target." At least he had that right, sadly we only had a connection to her because of the past or we would never even have to deal with her.

She was Charlie's birth mother not that there was any real kind of connection to her emotionally.

"I didn't know who he was, however, I do know who Katherine Hawthorne is. Have you dealt with her before?" I was curious how he had known about her.

"Yes, I have dealt with her, usually the only way a person knows her name, is most refer to her as the lady in black and usually they shake from the rumors that float around about her.

Most vampires or other creatures never deal with her unless she wants something from them, or they simply mess up and get in the way. My name is Drezin... and yours?" At least if he was sharing his name, I guess it could be harmless to share mine.

"My name is Jacob." Shaking his hand, he made no move to threaten me.

"So, what is your connection to her? How did you manage to mess up?" Drezin asked me.

I guess I would have been curious also since I was rather young for knowing her let alone the fact that I hadn't acted afraid or phased when he mentioned her name.

"She happens to be my wife's great-grandmother. We don't deal with her unless there's something she seems to be messing around with. I can only guess there's something she seems to think we have that yet again, we don't. it would be much easier if we were not related to her." I had wanted to make sure he understood we were not close to her in case he hated her enough thinking he would get at her by attacking us.

"My only connection to her had been to protect my family from her. However, I have a feeling she had been breaking our deal. Mind if I come with you then? If my guess is right, Charlie should be meeting you then? I haven't seen him since I was seven years old." As he smiled at the thought it was difficult to see him as a threat but then I also had to be careful.

Nodding, I figured there would be enough of us together in case it turned into a trap. We could handle it, not that I wanted to bring trouble with me, but then maybe he could help me travel there quicker if we have another one of the lady's death agents ambush me again.

Taking off, he kept rather close and thankfully we hadn't run into any more vampires who hunted me. Still being careful watching out I noticed that Drezin was dropping something on the ground behind us as we would run. I wasn't sure right away what it had been other than to notice it had a rather strange scent, not one that stuck around, then I realized what he was doing. He was covering our scent so no one could follow us or pick up on the fact we had come through here. He was an experienced vampire. After running for a while, I could tell I was getting tired since I wasn't running as fast as him, not that he ever complained. In the distance, I could see the little white house tucked back in the trees. One main thing about our homes. We were usually in the middle of the woods, surrounded by mountains or perched by the ocean, which always made it easier to get away to safety in case it was needed.

As a vampire living for so many centuries and with humans moving in closer all the time, we needed to take all the precautions that we could. Not that we couldn't keep ourselves safe. It was a matter of keeping to ourselves and protecting our identity. I could see the shade being pulled back from the window. Slowing up before I reached the house, I wanted to give them a chance to decide if they wanted to stick around once they saw Drezin with me. I still had no clue who he was other than the short friendly introduction he gave as well as the help that he gave me. Not that I couldn't have protected myself against one vampire, however, when the other three had shown themselves. I knew I never would have made it on my own. Charlie, Sophie, Dinah, Rose, Lily, Nichole, and Anthony came out of the house, all surprised, but questioning looks on their faces. Maybe they were wondering why I had this person with me, either that, or they were wondering what he had wanted and did remember him?

"It's been a long time Charlie, not sure if you remember who I am? I've changed quite a bit." Drezin had been the first to speak.

I was beginning to wonder if Charlie would be able to, he kept looking as if he was going to say something except that he just had not figured out how to word it.

"Prove who you are, we've had enough surprises lately, if you're alive, why show up now?" Dinah had been the first to speak.

Just hearing her tone of voice, Goseck had come out of the door not sure what was going on, he was just as lost as I was. The others were standing in front of Lily protecting her and I started to wonder just who I had brought to the family. Then Lorah had also come out, unlike the others she hadn't hesitated at all as she ran out and grabbed a hold of him hugging him. At least she didn't seem concerned about it; she knew immediately how she wanted to react.

"I can't believe it's really you, I heard you were killed a year ago. Where have you been hiding?" Lorah acted as if she could barely contain her excitement.

"You heard he died a year ago? Wasn't it several years ago that we found out he might have still been alive working for Katherine?" Charlie seemed shocked by Lorah's comment.

"Actually. I faked my death a few years ago and yes, I was somewhat working for Katherine except not exactly in the capacity that you might assume." Both Lorah and Drezin were smiling rather excitedly since they had yet to let go of each other, I wished I knew who this person was.

"Can someone explain since I seem to be missing something?" Sophie at least voiced what I was wondering also, she looked rather bewildered so I could only assume Drezin had come before her time.

"I am Drezin, one of Charlie's brothers. I was supposed to be dead however it was a deal that I made so that Katherine would leave the family alone, and I went to work for her. Once she separated from the council, she formed her group which I hate to say I was a part of for a while. Then later I split. However, I never had the same connection vampires get when they have been changed by someone. I was still human and quite healthy while the rest of the family had come down with an illness that almost wiped them out until Katherine changed many of them. I was on my way home from school with my friends and a vampire had taken us into his home, raised us, and changed all of us. I hadn't seen my family since, I had even wondered if I would recognize them if I were to see them later?" At least now it explained the shocked look on Charlie's face.

"I don't know what to think?" Charlie was still stunned

as Sophie stood near him offering him support, not just emotionally, he seemed as though he was leaning against her in shock.

"It's okay. I never expected a huge welcoming, I wasn't planning on running into you. I was helping this young man out when Katherine's men attacked him. From the deal I had made with her, she's breaking it which I guess shouldn't surprise me, after all, when can a person trust an evil demon, who has no real personal ethics unless it suddenly suits their purpose?" No one had spoken for a while; it was apparent everyone was getting more uncomfortable by the moment.

"While everyone is deciding how they feel, I need to borrow Lily. Lucian isn't getting any better while he waits. Besides, I have other matters that need to be taken care of before Katherine hurts another person." Lily had already started walking over to me as Drezin started to talk.

"If you want help, I would be happy to make sure you both make it back wherever Lucian is, in case Katherine's men are still waiting for you? Then I need to take off on my own. I am supposed to be in hiding still, after all, right now I'm a walking dead man and I would like to keep it that way for my personal reasons. I can't explain right now." For the first time, Drezin seemed uncomfortable.

As long as I had known Charlie, I had never seen him like this before except hearing Lucian's name, he seemed to snap out of the fog he was in.

"I'll come also. I want to make sure Lucian is alright, you're welcome to come along Drezin, we can always use more help." For the first time, Charlie seemed to be lightening up almost smiling as Drezin nodded in his direction.

It was interesting traveling with a guardian; they had an unusual way of traveling. Instead of the speed we had when running, they simply used the wind and air pressure around them to propel them forward and at times faster than us, as she had to keep slowing herself down so she would not outrun us. As I led the others, I tried to keep up a fast pace since none of the others were hindered the way that I had been. Lorah had stayed behind since she had other matters to deal with, her and Valafar worked together and were tending to the council being in power again, at least publicly. Only Drezin, Charlie, Lily, and I were headed off to help Lucian. Lewis was going to join us once we were there since he and Evangeline were not that far away. I was thankful that we were never attacked on our way back and Drezin continued to cover our tracks, which seemed to surprise Charlie at first until he figured out what he was doing. We had made it to the cabin rather quickly but then it also helped when I would start to tire, Lily would help add pressure behind me and lighten my feet with air making it much easier to run and keep up, I knew it wasn't as if the others would outpace me. I was the one who knew where we were heading. Once we were there, we made our way down to see Lucian. Looking at the corner where I had last left him, I felt my heart sink into my stomach as I worried maybe Katherine had found him or perhaps he went looking for the girl in his condition?

"This is where I had left him, his blood is still on the cot, there is no way he could have healed this fast." I was shocked as we all searched around the cabin looking for him.

Not that there were very many rooms to search in except there were no clues as usual as to where he had gone or how long he had been gone. Even Lewis had shown up hoping to help, thinking he might have missed us when he came in and hadn't seen Lucian. Instead of attracting attention to Lucian's cabin, we made our way over to the next town where Evangeline and Lewis lived. Unlike the town we had just been in where humans made up the population. The next town over was heavily populated with vampires. Being here during the daylight Charlie was careful about traveling in the light. Amanda was playing outside with the wolves, not that they were wolves, they had been younger family members who preferred to stay in their nonhuman form and happened to be from Lewis's side of the family. As soon as she saw them coming back Amanda ran over to Lewis as he picked her up. She had still been a little kid, after so many years I had a hard time remembering she was older than her looks. She had been changed as a child by a very cruel vampire who had been destroyed by the council. She had already been around for over twenty years; her cousin had continued to grow not that she was a natural-born part of the family, she had been inherited from her parents who were fearful of raising her and wanted her safe and protected from the world and the council who originally sought to kill her since she would never physically grow to look any older than ten years old.

"We get to have company?" She seemed rather excited to see someone new as she looked Drezin over.

"We have company for a little while; I want you to stay out here with your cousins and play longer. We need to have a private talk inside." Kissing her on the cheek Lewis set her down as she went back to playing with her young cousins.

The rest of us had followed into the house.

"If you don't mind my asking, does the council know about your daughter?" Asking just out of curiosity Drezin found the others staring at him with concerned expressions.

"Why do you ask?" Lewis was quick to answer back with a rather stern tone.

"More out of curiosity however more just to warn you how strict they are about it; I would never let them know. I think it sucks it happens except I still don't think the child should have to pay their life because of a vampire's stupidity or selfishness. I still don't agree with the reason I was changed myself, and I was older, the only difference is that I was fortunate to age. I'm sorry if I made you uncomfortable with my comment." Drezin had stepped back a little after making his comment.

"I missed who you were." Not sounding like a question, however, more like a statement.

Everyone was acting rather tense.

"Maybe it would be best if I took off, I don't think my finding you was the best timing. Jacob if you need me, you have my number, other than that I'll be laying low myself. Charlie, it was good seeing you again." Giving a light wave everyone was watching as Drezin was about to take off.

I couldn't help it, but I wanted to know something before he had taken off.

"Drezin, before you take off, I want to ask you a question. When you said earlier you made a deal with Katherine to leave your family alone and you worked for her in exchange, how did you make that arrangement at your age? I'm not trying to put you on the spot I'm just curious." I had hoped he hadn't thought I was making things difficult.

I wanted to know except I guess I could have waited to call but then I wasn't sure if he would take a call from me or not considering the current circumstances.

"That's fine. I don't mind answering. I was at a friend's house when I found out they were vampires. Their father was Doc Denthre. His family didn't die of natural causes, they were experimented on and killed by him. He was having an affair with Katherine. She was over one of the nights and I couldn't sleep so I listened to them through the wall. Charlie was given a gift so that the council would not find it, when they had searched her and couldn't prove she had done any wrong they let her go calling it a mercy gift. She came back to wipe out the family, so I took the charm without Charlie knowing about it and hid it rather well. I had the magic moved to another object which is why I'm obsessed with some forms of magic. I told her the magic itself would be destroyed if she killed the family, I had put a charm to protect the family, and I had a higher-level magician help me with it. She didn't know I was bluffing, however, to make sure I didn't get away from her, she took me, leaving me with another vampire who changed me and a few others. It's the necklace she's no doubt looking for now that Lucian no doubt gave to this mystery girl without knowing. If you have one of the guardians use the necklace, along with the bracelet and the gift of the stone then you can do some amazing things. A former friend of mine was a seer; the things he showed me. My favorite is the ability to create worlds within worlds. They could help Amanda age and many other things; it can even bring back the dead however not the same as before." Even though he had everyone's attention they were no longer looking at him as if he might attack them at any moment, they were listening intently to his every word.

"Do you have to leave so soon?" Charlie had asked rather quietly.

"I need to hide a few other people myself; I might even die this time, and I don't want the council breathing down your neck, however, I would make sure I leave instructions with Lorah on how to help Amanda if you chose to, I'm not worried what you would do with the power. If I had to trust anyone it would be you, Charlie.

"Drezin, one last thing before you go, thank you for your help earlier with the other demons." Not saying much other than a nod of the head I had wondered if we would see him again other than the fact that I was sure he might be able to help Amanda.

We all listened as he was leaving, but before he could go far, he was stopped by Amanda herself. At first, we thought she would ask about aging however her concerns were still more innocent than that thinking of others.

"You upset my parents." It was all she had said in a stern voice.

"Biological or not you certainly take after your parents; you fit in just fine with this family. I am sorry for upsetting your parents and I certainly owe you an apology for upsetting you." Smiling back at him Amanda never held a grudge as she went back to playing with her cousins.

Then as we watched Drezin was out of sight in a split second. I had to say he officially won at being the fastest family member. We assumed he was heading off to speak with Lorah even though we all wondered just how Lorah had known he was still alive and knew what he looked like.

"Maybe if Amanda started growing up or at least aging maybe she might break out of her mentality a bit, I know others would treat her differently. I just don't know if we can trust something like that or want to risk it. It would have to be her decision, and that is if any of these items could even be found." Lewis placed his hand under his chin as he always did when he was considering something serious.

"Let's not even talk about it yet until we know something like that can happen." Evangeline sounded worried even though she was more worried about getting Amanda's hopes up in case it couldn't happen.

Everyone was looking over at Amanda as she made her way with her cousins in tow.

"I know everyone is talking about me, I already heard what that man said. If I can grow older, I want to, I won't get my hopes up but if I can be more like my cousin Larissa then I want a chance." Not saying much after that she had gone off to her bedroom to read.

At times even if we forgot to age her, she had the intelligence of an adult however she was so carefree she fit in with her little cousins so easily it was difficult to remember, she was only playing with them the same way we would have.

"Jacob, I want you to stick close to the cabin in case Lucian shows up again, make sure you watch your back. I'm positive Katherine hasn't given up looking for either of you. I'm heading back to see if Drezin is still talking with Lorah. Lewis and Evangeline will be here in case they hear anything." Just before taking off, Charlie stopped to say goodbye to Amanda.

I simply had gone back to the cabin with Lily, at least if anything happened, she could transport herself out. At least I knew where Drezin had gone. He was waiting in the library looking through the multitude of books that Lucian had collected over the last century, and those that once belonged to Charlie and his family. Looking up at me with a book in his hand not acting surprised.

"I heard you come in. I hope you don't mind that I didn't wait outside for you. I wanted to finish speaking with you privately. I wasn't sure if the family would trust my being alone with you quite yet." Setting the book down I watched as he went over and sat down motioning at the other chair.

"Is it true you can help Amanda?" I wasn't going to like him if I found him promising things he couldn't deliver on, especially something as important as this.

"I will say it doesn't work for everyone, just like a shade might be able to heal others but they can't always heal themselves, Lily I'm sure you've found that even you can't heal everything. Perhaps an illness? Wounds are always a given, something simple however disease and illness are much more complicated beyond what your magic controls. Depending on what Katherine used on Lucian. I'm sure you will only be able to heal so much. Do me a favor and transport yourself to Lorah and tell her I'll be coming to speak with her, just tell her my usual place and she will understand." Looking over at me Lily wasn't sure if she had wanted to leave me here alone.

Giving her a slight nod of the head, I knew I would be safe. If he had wanted to kill me, he could have let Katherine's men do it. A white haze formed around Lily as she disappeared.

"What did you want to talk to me about? Charlie was on his way to talk with you and Lorah." I wasn't too sure what to expect. Why did he need to speak to me alone?

"How did Lucian get the necklace in the first place? I had hidden the one she gave to Charlie which she no doubts still believed he had; she must have thought it was safe to come after the family when she heard I was dead." He would have to ask me a question I wasn't sure of.

"I don't know how he was given it; other than I think his past girlfriend had possession of it. She was a guardian of the stone, she died a few years ago." Not saying much beyond that I was wondering what exact interest he had in the power. He might have been family except I wasn't sure how much we could trust him.

"Any idea who might have the bracelet? Originally, I had hidden the items with guardians; I felt they would be the best to keep them safe." Thinking it over I had no idea who had it except Harmony might have had both, I did remember her wearing quite a bit of jewelry.

"I have no idea even though Katherine only seemed to be asking for the necklace, she hadn't asked for the bracelet at all, she might even have it already." Shaking his head Drezin didn't seem to like the thought of that.

"You need to keep your guardians safe. If they are going to live out in the open the way they are with you, especially since she keeps coming back to you." As he spoke my cell phone was going off.

I almost expected Charlie to be calling wondering where Drezin was except it wasn't his number. The number was blocked and instead of a voice call, it was a simple text.

"Just a friend, nothing I have to answer right away." Nodding for a moment I think he understood without my saying anything.

"I'm going to join Charlie and Lorah before they begin to wonder where I am." With a nod of his head, Drezin took off.

As I watched I wanted to make sure he left this time. I wanted to make sure no one else followed me as I took off. Looking down at the text. I hadn't needed a name to know who it was. The text read, *'J, P&C PLZ, RBTL, wet soggy bread flies well."* Which translated meant, 'Jacob, this is private and confidential so don't share with anyone, read between the lines, I'm by the lake we hide at so get here before anything else finds you there.' Unless you text a lot you might figure out a bit of it except having it random enough, I knew I would be able to find the location, however, it was going to take me a while to find out which particular lake since there were two of them we used to hide at. Calling Rose on the phone I figured when I hadn't come back with Charlie she might start to worry.

"Where are you?" Just from the tone of her voice, I heard worry even though I was sure she was much more worried about her brother right now.

After all, she was used to the sort of trouble he would get himself into.

"I'm about to meet up with someone, I didn't want you

to worry but I'll be gone for a while. Tell Larissa that I love her and in about a week I'll be by the house. I have to take care of something." I knew Lucian wouldn't want me to say I was meeting him, or he would have said something.

"Charlie just arrived, and he seems surprised, where is Lucian? What's going on, is there something I can do?" I was used to her voice as it began to waver a bit.

"I promise everything is alright, Lucian is just healing, he did get hurt but he's going to be okay, and I need to do something before I get home. Tell Charlie that Drezin is running behind. He had to make a quick side stop and he will be there very soon." I knew it would only worry her more if she knew how badly injured Lucian was.

I was still shocked that he was able to move. For whatever reason he chose to, it must have been serious enough.

"I know you're not telling me everything, I can leave Larissa with Sophie and join you." Rose was just as strong-willed as her brother that I wondered how their parents ever lived through raising both.

"Please Rose; trust me it's safer you stay there with Charlie and Sophie for right now. I'll be home as soon as I can." For now, she seemed to accept it, however, I knew if this went on for too much longer, she would be stubborn enough to come looking for us.

As soon as I had hung up the cell phone, I took off looking for the first lake that we used to go to hoping I wouldn't have to travel to far looking for Lucian. With him, it was always a mystery until I solved whatever search I was working on. I knew eventually I would find Lucian and most likely we would simply be waiting until he was strong enough to join the rest of the family. However, I also felt there had to be a reason he still felt he needed to hide. Maybe Katherine knew he was the only connection to the girl who had the necklace, and he felt she would be safer if he simply hid. Either way, I was curious how the meeting was going with Charlie and his brother Drezin. Charlie has had enough strange events in his life; it would be nice for once to have a regular family life during one of these centuries. After traveling for a while making sure I wasn't being followed, it had helped using the powder that Drezin gave me to cover up my tracks. At least this time I knew no one would be following me. I made it to the lake in no time, as I had texted the number that had shown. Receiving the coordinates to exactly where I was to go, I had seen this cabin very similar to the one I had been at only this time it had been halfway hidden on one side by trees while the rest of it had been built directly into the side of a cliff with a very narrow pathway leading to the front door.

Opening the door, I was amazed at how similar it looked to the other cabin even on the inside. Even the library had been stocked the same as the other one, the only difference with this one had been the books themselves. They were all hand-penned by Lucian himself and stories he came up with either on his own or old stories from Rose. Moving rather quickly to the secret hiding spot there was nothing there. Looking around more I recognized something that only Lucian and I would have looked for. A stone design on the floor when stepped on in a certain pattern lowered itself down. Once down there. I walked through another narrow passageway. Down at the far corner was Lucian all crumpled up refusing to move anymore not that I wanted to risk him moving.

"Why did you leave, we had Lily there and she was ready to heal you. She may be the newest guardian; however, she is very capable, it's far too dangerous to have you moving around." I wanted him to know we were all concerned wondering what had happened to him.

"Katherine showed up and I had to take off. She has spies all over the town, it's too small to hide there and not be noticed. If the girl saw me, she would come without hesitating, not knowing it's not safe for her right now. I had left a couple of books and her favorite flower on her nightstand where she normally puts her books, which she borrows from me when her family comes. I hoped it might keep her busy so she wouldn't come to the castle to see me. At least she calls it a castle; I guess my idea of a cabin had become a bit warped."

"I take it we are waiting here for you to heal, let me at least take you home so we can help you." Shaking his head no, I hardly had to be told that Lucian had other plans.

"We can't risk calling or going home right now, Katherine will keep coming after us since we are the only real connection to the girl, and we need to keep her safe. When you leave, I need you to promise me you will keep an eye on her, but don't let others know you are. That way she will just blend in with any other human who would be vacationing here. When I'm healed, I'll get the necklace from her, that way I can keep her safe and I'll either destroy it or see what Charlie wants to be done with it." At least I could update him now on the necklace.

"Charlie has a plan for it, only we need to find the bracelet also if it's going to work, it can help Amanda age." That was all I had to say to know Lucian was agreeing with it.

Now as we sat, we waited for Lucian to heal. I had only gone out for a few items, every so often getting food or other needs, each time covering my trail being careful not to be followed while taking care of Lucian. I knew Rose would be worried since I had been gone much longer than planned and this time no one knew where either of us was. I had finally found the girl and kept an eye on her a few times, which wasn't easy, it was almost as if she attracted danger. If I hadn't been used to protecting Rose, this would have been rather overwhelming.

Chapter Three

Drezin

Getting anxious while looking around, Charlie had been waiting for Drezin to show up as he said he would. Lorah wasn't at the house and Rose had left an odd message for him from Jacob saying he had a place he had to stop at first and would be there soon. Pacing almost driving himself crazy waiting, there were so many things that he wanted to ask Drezin. All he could see was a slight blur in the distance assuming it had been Drezin. Not sure how to feel, Charlie was slightly excited about having his little brother back but then also hesitant since he hadn't attempted to contact the family this whole time, as well as working for Katherine for so many years. As the rumor had spread, he had also become rather prominent with the council, which is a rather dangerous group of vampires who ruled the vampire world with at times an iron fist to keep order.

"Just when I think I finally have my life in order and figured out; someone shows up. I never thought I would see you again, I was positive you were dead." Charlie still had a look of disbelief on his face.

"How many have you had come back from the dead?"

Drezin seemed a bit surprised by the way Charlie had reacted.

It hadn't taken longer than a minute before Charlie had finally come over to hug his brother.

"Why didn't you try to contact us before?" Charlie seemed surprised that his brother, after all this time, still wouldn't have searched or tried to contact them.

"I didn't want to be a danger to the family. I knew you were safer without me. If I had known Katherine was threatening the family, I would have found you earlier. The only reason I found you now had been from helping Jacob when he was jumped by a few of her men." Nodding his head Charlie understood at least and accepted it so far.

"What have you been doing?" From basic curiosity, Charlie had asked.

"I was raised by Railar, another demon who had changed me and a few friends. We were heading home from school when he attacked us, it all happened so fast before we even had any idea what happened. We were not allowed to contact the family, as he was raised, I learned a lot of things that quite frankly ruined my way of looking at the world. Then I worked and was trained by Katherine who later turned me and my friends over to the council to serve. We were put in rather powerful positions working for the council. Especially Langston and me. We were right-hand hit men for the council. I must admit I didn't hate most of it. When the council went into hiding, we were used the most during that time, it was their main plan for changing us. We had purposely been handpicked. It only helped to have such strong power behind me to keep Katherine from killing off our family." Taking a breather before finishing Drezin dropped more of a verbal bomb that Charlie had been shocked he never knew about or that Lorah had kept the secret for so long.

"Except things happened that I needed to protect some of my inventions and my new family, I had rather gone into hiding and Lorah has been rather helpful at keeping the truth of my death secret. I only ran into her a few years ago and it couldn't have been better timing. I found out a few people from the council were planning on killing me and they still want to take over the council, there would be no chance at freedom. The new rules don't leave anyone immune, if they want to destroy you or your family, they will do it. Our family would be the first to be destroyed because of the children, no questions asked. Don't get me wrong, I supposed the council, otherwise, you know how we vampires get when we've isolated ourselves too much and know there are no consequences."

"I would love to know your family, even to meet everyone. There are many of our siblings I haven't seen in a long time. I never once thought I would say that. I still can't believe I'm looking at my baby brother, the head of such a wonderfully huge family. I bet you never saw that one coming?" Smiling at the thought, I guess life had surprised us all; however, it wasn't anything either of us could complain about.

Looking at Charlie waiting for his response, not that Drezin expected what Charlie was about to offer no matter how caring it was.

"How long do we get to keep you here?" Charlie was hoping to find out more about his brother except sadly this wasn't going to be the time.

"I wish I had more time but it's something I seem to be running out of. Lorah is already helping and meeting me. You won't be seeing her for a while, she and Valafar will be part of this and sadly I can't explain too much. I don't want to put you at risk. When I can. I promise I will come to see you again. You have no idea how much I have missed you. I really must get going; Lorah might worry about what is keeping me." Giving Charlie a rather firm hug promising again he would do his best to come back after things settled down.

Charlie watched as Drezin had taken off again however not as far as he would have assumed. Drezin had noticed something he didn't quite care for and before he could leave his family, he wanted to make sure they would be safe for the time being.

In the distance attempting to hide, however, not as

careful as Drezin had been he followed a few men who were hiding another creature in the center of them. As long as he had known there was one main person who traveled rather quickly and this secretly. Katherine was making a visit to the family again and Drezin wanted to make sure he was there for this one.

Following the group at a safe distance watching to see what they were planning. Charlie had already gone into the house with the rest of his family. As the large group circled the house, they had not wanted anyone to escape. If I had a way of warning Charlie, I would have. The briefest view of the lady in the center had shown itself and my guess had been right. It was Katherine and she was extremely angry. I had seen that look on her face many times and each time it led to several deaths. I wasn't going to risk that happening to Charlie and his family. Being careful I moved rather slowly behind the house before the men there even knew I had been behind them. Shooting at least two with a poison dart that killed them instantly leaving only two more to chase after me. Racing off into the woods behind leading them with me I loved the chase, and it was even better when I had the chance to be the rabbit. I always found it much easier to pick off my enemies when they raced after me. Not that I had to run very far, just far enough to reload my dart thrower. I had made my special brand of magic tips that would take down a vampire quickly. I could either knock one out or bury one ten feet under, facing down and waiting to see if they ever figure their way out or outright kill one. It had all depended on the demon for the choice I had made. For these that traveled with the lady. I killed them.

After taking out these two. I noticed the others knew something was up when the other two were not coming back and they had already checked on the ones that were laying on the ground dead. Being more protective of the lady, they were trying to figure out who had attacked them before bothering Charlie and his family inside. As Charlie peeked out the window, he knew something was happening. Not that anyone could have missed it with the rather large men standing outside their home.

Acting a bit cockier than I should have. I ran up behind the lady ready for her lightning bolt of fire, she shot it straight out as I moved out of her way. I was used to her usual forms of fighting techniques. I let her get a real good look at me as she could have truly died in the spot she was standing; she hadn't expected to see me either. Charlie had opened the door coming out himself only, as the rest of the family looked on in curiosity for now just in case, he had called them for help. It had been far too confusing for the lady to see me since she had assumed her attack on the family would go unpunished thinking, I was dead.

"I'm sure you weren't expecting to see me, nice to see you though." I couldn't hide the smile on my face even if I had wanted to.

A quick peek at Charlie I could tell he was confused but then he had, after all, thought I had already taken off and probably not sure what the lady had wanted or the fact that she was stopping momentarily.

"How is it possible?" Were the only words she seemed to be able to utter.

"Same reason you're still alive my dear. Now you know how I get when a deal is reneged on." Not taking my attention off from her I could see her giving the others signals that I was still quite familiar with.

"I highly doubt the council knows of your condition." Using this as if it was a threat, of course, they didn't know, however, she didn't if they did.

"You can forget about your little signals to besiege me with your hounds, after all, I know all of them, or did you forget I created a few of them for you myself. Besides, how do you think my death was so convincing if not for the council?" I loved those rare moments I could make someone as powerful as the lady shake in her place.

"You're bluffing." Not that she tried yet to prove her theory.

"Try me; I would love for someone else to call the council for once. I'm sure they would love to know what you've been doing to my nephew; I suggest you never go near him or the rest of the family again. I'll be watching no matter what rumors happen to be going around." Not changing my expression or stance I was going to make my point.

Just a quick moment of panic ran through her as she sent a signal rather quickly that I still caught. As she shot out between the two guards only one followed her as the other three rushed at me. Charlie was ready to charge to help as I held my hand up for him to stop. Standing still not even moving yet the first two were quick as they approached from the front and the third rounded behind thinking he would be sneaky coming up from behind. I knew for a fact he would be the first to go. As I let the man from the left grab my wrist. I twisted to the side as his friend from behind had impaled him, as he was slightly leaning forward momentarily being stunned by the fact, that he had just done that to his comrade. I used my right arm to grip around his neck quickly not only twisting it but severing it from his body, throwing it to the ground. He had died and dropped before the one that had held me. The third seeing that the lady was far enough away started to run off as I ran to catch up to him shooting him with one of my special made darts only to watch him drop to the ground. Charlie stood there shocked. Gathering the bodies, I knew my brother would never have the heart to do it, but if it wasn't done, they would keep reforming and attacking until Charlie's entire family was wiped out. Setting them on fire, there wasn't anything else that needed to be done.

"That was nothing. They were barely trying to fight, I would have to guess they were newer recruits, she probably didn't think she even needed them when she came to get revenge on you. Now I need to get going, don't worry I won't be too far off." This time I had taken off now that I had felt my brother and his family were safe for now.

Pulling out his cell phone Charlie had hoped Jacob would answer his phone, instead, he had heard the automated message service. Either his phone was turned off or he was out of range somehow. Not knowing where Lucian had decided to hide or take off to and knowing Jacob would soon disappear with him. Charlie had only hoped both would eventually come home safe.

Several miles away Drezin was busy hiding a special family member which is why he understood the special need to keep Amanda safe. Not for the same reason, however, the council seemed rather interested in her and he had wanted to protect her. Knowing if two of the members of the council had their way, they would wipe out every family member he had, just to get to his one daughter and her special gifts, with them it would make it so much easier for them to take over the council entirely making the rest their servants. I hoped she would have a chance at a normal life and not be influenced by anything before she made her own choices. Drezin had no idea how the life stone had been kept so secretive let alone the fact its existence was real and no mere myth as many had believed. The very few who had come into its power or knew of its existence had kept silent about it, either fearing for their own life or the sheer respect for it and those who guarded with their lives for it. A few months had passed and still no sign or message from either Lucian or Jacob. Knowing what kind of condition Lucian had been in. For the others to know, would not have helped anyone. Charlie had decided to keep that to himself other than trusting Lucian knew what he was doing and hopefully would come to the family if he needed help.

Drezin placed a few trusted spies in the area, to keep alert over Charley and his family. He wanted to be informed if anything happened. The first piece of information Drezin was given had been Charlie's family was searching for someone. For the next several months' things started happening along with hearing someone was looking for them or rather Lucian and she was human. It wasn't the same girl everyone else had been interested in, however, Charlie had hoped no one would harm her thinking she might be. Searching for any information they could find on her. The only connection they found had been that she worked at the nursing home where Harmony died. But then that alone could place her in danger as well. She seemed to be moving around quite a bit making it harder on the family trying to find her, so they hoped she just might find them instead. Of course, without the family knowing I had already done a bit of research myself, not that I could do too much openly. After all, I was supposed to be dead myself, my main purpose had been to lay low while allowing my daughters to blend in with the world around them where no one would be finding them.

All that changed by a chance meeting with Jacob and finding my little brother, I couldn't turn my back on them. I had nothing else I could do right now, for now, I would help things happen. I wasn't too worried about Katherine saying anything about me to the council. She was much more intelligent and conniving then that. She was herself supposed to be dead and had been enjoying the benefits of it, both of us had our concerns before we could deal with the council. The woman who had the piece we needed was going to be difficult to get to. She had her special protection from her ancestors that might not exactly welcome a vampire coming near her. As for the girl, everyone else was looking for had been a blonde fair-skinned woman while I searched for a Hindu woman. I had decided I was going to accomplish this by staying in the shadows unless I was needed, after all, there are always ways of encouraging things to happen and sometimes you must do something to make that happen. The first thing I had to do was find out where Harmony had lived and where her last days were.

For a long time, I lived out in the open, no one had a clue it was me. I admit as an adult and from the things I've lived through, my physical appearance isn't what they would expect. I hated hiding. Now I had to get used to it, which I had never done before. I had nothing to hide from other than people finding out I wasn't dead. I would prefer to face something head-on rather than hide from it.

Taking off for the nursing home. I found she had been registered under her original birth name. Only the years and dates were changed so no one would be suspicious about her name, nothing new to vampires. The place had been rather protective of its residents making it a little difficult to break in at night to find anything. There was a new resident in her old room not that there would have been anything left in there from her. Checking out the office there was one single file on her. It had been as simple as possible which of course meant no real leads to follow. On the workers' schedule one of the women was taking a month off for vacation and it had listed on other papers that she had signed out personal items that had been left by Harmony. Finding her address hadn't taken too long; with the internet, it was much easier to find any place now.

      Following the instructions, it hadn't taken too long, the town was rather small and thankfully dark at this time of night. All the bars had been closed or at least closing so very few if any people were out this late, not that any seemed to take notice of me. Being careful not to be watched for too long. I made my way to a small apartment complex. The front door had conveniently listed all the tenants next to their apartment number. Not risking ringing any numbers. I simply counted from the outside to see which one would be hers. There were only six apartments however several cars, not that I would have known what she drove. The lights were all turned off from her apartment as I climbed the outside building, using the patio furniture below to get on her balcony. Apparently, she thought it was safe to leave her sliding glass door unlocked from up here which made it much easier for me to let myself in. Being careful not to wake her in case she was still home. I took my time looking around. Each room had been empty, at least there wasn't anyone that would notice I was in the apartment or that I would run into. Not that I needed a light to look around, I could see in the dark just fine. Each room was rather neat and very organized making it easier and much quicker to search through everything. Still finding nothing and not even a destination or at least not until I read her journal, which she had been rather detailed about her conversations with Harmony as well as her planning an adventure to return an item she had placed in an envelope for Lucian. Out of habit working for the council, I had taken the journal with me not just to use as a reference, but to hide so that no one would know who and exactly how our world's secret was introduced to the eyes and ears of a mortal.

Sadly, the piece she was trying to return had simply been only a part of it, there were two pieces that made up the bracelet. The one piece that connected it to the necklace, she had a rather intricate design of the necklace drawn in her journal along with another small piece on the side, if she had only tried setting the one on top of the other it would connect on top of the bracelet as well as connect to the necklace, if it was set on top of the centerpiece of it. She only had part of the bracelet; I could only assume the part Harmony had given her as a gift was presented separately to make it look as if there were two pieces instead of one which would have made it much safer. Reading part of her journal I tried to figure out what she was doing or where she might be, she seemed to document her events in her life rather well including her childhood, skipping much of the personal script. I found what I was looking for or at least something that might help.

July 17ᵗʰ,

I worked at the current nursing home for the last ten years which I hadn't minded; I certainly wouldn't complain. I loved getting to know the residents. True, some had been cranky but then I guessed I would have if I had people telling me what I could or couldn't eat. What medications to take and asked me if I had gone to the bathroom. Especially when loved ones promised to visit but knew the next time they saw them, would be when they were in their coffin crying wishing they could have seen them more. Other than that, I got along with the residents rather well and I loved hearing their stories from childhood and as they had grown up. One thing I had not cared for would be if I were visiting with a resident and sat down before looking, feeling a wet cold feeling soak through my clothing rather quickly. Someone had an accident on the chair and sadly I should have known better by now than to have sat down without looking.

One of the residents I visited I enjoyed the most; she always seemed to be in a good mood no matter what was going on in her life. Sadly, she never had any visitors after her first two weeks of being admitted to the nursing home, however, her explanation of this had always been she understood and would never once judge any of them, after all, they had a life that could not begin to be explained. There had been times she would tell me of these wild stories, and I wondered if they had been true or taken from a book, she read at some point getting reality mixed up with them. Many of our residents were capable of taking care of themself but were not able to live on their own. We had some that simply had no grasp on reality any longer. Even though her stories regardless of whether they had been true or not, always caught my attention. I had spent so many hours with her even after my shift was over just because I wanted to hear more. Especially for the very reason, she wound up in a nursing home, to begin with. She was convinced she had been a very powerful shade that was bitten. Sadly, the venom had not reacted well. At least it had not killed her, however, it accelerated her aging causing her to be almost human again.

It was difficult to tell if she knew if I had believed her or not, but either way she hadn't seemed to care. She was just happy someone was finally listening to her, which I did with great interest. The way she described the places she had gone caused me to research many just out of curiosity, which they had turned out to be real and exactly the way she described them, which made it even hard for me to distinguish what had been real and what was not. After a while. I found myself wanting to believe in her stories especially when she told me about the young man she had fallen in love with. Her very first love and sadly because of certain events chose to leave him to keep him safe. Yet from the outcome, she had always maintained that it was best for both of them the way life had worked out. She never regretted the choices she had made she just wished she hadn't hurt such a wonderfully loving and honest person. She was glad he wasn't watching her grow old and die even though she felt at times he still watched her from a distance.

Over the last three years that she had been a resident. I had *started writing all of the stories she ever told me down on paper, when I would be home, I found myself always thinking about her. I had wished I could have known her when she was younger. She had already been living in the home for the last eight years. Even to the last moment when I had my day off, I had come in to spend time with her, which I was very thankful that I had. When she was telling me one of her last stories, I had been the last person she spoke to. All she had was one simple request for a letter with a small piece of jewelry inside to be delivered for her. Not that anything else had been expected, she had simply smiled and as she was talking her voice grew softer and slower until she passed away in my arms. After she passed. Unlike any other residents. I had a very hard time getting over this one. I had cried for several nights at home even while reading over many of the stories she had told me. I had a few pictures of both of us on my wall at home, on my computer as well as at my office at work. I had decided that I needed a bit of a change myself. Her stories were inspiring so that I needed a change no matter how minor and how it had turned out, at least I would have something to tell myself one day. But first I wanted to carry out her last request. Looking at the address that had already been on the letter she had wanted it hand delivered and not mailed in case it was lost or destroyed.*

After reading her comments about Harmony. I looked at the front and back cover of her journal looking for any more information on the woman. She had her name on the inside cover, it was listed Avani Isha, at least now I had a name and even a picture to go on. This was where vampires and mortals were extremely different. Mortals seemed to mark their belongings and leave photos of themselves everywhere, vampires kept it extremely limited where their names and pictures appeared, even on personal items just in case someone were to find out who and what we are. I didn't quite have it planned how I was going to get the other piece from her, but then I guess I could just let her deliver it herself. Unfortunately, if Katherine was still watching Charlie's family she might not let any strangers near them without searching them first. It's not like anyone was looking for her, they were all busy searching for the other girl. I always preferred being the one chased however searching for a human was simple enough that I didn't mind being the pursuer this time. At least there were a few hotels she was planning on stopping at on the way. It should be easy to find her; it was a matter of catching up to her and deciding the best plan of attack.

During the day I had to stay in the shadows which slowed me down and depending on if she had left on time, she was at least a day ahead of me. Being cautious when traveling I had noticed a few familiar creatures; thankfully they were too busy with something else to notice me. I had even seen Jerome one of the council's lead hunters, he had been the only equal to my best friend Langston. We all worked for the council until my wife Thea, and I separated from it preferring to be on our own rather than under their leadership. I only had to wait till she had stopped at her first hotel to catch up to her. It was almost too easy and if she hadn't been mortal, I would have assumed it was a trap. Walking into the front of the hotel doing my best to avoid the security camera, not that it would have picked up on my image other than to look like a blur. Standing at the desk was a very tired-looking employee. The more tired she was the easier it was going to make this.

"Hello, my niece is staying here, and I was supposed to see her except I can't remember the number, I didn't want to bother any of the others. Her name is Avani Isha." Usually, this excuse worked.

"Isn't it late to be paying a visit?" She may have looked tired however she was still with it enough to ask a question.

"Yes, it is late however we both usually work night shift, so we are used to talking to each other at night. If you can just call up to her room or give me the number and I'll come back tomorrow before she leaves. I believe she should still be scheduled for checkout tomorrow?" I hoped this might convince her that I was meant to be here.

"I can't let you through to visit this late, but you can call on the phone to see if she is still up." Handing me the hotel phone she gave me the number to type in.

She was in room three hundred and fourteen. Tipping the phone, as I put in a random number, I had thankfully picked one that no one was answering.

"Thank you for the phone. I'm guessing she went to sleep early since she's on vacation. I'll be back in the morning, have a nice night." Smiling and being as friendly as I could, I walked out of the hotel lobby to the parking lot.

Walking to the back of the hotel. I scaled the wall being careful not to be noticed. Not that I could get away with walking the inside hallway to find the room. I noticed from the inside lobby where the numbers had been, guessing where her room was, it must have been the third floor, far end of the hotel in the back. At least this way it made it much easier to find her. The light had been turned off so I could sneak in, not that I had made up my mind what to do. It was much easier to just take the item however I had to make sure she still had it with her. One thing I had noticed with mortals was, very few locked their sliding doors when they were on the second or higher floors. Sliding the door open I walked in rather easily. She had left her purse on the couch as I made my way quietly to it. I hadn't seen any lights coming from the bathroom or bedroom, then I could hear her faintly breathing, she was asleep. Dumping out the contents of her purse searching through everything I had found the envelope, except it was empty other than the handwritten letter inside. There wasn't anything in her bag either.

"Is there someone out there?" Her voice was so light I assumed something I had done woke her, even though I was careful not to.

I had always been extremely good at breaking in without being caught. Then it hit me as I saw a haze come out of her room. Her ancestors must have awoken her. There was a rather thick fog forming in the room before she slowly had come out stumbling half asleep looking around trying to figure out if anyone had entered. I had been careful to close the sliding door when I came in, hiding in the restroom as she finished looking through the main room. Picking up the phone I was worried she was going to call the police.

"Can you send up someone, it's rather foggy in my room and I'm not sure why, I think it's what woke me up?" Hanging up the phone and sitting on the couch, I knew I needed to find a better hiding place than this.

Another person was only going to complicate things more. Sliding the bathroom window up and climbing out. I stood outside on the barely usable ledge closing the window behind me hoping their checking the place out wouldn't take long. I had to find out if she had the piece. Watching as she walked around there was nothing special she was wearing. The employee couldn't explain what the fog was coming from, so they moved her to another room. She didn't have much to move. Once they were gone, I thoroughly checked out the room in case she dropped it. Now I made my way over to the other side where they had moved her. She flipped the television on watching it until she had fallen asleep on the couch. Letting myself in being much more careful. I had searched through the tiny bag she carried from her bedroom. Then I noticed where it was, and I knew it was going to be more difficult getting to it. She had a small pouch attached to the front of her shirt no doubt thinking it was a fashion item. A medium-sized medallion and sadly right out in front where anyone could see it to go after it. I wasn't going to be able to retrieve it without waking her. I just had to wait for now until she changed her shirt and hopefully doesn't wear it with every shirt.

The next morning, she had woken up early enough still; after paying and leaving in her pickup truck she had the same shirt on. At least I wasn't going to lose her, I had laid underneath the dark blue tarp in the back of her open-bed pickup truck, occasionally being tossed around a little however it could be worse. I only had to fend off one demon who realized what she was wearing, they must have thought they could stow away until it was dark enough out to spring at her, attacking for the medallion. The look on the demon's face was just priceless when he saw me already under the tarp; his eyes bulged so far when he had seen a twice-dead vampire. Grabbing ahold of him rather quickly, during his surprise, I separated his head from his body preventing him from making any kind of noise or directing any kind of attention to us. As soon as we were back on the road, I carefully dumped his body out the back watching it roll down the side of a hill. Getting comfortable again. I felt it might just be easier to make sure she is safe dropping it off rather than stealing it from her. I couldn't help but let my mind wander to my nephew Lucian, and I hope he was safe still and healing. I was sure Jacob would be protecting the other girl and hopefully collect the necklace from her before it put her in any more danger.

Chapter Four

Convincing

Leave it up to a mortal not to take the situation seriously. After all, this could mean her life. Not that anyone has had a chance to explain it to her. But then why would they unless they were after her to kill her to get it. The medallion had been added to the center of a bracelet while the other piece of the medallion had been placed on a necklace to keep the two pieces from connecting or being found with each other. At least now it was safe to say she only had one piece and the coin she thought was important had no real importance to it at all, it was simply a collectible coin placed in an envelope no doubt to distract others from it. Harmony understood more of what she was doing when she died than she had let on. I had no patience for mortals, which is why I preferred to live far away from them as possible. Apparently, she wasn't in a hurry to hand over the envelope as she had made it sound in her journal. She was acting the tourist part as she kept stopping at roadside souvenir shops as well as little towns along the way.

If I could just snatch the item from her without her knowing or seeing me, I would and I kept my attention for any available moment to either steal it or get her going. The nighttime had been the worst for her to stop, no gas station opens right now along this road, and I had hoped since she kept driving, while it wasn't safe for her, I wasn't worried about myself. Having grabbed an extra gas can filling it earlier not that it would hold very much. At least in an emergency, I could fill the tank while she was occupied driving.

On the way, she had stopped at a festival. It wasn't too difficult keeping her in my eyesight but then after walking around the several tables and countless people coming and going, I also spotted a few others who were watching her. Hiding my appearance, I had died my hair in her bathroom while she slept at the hotel as well as let my hair hang down hiding most of my face, usually, I kept it swept back in a ponytail at the nape of my neck. I felt going from dark black to a light blond was change enough, at least I can change it back when all of this was over. So many people around were unaware of how many vampires right now were walking among them. As the kids were excited on the rides and their parents watching, others played games at the tables. Following close by. I knew if she went on the Ferris wheel alone, she would be paired up with another and I could see another vampire had the same idea trying to stick close. Making sure I stepped in front when she went up, I wound up going on the amusement ride with her. There were so many other things I would have preferred doing than this. I felt as if I was babysitting her. The higher we went up I could see others around below just waiting for the opportunity to grab her when she was down on the ground. I had to make sure that didn't happen.

I never liked risking magic in front of mortals especially this close however my identity could be spotted by far too many other creatures right now and she was taking far too long getting to our destination. This situation however demanded that I do something quick, it was just a matter of convincing Avani to go along with it. She seemed to enjoy the ride so far even being friendly enough to say hello to me which I reciprocated to her. We only had a few more rounds to go around before we were going to be getting off, so I had to move faster.

"My name is Drezin, I'm just visiting, and you?" I was hoping to at least get a conversation going otherwise I wouldn't be able to hand her what I needed to in order to do this.

"My name is Avani, I'm on vacation here also, this is a very cute little town, I didn't know it was here until I almost drove past it however the music and lights from here caught my attention." At least now I know why she had the urge to stop at this place after only driving for a few hours.

"Do you like magic tricks?" As long as she said yes, I could slip the powder into her hand, hopefully if she was willing, and do something few thought only the stone could do.

True it can, however, with a bit of the right mixture I can bring us to only a few places and one of those places would be a bit out of the way however with my travel I could make up for that in no time.

"I like some magic tricks, nothing that tests human ability, but I like the sleight of hand tricks." Smiling as she told me, she had no idea what she was about to get into.

At least her ancestors were not giving me any problems so far but then they no doubt saw what was waiting for her below and there was only so much they could do to protect her.

"Hold out your hand, I have a trick my wife loves." Hoping she would accept that explanation I had taken powder out of my jacket pocket now dropping it into her hand.

As she looked at it, I made sure at least a part of myself was touching her as I enchanted a few words causing a cloud of white smoke to swirl around us. As our seat came to the bottom for the conductor to let us out, he was astonished as well as those who had waited for her. Neither of us was sitting there, leaving the seat empty with only cold prints where we had sat almost as if someone had quickly rubbed it with an ice cube. Now was the hard part, explaining to her how and why I did this hoping she wouldn't fight it. I knew she would be a little confused when she realized we were no longer on the Ferris wheel ride let alone the park itself. Looking around in confusion she hadn't seemed angry or at least not yet. Backing up from me just a little before asking she looked as though she was getting the idea of what just happened.

"Where are we, how did you do that?" Now she stared intently at me.

"This is my office of sorts." I hadn't planned on what I was going to tell her once we were here; I was never good with conversations.

"Are you kidnapping me?" As she took another step back away from me backing into the wall, not sure why however I almost expected her to pull out a can of mace from her purse and start spraying it at me, not that it would have done much, she had a small can in her purse.

"Not exactly, you're not a kid and it's not entirely against your will or your ancestors would not have allowed it, besides, you're going where I need you to be except your just taking way too long to get there so I hurried it up a little and to be honest, there are others who were waiting to kill you." She was looking at me as if I was crazy.

"What do you mean my ancestors? How can dead people help me if you're holding me hostage?" Still not trusting me I hadn't made one move towards her yet.

Not that I had to wait too long for them to show themselves, the room started getting that smokey haze look again. Pulling more dust out of my pocket, I blew it in the air as it showed three people standing near her that she could see. At least she hadn't freaked out when she saw them, not that she seemed to believe what she was seeing with her own eyes.

"You have an envelope from Harmony. A patient of yours that you're delivering to my nephew except it's not exactly what he needs, it's nice for emotional reasons if he still wants to go down that road, however, it's the medallion you have attached to your shirt the family needs back, that's why I'm here. I was trying to either collect it from you or help you get to the family except you just take far too long to get there and I can't keep protecting you and keep myself hidden. I'm not even supposed to be here." As I mentioned the medallion, she placed her hand over it.

"You don't have to protect me. I can do that myself." She sounded determined.

"That's nice and all however you've been attacked twice now and had another group ready to kill you for the medallion back at the carnival, which is why I had to drastically move you, I would have let you arrive there naturally, but things had to change." While she was still trying to figure this out, I started looking out the door of the barn making sure no one was around.

"Who are you hiding from, the police?" Apparently, she thought I was a fugitive if I was trying to stay hidden.

"Definitely not a fugitive, the police have no idea I exist, there are creatures out there I'm hiding from, and no I haven't lost my mind, however, neither have you. I know you talk to your ancestors and have a strong bond with them, that's a good thing, I won't judge you for that. I don't have time to explain it all, hop on my back and I'll explain it when we get there." Turning I had hoped she would just listen except I guess I'd have to convince her more.

"I'm not hopping on your back or going anywhere with you, how did you get me here in the first place, where is here?" She stood her ground as I tried to think how to answer her.

"I can't exactly tell you where we are, this is supposed to be a secret, it's my office or at least the entrance to it, and I don't have any other way to prove to you that you're safe. I have no intentions of taking the time it takes to form a bond with you, I need the medallion and if you give it to me, I can drop you off anywhere you want or you can just walk out of here on your own. If you take off with the medallion there are several out there that would kill you. I do value life to a point however you're getting to the point I'm ready to do what I need to in order to get it, so is it going to be easy or hard?" As I had said before I had a short fuse when it came to mortals.

"How did you get me here? Besides, how do I know you won't just kill me anyway?" At least she was making a valid point.

"You don't know if I will or won't kill you however in my best interest it would be best to kill you, I'm supposed to be in hiding and you could ruin that, I'm just helping my family right now and you have something dangerous that belongs to them. Or at least what belongs to the guardians. How I brought you here was with magic. Not hocus pocus crap, real magic."

"I'm supposed to believe you can perform real magic, if you have magic then why not advertise yourself?" She crossed her arms in a defensive position.

"If you had magic or any kind of gift this powerful, would you advertise yourself? You don't exactly know what you're advertising yourself to. There are a lot of good people out there with good intentions and there are evil people as well with their intentions. Even good intentions can be harmful. When someone has a gift as we do, we guard it with our lives to protect not just ourselves but for others as well." This was already taking longer than I had cared for.

I hated killing however I had already killed enough; it's why I had left the council. I was tired of carrying out execution orders.

"If you have powers like that and so do so many others, why don't they do good or make a difference with it?" Hanging my head down for a moment, I was tired of getting asked this question, century after century I get asked this.

"Some of us do use it for good; we just do it unannounced for many reasons. The magic I performed to get you here should have been proof enough." I started pacing since she wasn't going to end with the questions.

I had to admit I had mellowed over the last several years since leaving the council. Working for the council had numbed many feelings and senses. If it had been anyone else, I would have felt bad for an innocent person dying. I would have made sure she was buried well, for some reason I just couldn't force myself to lay a hand on her but then it could have been out of the respect for those who were watching over her. It was hard to say.

"Why would you hide something like that?" She seemed genuinely interested.

"Simple, there are a lot of crazy people out there that might not want to use it for good; there are very evil uses to our gifts as well if it's used for that. We have what we call our Presidium, it's a group of long-time vampires who control our world just like you have your government to control the safety of your people, or at least that's its intent. However, ours is for the most part not as strict, we only have a few main rules and again it's to protect us as it is non-magical humans.

"Isn't a presidium under something? Sort of like an administrative committee, so who is above them?"

"The presidium is a group of very powerful people that are still not to be taken lightly or underestimated. The council which is the absolute above is a group you should make sure you never meet."

"Are these the only groups presiding over those with magic?" Even though she wasn't walking away from me anymore she was still having a hard time believing me.

"No, they are not the only ones, there are different groups out there and some even more ruthless than ours and very few that are rather humanized except they do not last very long. The groups I used to work with have made it this long because of how powerfully strong they are with a variety of gifts and creatures at their disposal., over the centuries, we've learned to blend in. there are thousands of various creatures around you but if you don't know what you are looking for, a human would never know they were there." I stated bluntly.

"Have you ever done anything evil with it, your gift that is?" She swallowed hard.

"Yes, I have" I had no reason to deceive her; after all, I had been rather evil for a long period of my life.

"What have you done?" I could tell she was picturing something that made her shiver.

"That would be my business to know, I won't share it, just like I won't share my beliefs, and neither is up for interpretation or discussion. I respect yours however I don't need to know it. No more questions. It's time to go." Grabbing a hold of her rather forcibly I pulled her over my shoulder onto my back as I rushed out the barn with her not quite at the fastest speed.

I wanted to wait for a little before I broke out into a full run for when she was slightly used to it or over the shock of traveling so fast. After running for an hour, I stopped setting her down letting her catch her breath.

"If you need to bring me somewhere, why don't we poof there as we did before? Why not use your magic?" She seemed more surprised than afraid.

"Magic leaves prints, and it affects many things, far too easy to be found and we need to cover any trails we might possibly leave. Besides, that sort of magic is very limited, I need to bring you somewhere my magic is not connected to yet. My magic is still in its experimental phase."

"How much further not that I have any idea how far we've gone. I couldn't see a thing; it was all a blur." She asked.

Looking around I hadn't wanted to tell her just how long it was going to be. If there weren't other demons watching the family, we would be there in a short time from now except there were trails I was picking up on from other demons.

"There are other demons in the area so we need to be careful, it's not a matter of how close then it is avoiding other demons, I can defend myself however if there are too many it would be harder keeping you alive. I should have just taken the medallion from you except if I had left you there, they would have killed you anyway because you had it in your possession. Killing you would have prevented you from talking about it or going after it again." Stepping near her I was getting ready to make another quick sprint.

"When we get there what are they going to do with me?" Looking nervous she asked with a certain right.

"I would be done with you once your there, it's up to them what they do with you however I can promise you will be very safe with them; they would prefer not to kill you and to keep you safe, they haven't had the same training and morals that I have. They might look at you as a pet or try to add you to their family," I knew it came out a bit sarcastic, but my family wasn't your average vampire clan, I promise they will keep you safe and help you figure out how to get the others disinterested in you." Reaching over my shoulder to hold on she asked one last question.

"If you're not mortal, what are you?" As she held her breath for a moment.

"A vampire my dear, nothing very special just a very clever calculating leftover form of a human that used to exist. Harmony was human like you, but she was given the gifts of a shade." Not saying anything else I had quickly taken off with her heading off in a slight detour avoiding many of the scents I had been picking up on.

Even though Katherine was being careful with her men watching the family she certainly had enough of them keeping an eye on them no doubt hoping to find the items before they could make it to them. I took Avani to the nearest hotel. I had her check in asking for the highest floor, it made it much easier to sneak in from the outside. That way I could come and go as I needed to. Somehow, I would have to bring Charlie to us, but then that would end up putting him in danger if he traveled with a group. He would be safer except it would just endanger the others and alert Katherine's men that something was going on. I couldn't get rid of that nagging feeling something else was wrong. Watching out the window I could see two demons lurking around outside the hotel. The first thought I had was they found me. I hadn't thought for a second that they would have traced her here somehow. I know how I travel, and I was cautious not to leave any kind of a trail. There had to be something else, or someone tipped them off somehow. Either way, I had to find out. Not that I was going to be waiting for very long.

Avani was already in there taking a shower; she had

taken her clothes in with her as I watched out the window. The others had already worked their way up the different floors of the hotel. Leaving our door opened a crack I was hoping to tempt them enough to lure them in without doing anything. Not that I would let them anywhere near Avani but then I also hadn't any intentions of allowing them to leave either. Standing in the hallway. I could still hear the water running so I would have to keep the noise down, after all, I didn't want her walking out into this. The first one cautiously walked in looking the room over as he started flipping through the pockets of the four shirts Avani had hung. The second had walked in following the first, not doing anything and letting the other test out the waters in case something happened. At least I knew who my first target would be. Using a favorite trick of mine I made it sound as though a sound came from behind the couch. As the first raced quickly to snag whatever he assumed he was going to find, the second stood back intently watching him. As he did, I stepped behind him quickly severing his head from his body carefully knocking him back so that he would only spray blood into the open duffle bag not that it would hold it for too long. The first realized he was too late to protect the one that had come with him; instead, he searched for a way out.

"I wouldn't recommend taking off. I have a few questions and if you don't answer them, I'll hunt you down and kill you." I thought I was being fair enough while keeping my voice down.

"You're going to kill me anyway so why should I tell you anything?" Still apprehensive I could tell he hadn't been around for too long or at least not got into any trouble I would have dealt with him before.

"True, I will kill you anyway however if you answer me, I'll be nice about it." Giving him a rather evil grin, he was getting a rather good deal.

I could hear the shower being turned off. I had hoped to be done with this before she came out. Grabbing the bag with the head, I tossed it out the window into the shrubbery below along with the body. Hopefully, no one was watching.

"What is it that you want to know? Maybe we can work something out and you can let me go?" At least he seemed hopeful, plea bargaining was never a good idea with a vampire who just admitted they were going to kill you regardless.

"Are you working for Katherine and if so, what are you looking for around here?" Short and to the point, I made it rather easy on him.

Unfortunately, as I finished asking Avani started coming out of the shower. Making my move quickly I made it clear to him not even to attempt to go after her. If he had managed to kill her at least I would have him dead also and I would be free to leave with the medallion. Avani looked rather surprised to see another person in the room as she looked from him to me trying to figure out if he was safe or not.

"Who is the girl?" Before answering he was eyeing her over and then taking a closer look at me.

I knew it wouldn't be long before he figured it out. I hated to do this in front of her, but I knew there was no other way, or they would find out I was alive. I trusted Katherine not to say anything however her hunters were not under the same obligation since most were independent workers.

"The girl is none of your concern, your time is counting down, finish answering my question or die now." As I spoke, Avani took a step back almost as if she thought he would go after her or she would end up in the middle of it.

It never hurt to step back out of the way, after all killing was a bit messy, even when it was just a vampire.

"No, I don't work for her however my former friend did, he was traveling through, and he thought he saw something he wanted coming into the hotel here, so we looked. I don't know what he was looking for. You look familiar; I think I've seen your picture in the office of the presidium. I was being recruited recently but said I needed a lot more training." As he tried to figure out who I was, I knew this was going to be difficult since the presidium would not let go of their recruits being killed.

I could hide him for a while except that would still get

them asking about him. If I let him go I could in serious trouble.

"Don't leave the room at all until I get back." As I told Avani, now racing for the other vampire I grabbed the powder out of my pocket transporting us both to my office.

Most vampires were not used to traveling this way, it was rather unusual, and I had learned from a creature that performed exclusively black magic. Grabbing him I had no other safe place to detain him other than my empty vault which I no longer used since I had moved it to a larger one elsewhere. Closing the door making sure no one had seen me. I made my way back to Avani. I wasn't worried about the vampire breathing, there wasn't any need for air in there, and for some reason, if I could find a way of covering his death I would do it. Right now, I can just hide him until I can figure something out. Then I noticed something strange about those who were around in the area. They were not just men working for Katherine; of course, there would always be a few free agents who worked for themselves. There were death hunters from the council as well as basic hunters from the presidium. They were not all here keeping an eye on Charlie and his family however they were getting curious about the others and why they were.

Apparently, my best friend and close enough as a brother Langston was running from them at the moment. The rumor seemed to be that he had been up for execution and ran however another rumor had been that Gerard a member of the council had worked a deal with him promising him death if he finished another assignment for him. I didn't have to guess it had to do with my family and why I was hiding. At some point, I needed to show myself to him. I just couldn't do it yet. As soon as I could I had to make sure she was safe. I have no problem being responsible for my actions however I never did like others to suffer from my choices. As I watched the one, I felt my feet flip out from under me as I hit the ground, one of the rare times I took my attention off from my surroundings even though I had recognized the scent. There was no need to fight back.

"That was far too easy, good thing you have your kids

being raised elsewhere." Letting me up as I looked at her.

She had bailed me out from several situations when dealing with humans, in a way she had softened both my wife and me, we had met very few out in the world that were like her and her family.

"You know I have a hard time learning from my mistakes, I hate to say I might end up in this situation again, if I don't attempt it then how will I ever know if it might work?" I never understood my obsession with it myself.

Unlike others I knew who worked with magic they could control their emotions, on the other hand, I didn't control my emotions, and I let them run wild. Not exactly a good combination. Being a vampire was difficult enough then to hide magic also.

"Did you need to go this far with it? Did you ever think about the girls and what they might want or the fact they didn't want this at all?" I had thought about it, and I knew what I had wanted but then I knew I was also being rather selfish.

When I had first presented the idea to my wife Thea, she was rather excited to expand our family however she wasn't thinking in the direction I had been. Not that we planned on infecting a child into a vampire life. Thea couldn't sustain a child any more than I could. Thea had come from a long line of witches and mine; we simply became the first round of vampires however I was not changed by the same as the rest of them. She certainly hadn't been happy with the way our family came about. Not that I had originally planned it this way until it had hit me the magnitude of the power the children would have and when Gerard had mentioned having them all raised and trained directly with the council or rather under his direction. The children were never meant to be conceived this way; it would have been overtime having a surrogate helping us. Instead, to make sure the children were safe, I found families who wanted children making a deal with each one. Oddly enough not one couple turned me down, they knew what might happen one day, after all, they had the right to know the children would not be normal and I had to know they would be safe. Then the strangest thing happened even beyond my planning, all six children had been born on the same day within a few hours of each other, the reason for the seventh not being born yet?

We had wanted to raise her still however our surrogate died after childbirth, and it brought attention from Gerard since he thought I had destroyed all of them. At least that's what I let him think and had shown him. Then I had to finally hide my last daughter with the help of Lorah. I knew once she was born things would start happening for the other girls. Lorah had only known about the one daughter, only Gerard had discovered there were three, knowing how magical of a family my wife's side had been. He never assumed there would have been more than that.

"Do me a favor Lorah, kill me now, Thea won't get mad at you, and I know she would understand." Kneeling in front of her bending my head over as if I was offering it to her.

"That would be the easy way out for you. You're going to fix this, besides your daughter is going to need you. You started this and you get to finish it. Besides, what makes you think I want to touch you?" Now that Lorah had already taken me by surprise I kept my attention on our surroundings.

"You already touched me once when you tackled me. I have someone you should meet." Making our way back to the hotel I found Avani hiding in the closet with a can of mace ready to spray.

Not that it would have hurt if she had sprayed me however for her sake it was better, I announced to us as we entered, especially after the situation earlier. Helping her out of the closet she stood staring at Lorah.

"This would be Avani; she has a letter for Lucian and the medallion on her shirt is the very one Charlie is looking for." Stepping aside Lorah came right over and instead of a handshake she gave her a light hug or at least as light as a vampire can give.

"I'm Lorah, Lucian is my nephew. How is it that you know him or have a letter for him? He's not exactly available right now but I can leave it for him." I wasn't sure but all this time I could have asked those questions also.

It came much more natural for Lorah to ask but then she was always good with mortals.

"My name is Avani Isha. I worked with an elderly lady that was brought into our nursing home, and she had this letter she wanted to be delivered. I didn't know what to expect but after what I've experienced, I believe her stories now. I thought I would have an adventure except I didn't plan anything like this at all, I just wish I could go home except I don't think it's an option anymore?" Both of us could tell she was feeling overwhelmed.

"It would be easier if she was out of the way, and we can hand over the letter and medallion for her." I was always thinking of the easier way.

"Valafar is close by, we could bring her home safely, and how are you going to explain to Charlie that you have the medallion? He's already not happy that I've hidden the fact you're alive all those centuries. I knew he would have been very hurt if he knew anything about your childhood. Someday he's going to find out, hard to hide it when you keep getting yourself in trouble." Shaking her head, I knew she was slightly disappointed in me herself.

All I could think had been the fact I wasn't ashamed of the way I had been raised. It was nowhere near the way the rest of the family had been raised. This was our life. It was the way vampires had lived for centuries. Maybe by human standards, it was harsh and possibly something to be remorseful over. However, I had no regrets other than missing out on my siblings growing up, but I was lucky I wasn't alone. I had my best friends with me.

"Avani, will you give me the letter and medallion? I can deliver it safely; you won't have a chance if we get ambushed. You must promise not to say a word about any of this or who we are that you talked to." I had hoped she might go for it; this would be much safer for her and easier for us.

"Will other vampires come after me?" At least it was a valid question.

"They will if you're caught with us. Right now, no one knows about you and the only two that had any idea that you had the medallion are dead, I took care of that already." I already knew I didn't want to look at Lorah, I could almost feel her frown.

"Hopefully you didn't do that in front of her, we don't need to scar her for life or make her think vampires are all vicious nasty monsters." Lorah was always rather adamant about this subject.

"No, I haven't killed any around her, besides I still have to pick up the body of the one if no one has found it yet, and I have another live one I still have to deal with, I moved him out of sight." I had tried making it sound as if I had done a good thing except, she still looked upset with me.

"You will release that one and not kill him?" Lorah had crossed her arms in front of her showing her disapproval even more.

"I can't promise anything but if we are going to do this we need to get moving before we run out of choices." I wasn't in the mood to get lectured by Lorah and I knew it was coming very quickly.

Once she was on a roll, she could make the worst demon feel bad. Taking the medallion out from the mini pocket Avani had sewn onto her shirt she handed it over to me. Lorah had called Valafar on the cell phone and he was there within seconds. She was right he wasn't that far. Giving each other a nod of the head, I had known him for a long time, after all his family had been the ruling majority on the council. The only reason I hadn't feared him had been the simple fact he had separated himself from that life. He was neither a traitor or a spy and he had my respect. If he ever needed help, I would assist without hesitation. I watched as Valafar held Avani on his back. I explained where we left her truck. Lorah was going to collect the truck and bring it back to her home.

As both took off, I was starting to head towards Charlie's home except from previous experience with powerful magic or gifts. I knew one main thing that I had seen happen every time. Others would kill by any means possible to get the object of their obsession and I was thankful not to be that deranged yet. I wanted to protect my family and keep the medallion around for when they needed it except, I couldn't get myself to risk their lives with it yet. I was supposed to be permanently dead so it would be best hidden with me. For now, I took it with me and went back into hiding with Thea. I knew if I had the chance to explain to Charlie he would understand. At least I hoped he would.

While all of this was going on Lucian had his problems he was still dealing with as Jacob stayed with him. He couldn't risk seeing or calling the family or he would have given the easiest path right to them.

Chapter Five

The Other Girl's Vacation

I have very few memories that stand out and the ones that do. My parents always told me that I imagined them; there was no way they ever could have happened. My father liked to tell me that I was just very creative with an overactive imagination. In my earliest memory, had been when I was four years old, I would be starting school early even though my birthday had been in December. As my parents were bringing in our luggage, I walked out on the screen porch following our dog. I wasn't paying attention to where we were until I heard her bark and runoff in a certain direction. There was no way that I could even keep up let alone remember all the turns we had taken to get back home. I was completely lost at that age. I didn't know to stop wandering. I kept hoping I would find the cabin. I never had any idea just how huge the forest was. As I was walking. Something almost ran me over. Not that I could have seen it, whatever it had been passed by in such a blur except it had been the only thing that made me finally stand in place looking in the direction that it had gone. Not having to wait for too long the flash of wind I had felt and the slight blur of blue and black showed itself again. Standing in front of me. I stood frozen in place. I had never seen anyone look like this. He wore a long black jacket, black slacks, and a dark blue shirt. His feet barely touched the ground when he ran. His hair was jet black and very long. However, unkept. I wasn't sure what exactly had possessed me to react in the way that I had other than the fact when I was a small child, I had no fear. I pulled out a comb from my pocket which my mother had given me. She had made it clear if I wanted long hair, I had to keep it combed or she would cut it. Reaching out so the stranger could take it I said to him.

"So, your mom doesn't cut your hair." He had given me a rather strange look when I said this to him.

"Does your mom even know you're out here?" He almost looked as though he was trying to figure out what to do with me.

His voice had been so calm I felt safer with him than with anyone I knew. All I could do had been to shake my head letting him know my mother didn't know I was out here.

"Do you have a name?" As soon as he said this I smiled and nodded an affirmative yes.

"Can you tell me or is it a secret?" Smiling more he sat on the ground not too close to me.

I knew he wasn't going to do anything from where he sat. At least as young as I had been, I didn't know how fast he could have moved from a sitting position if he had wanted to.

"Teddy" I had beamed rather proudly when I answered him.

"That's nice you want your teddy bear, but I would like to know your name." Never raising his voice, he still sounded patient and soft-spoken.

"My name is Teddy. Mom and dad call me Teddy." At this age I had been surprised he questioned my name.

"I'm sure your parents are looking for you. It's rather late and dark for you to be in the forest alone, besides it smells like you rolled in a field of flowers, lily of the valley, at least it's a pretty scent. Want me to take you to your parents?" I had always been taught not to speak with strangers but then I broke that rule when I had spoken to him.

Oddly enough he used my comb which I was happy with. Handing it back to me I was rather proud of the fact someone else had needed it more than I. Not answering verbally, I nodded my head. I gave into a slight shiver as I raised my arms for him to pick me up. Removing his jacket, he wrapped me in it explaining he was going to be running rather fast, and it would only get colder. He was right. We took off so fast. I barely remember much of the ride. I couldn't see a thing until we stopped. I could hear my new puppy barking in the distance.

"That's my dog" was all I had to say, and he was off in the direction with me following the dog barks. I could hear my dad yell for the dog to quiet down with no lights on in the cabin, they had obviously not known I was even missing. I was feeling sleepy myself as the stranger carried me quietly inside the cabin and to my room I pointed to. I was the only one sleeping upstairs. All my stuffed animals had been laid neatly in a row along the wall with my bed still made. Pulling the covers back I climbed into bed as he put his jacket back on. Covering me up, he kissed me on the forehead.

"Goodnight, little one." Had been the last time I had heard his voice or seen him for quite some time.

At least at my age, it had felt like a lifetime. When I learned that my parents were not going to believe me, I quit telling them when I would see the stranger. Mainly he was nearby to shake his head no and motion for me to turn around and go back to the cabin. He didn't want to risk me getting lost in the woods again. One thing he kept telling me had been that I smelled like a certain flower not that I ever smelled it. I simply took his word for it. After a while, he would bring me a handful of lily of the valley. I had fallen in love with the flower. When we had left at the end of the season, he had been waiting for me at the bridge to say goodbye. I cried all the way home. I hadn't wanted to leave. The following summer I had been so excited knowing we were staying at the same cabin, this time I was five. I had memorized the path heading off to the park. When mom and dad have others over, I would sneak out and go to the park. He would be there to push me on the swing or just watch me play making sure I didn't get hurt or no one else tried to bother me. Some even thought he was my father, which I don't think he minded at the time, at least not until I had started to get older and started changing. I took a deep breath in and sighed rather loudly not that anyone was paying attention, which had been so long ago.

Throwing one bag on top of another bag into the trunk of the car, not worried whether the suitcases were stacked right. This was supposed to be a fun weekend in sunny Cozumel with my friends. Instead, I'm getting into the back seat of an old station wagon with my parents still taking our annual family trip even at the age of twenty-five. But what was I supposed to do? I was broke and not allowed to stay home because my parents were worried that I would have a drinking party and burn the place down while they were gone.

First, I have to say I have not been all that motivated to move out of the house, not that I could afford it yet and up to this point. I have done pretty much everything my parents have asked of me. I've never smoked, drank, or done drugs. They even like my friends, which in many ways does make me feel older than I am. Not that it's a bad thing they like my friends but somehow, I would like to give them a real reason to actually distrust me for once. Of all the times I could have snuck a boy into my room, and they never would have known it.

I should mention my friendships are a bit limited, I admit I'm not that outgoing or social of a person, I would personally love staying home in my room working on my projects or just plain getting comfy in bed reading a good book with Max my Siberian husky sleeping on the bed. Max seems to be under the impression that he's a small lap dog. Either way, my two friends Beth, Arianna, and I had planned on a nice vacation so instead of wondering what bathing suit I would be wearing, now I would be wearing a rain-slick over my clothes and occasionally a coat and hat. My parent's vacation had to be up north at an old cabin with cold drafts and a permanent leak above my bed that the owner always says they intend on fixing. I'm pretty sure after twenty years that's not going to happen.

Enduring the road trip, I couldn't wait to lock myself in my room at the cabin. I could only handle the license plate game for so long. It was as if I was five years old again. My parents would insist that I would fall in love with the place again and try to remind me how much I loved and looked forward to it when I was younger. If they had only known the truth of why I had loved coming. Most of it started when I had met this older man our first summer here when I was five and I could only guess he had been in his forties? It had freaked my parents out when they had seen him talking to me at the playground. If he had wanted to hurt me, he could have done it the first time we met except he hadn't.

He wasn't trying to lure me anywhere or give me anything. He was trying to talk me out of standing near the creek. He was worried I would fall in and get sick from the cold water. I had seen him every year; he had even managed to give me a gift for my birthday. At the beginning of summer, my room would have vases of lily of the valley that my room would be so potent with it. My parents always thought it was such a nice thing the people did for me that rented it out to us, at least I knew who did it and I loved it. Then the last ten years I had not seen him; his place was empty with no hint of where he had left to. The entire place was empty except for one room, the library with all the books. Even though he was gone I still went up to the old castle out in the woods just to check hoping he would be there.

The most we ever talked about had been about the woods there, or how old the castle was, and his experiences of traveling the world. Even as I had become much older, I wondered how one person could have experienced so much but personally, I hadn't cared too much. I loved listening to him and most of all he listened to me when I spoke. I never felt uncomfortable, I knew I was safe. I knew I was much safer with him than my parents or anyone else for that matter. I never doubted in my mind for one second that my time should be spent with him. I just could not explain it. When I was younger, I sat on his lap and as I grew bigger, I sat next to him as he would either read a story to me, work on a craft project or simply race through the forest and he would carry me. I had to admit he did start to be different as I was getting older. I wasn't sure if he noticed but I realized that he was not only different, but the simple fact he was male and very handsome. I had finally started to notice him. He was the one obsession I had, my one and only true flaw, but I loved it. As I grew older, I hadn't risked telling my parents about still seeing him and I certainly wasn't going to tell my friends, or they would have thought I was crazy. The one thing I had to admit might not have been technically the smartest or safest thing, I never once doubted if I should or not. He was the only reason I had ever looked forward to this trip. Not that I ever expected him to suddenly appear again. I just wished I had known where he had gone to, and hopefully he was safe, he was an amazing friend.

As we arrived at the cabin the rain was down pouring incredibly hard. No carport or garage to park in. We had to make a quick dash to the front door. Pulling our suitcases over the seats, each of us grabbed a few bags; I wound up taking three since my duffle bag strap looped over my shoulder. I was never into packing heavy and pretty much wore the same clothes day after day. I preferred being comfortable and if someone felt it was laziness, I was fine with that. I wore nice clothes. I just wore them a lot. Not bothering with an umbrella, I ran as fast as I could beating both mom and dad to the door, not that I had to wait for a key, the cabins were never locked. At least not until we moved in. Living in the city mom and dad insisted on locking all doors and windows to the point we had bars on all the lower windows. Being the first one in I knew not to go in too far or risk getting scolded for dripping all over the wood floors making them a safety hazard.

Leaving the door open I had taken off my shoes leaving

them by the front door and set the two other suitcases down next to them. Then I walked over and up the stairs dragging a towel behind to mop up any water that could have possibly touched the floor. My parents were compulsive about being clean and organized to the point that I like to call it insanity. Most of the time our house looked more like a show home with no evidence of anyone living in it until you were to see my room, whereas my mother loved to say a bomb went off. At least after so many years, she gave up threatening me to clean my room. I just had to keep the door closed. My room may have been a mess, but it was an organized mess and at least the only important person could find where everything was and that was me. My parents always stayed on the main floor feeling I would be safer up on the second floor. The main reason they had thought I would not be able to sneak out without their knowing it. Not that there was ever a place where I would want to sneak out to. There was a second room upstairs except it had been more like a library or study room with a very old desk and oil lamp. I liked the oil lamp usually great lighting to read scary stories next to when the rest of the room was dark.

It was far too cold to hang out at the beach, and I certainly wasn't going to spend time shopping. I had a full-time job, and I put away every dime I earned into savings. Usually, I wound up taking long walks along the trails but since my friend disappeared without explaining if he would ever be back. I mainly stayed in my room just as I would have if I had been at home. Occasionally there might have been a good movie to see except that wouldn't last all summer. I hadn't bothered to unpack. I left my duffle bag by the side of the bed. When I needed something, I would reach in for it. I never ironed so I never bothered buying any clothes that would need ironing. The only thing I was waiting on now had been the bed sheets and blanket that were now running through the washer and dryer. They were supposedly set for this summer however my parents always insisted on washing everything again just in case. Mom was always positive that someone had sex in all the beds just before we arrived, so she made sure everything was rewashed. It's what I call her paranoia coming through. Pulling out three good books I placed them on the nightstand hoping I might be able to stretch them out all summer even though I was sure I would have them all read by the end of the month. At least they had a nice size bookstore here.

Standing next to my window I watched as the rain kept pouring down, I couldn't see the tree that I would normally climb out onto at night. At least I won't be trying it tonight. There was a spot I liked walking to and not many knew about it, I had been shown by my old friend Daniel. Sitting down now on the edge of the bed flipping through the channels on the television, at least nothing has changed. It hadn't worked the first time we were here and still doesn't work. The bed was damp in the center, pushing it to the other side of the room. I hadn't cared if it was directly under the window. At least I wouldn't be dripped on. Not waiting long my dad knocked at my door. Mom hadn't wanted to risk seeing my room even though it was too early to mess it up yet. Walking over opening the door, I accepted the sheets and blanket closing the door behind me. My dad and I never did talk but I still felt close to him. We kept it simple. Besides, I knew if I ever had a problem, I could talk to him. Both of my parents pretty much gave up on getting a conversation out of me when I was little, it's not that I didn't have anything to say or was shy. I just saw them every day, so life gets a bit familiar and boring, just nothing new to share.

After making my bed. I opened the door again letting Max in, he always slept with me every night instead of staying in his crate to sleep. In any other room, he would get bored chewing everything from chair legs to wall paneling. He was a pretty good dog just a permanent puppy mentally. In my room he only chewed on my socks, I never blamed him. It gave me the excuse never to have to wash them. Lying down on the bed with my iPod, I turned it on playing my favorite music as I watched out my window. I just hoped that tomorrow it might not be raining, and I could go walk to my favorite spot. I didn't even have to look down to know Max was trying to get comfortable after circling so many times, he finally just plopped down on my legs and was soon snoring, at least I could feel the light vibration from his body on my legs. Not that I could have heard him or the rain. I had my music up loud as I kept my eyes closed.

I wasn't sure why but for the last few years I had only been able to fall asleep this way, or I always seemed to hear voices that just were not there. I could barely understand what they were saying, and it always seemed as though one hated me intensely and blamed me for everything while the other was trying to get them to understand something. For the most part, it's what I had guessed. I was probably wrong about the whole thing. Instead of judging my sanity. I preferred to drown out the sounds than deal with them.

I had slept in until noon the next morning. At least my parents hadn't tried waking me but then they knew me by now. They were probably up extremely early as usual or as they liked to say. 'The early bird gets the worm,' they wanted to take advantage of a full day and not risk missing out on anything. This would seem fine, but I always felt if something happened, and they hadn't been looking for it, they never would have seen it anyway. Sitting next to the door whimpering a little. I knew Max was ready to get outside.

I never bothered to change the night before, so I was wearing the same outfit that had been damp from the rain and finally dried. Putting on my shoes, slipped my lighter into my pocket and attached his leash. Max pretty much dragged me out of the cabin. Walking towards the main footpath we set off walking into the woods. At night we might have had a chance to see other animals but during the day we rarely did other than squirrels. Max seemed in the mood for the hike today as we passed several other paths that would normally lead back, he almost seemed like he was running after something. I guessed he must have spotted something he wanted to go after. Heading out even further I knew which trail we would be taking, and it went past my favorite spot. A large gap between the mountains where only a walking bridge connected the two, the distance down was rather steep. I would stand out here for hours either watching the stars, feeling the wind blowing through, or just watching the stream far below.

Not many bothered to come out this far or along this pathway as it started to be filled in with weeds and grass, even a few small pine trees started taking it over. Trying not to trip over the roots that jutted out of the ground. Max was still hyper trying to run as I did my best to hold him back. I wasn't sure if I wanted to catch up with whatever he was interested in out here. I knew it was still the afternoon, but the weather changed so drastically here at times it was getting darker but then I think it was only because of the dense woods. Then it also caught my attention something had darted rather fast in the distance, and it was tall. I doubted an animal would be that tall and move that fast. I wish I had known it was going to run by so fast. I would have tried harder to see it and figure out what it was. I hesitated for a second not sure if it was a safe idea or not, but my curiosity did get the better of me. Allowing Max to lead we followed in the general direction the figure had gone. Heading way off the path. I was hoping not to find any old mining holes that hadn't been covered or any other surprises. Not that I haven't been in this direction before which surprised me, the old castle was in this direction. I wondered if the thing we saw was heading towards it.

Not far in the distance, I could see the castle not that it was a rather looming one but certainly beautiful. There was a rather large rock if you were to climb over it and go a short distance. You would end up at the lake on the other side. This side was the only part of the castle that showed, and it blended in so if you did not know it was there you would miss it. The rest of it had been built into the rocky mountain. The trees around it had grown up a lot even the vines were covering more of it this time. Pretty soon it might just disappear from site since no one came this way. The only evidence that was left had been the vines that grew over the door. They were broken allowing someone or something through the doorway. Turning the handle and pushing what was left of the door, the inside was rather dark. Stepping in and closing the door behind. I reached into my pocket pulling out the lighter I had brought with me. Flipping it so it would spark I could see the mini torch on the sidewall. Taking it down I lit it, no longer needing my lighter I put it back in my pocket. At least the torches still had some use left, in other rooms there were oil lamps. Dust was everywhere and cobwebs were strung all over the ceiling and wall. I could spot a few spiders but nothing massive. We kept walking into the large room. I was always impressed with this part of the room. Straight ahead had been one large room with a very high vaulted ceiling not that I had ever measured but I would have guessed a twenty-eight-foot ceiling with a staircase on either side of the room directly along the stone wall leading to the upstairs. There were several rooms up there with only the one main one down here. Whatever it was that did not want to be seen, did not do a very good job at covering their tracks. I found two shoe prints right in front of the stone wall directly at the far end under the staircases. A rather strange place to find it. How could a human run that fast?

I knew I had just woken up but by now I wasn't that groggy? Taking a closer look at the footprints, they looked rather large, placing my foot next to them they were wider and much longer than my own. Touching the wall with my hands I knew Max wouldn't go anywhere. I dropped his leash as I tried to push the wall. Not that it looked like it could be moved but then there could have been a secret room in here and I might not have known about it. Daniel might have wanted to keep some secrets. Sadly, I couldn't even find cracks of any kind that would have indicated there was another room behind it. Walking back over to the base of the stairs I walked up the far-right side. Neither stair had led the same direction. Although both led upstairs, there was a wall that split the hallway in two. The bedrooms were on the other side. I preferred this side because of the personal library. The difference between these books and any other books around had been the fact I had never heard of these titles or authors before, let alone the simple difference that intrigued me. Each book had been handwritten. No printing from a store or factory, each one had its unique penmanship in some form of calligraphy. The walls were completely lined with books only with a few chairs and a table in the center, a harp over in the corner next to a very old pipe organ. I didn't risk touching the harp. All the strings had rusted. I didn't want to risk breaking one or cutting my finger on it again.

Thankfully I always carried a tissue with me. My allergies were being bothered being in here. The floors and walls were so dusty. I figured we came out this far I would take two books back with me and return them once I was done. As many as I had read it never seemed like I would get to the point where I read every book here. As I looked along the lower shelves I noticed a few books at the end, they hadn't been covered in the dust almost as if they were new. Pulling one out I hadn't recognized the name of the author. It was another mystery; those had been my favorite. Balancing the torch in one hand and stacking the four books from the end picking them up planning on taking them with me. I noticed something different. When the book had tapped the back of the bookcase that held it, I had assumed was rock, but the rock wouldn't make that hollow sound. Looking around me to see if I noticed anything else had changed, I noticed a heel mark, not even a full footprint. One other thing I noticed had been Max's reaction. The fur on his back was straight up as he started to grit his teeth with the lowest growl. Huskies are known for being working dogs, more of a sled dog but more importantly for their gentle friendly, and loving disposition. I had never seen him like this before so whatever was bothering him, he was trying to protect me from it. Next thing I knew something grabbed my hand. I had been resting it on the bookshelf. The hand was human, large, and extremely dirty. The only thing I could make out had been the skull ring with the bright red gem it had for eyes. Not sure why but more out of shock I screamed. It echoed around the room. Max leapt up and bit the hand that grabbed me. Letting go both Max, and I made our way down the stairs and out of the castle as fast as we could go, I didn't even have time to put the leash back on Max. I wanted to get as far away from that place as I could.

As soon as I wasn't in danger anymore Max treated it as a game. If I ran, he followed me occasionally running ahead of me. I had lost him before when he was off his leash mainly from his curiosity, he had taken off a few times exploring only to be brought back by my neighbors or someone else who had found him. We kept his name tag and information on his collar. As we made it home and I was almost out of breath. Max ran into the house and up the steps ahead of me. Standing looking bewildered had been my parents with guests.

"What is all the commotion for and why does Max not have his leash on? I don't want to spend all summer searching for him." My mother asked in her pretending to be concerned voice.

Not that I wanted to explain what had happened, otherwise I would be under strict watch or prevented from walking in the woods again. I figured it would be best to play it dumb.

"I took his leash off so he could go in the water."

"The water is freezing, make sure he didn't leave any mud prints behind. I don't want this floor dirty and why are you out of breath? Both of you shot in here rather fast and without introducing yourself to our guests?" Mom started crossing her arms giving me the signal I was rather used to when she was angry.

"His feet are clean. I just raced him back. I had a spider drop on me, so I panicked." I didn't care to meet their guests.

It's not as if I was going to spend any time with them and I had just stepped in. How was I supposed to know they were there? Not bothering to say another word I walked out of the room. I could hear my parents mutter to the guest they had no idea where they had gone wrong raising me, that I was a college dropout, no prospects, disobedient, and most of all disrespectful. Closing my door so I wouldn't have to hear them anymore, I could already guess what they were still talking about. I had heard it all before.

In my defense yes, I had chosen to drop out of college. I was only short of graduating by twelve credits. My parents wanted me to go into the medical field. Something I wasn't interested in; I had wanted something else. I just didn't know what. I tried to keep jobs but sadly they just didn't work out. The first job I loved but I found out after I was hired. I was only keeping the position warm for a woman who had gone on maternity leave. The second job was dissolved, and the next four jobs were worded slightly differently but with pretty much the same effect my bosses didn't feel I was happy and would be better off somewhere else. I had felt either they didn't like my level of performance; some other reason for dislike or one of their family members or friends were taking over my job position. I had to admit though they were correct about one thing, I hadn't cared about the job. It was just a paycheck to me and not something I planned on making into a long-term goal. Usually, I was always friendly to my parent's guests but when I recognized who they were I hadn't cared. I doubted I had ever seen the couple they were with ever smile. If they could have, they would have set me on fire in my place for the angry stares I was getting from them. But for the main reason, I just didn't care, my parents had wanted a boy, not a girl, which is why my name is Teddy or short for Theodore. They were determined to use the name and when mom couldn't get pregnant again, I had ruined it for her.

Now that I was finally relaxing, Max was now laying down on his side on my bed. I noticed the pain in my wrist. It felt like I had sprained it. Under the black mud that had dried to my wrist, I could see just how red my wrist had turned. The whole area was swelling up. Getting undressed I stepped into the shower to get cleaned off while being careful not to touch my wrist any more than I had to. Not bothering to get dressed. I toweled off and then put on my bathrobe closing it, the pressure from the robe was already heavy on my wrist not that the sleeve weighed anything. Keeping it covered. I worked my way down the stairs. The others were in the living room talking so I tried to slip in around the corner into the kitchen. Not making any noise I had taken the ice bag out of the freezer and sneaked it back to my room. I hadn't wanted to explain why I was using it. I had to shove Max back a little to sit on the bed holding the ice bag. I couldn't get over how huge it had swelled. Whoever had grabbed my wrist squeezed it tight.

There wasn't very much that I could do to keep my mind off the pain. The next few hours went by so slowly. I had already taken several pain relievers. As the swelling started to go down. The pain only intensified. At least I hadn't heard voices from downstairs anymore. I could only guess my parents had gone to bed and their friends had left about an hour ago. Not risking leaving the normal way. I had risked the harder path. Pushing up on the window with one hand and sitting out on the ledge. I did my best to use only one hand while climbing into the tree. The sad thing is I know I was old enough to come and go as I pleased so why did I keep feeling like I had to hide everything I did now? It would be much worse if I were to fall out of the tree and break something else and have to explain why I was going out the window. Not that I wanted to explain any of it, and I knew they would be listening for the front door now. Jumping down from the tree that last little distance I walked into town, not that it was that far away but still long enough to deal with the sharp stabbing pain in my wrist.

Relieved I was finally at the hospital I had signed myself in. The nurse was surprised that I had walked all this way instead of having someone drive me in. After several x-rays, I finally found it wasn't a matter of having a sprained wrist. I had several hairline fractures in the Radius, Ulna, and Carpals, basically the wrist bone. At least the doctor gave me the good news that once it was bandaged, I would be able to go. My wrist was expected to heal even though I could tell he hadn't believed my story about falling down a hill and my hitting my hand on a tree. I had figured that sounded the most logical. The cast covered my entire left hand up to the elbow. I was offered a sling, but I figured with it being chillier right now. It would be easier if I wore a long sleeve sweater to cover the cast. A sling would be a dead giveaway that I had done something. Putting the pain pills the doctor prescribed to me in my pocket. I made my way home. I wasn't about to climb back up the tree again.

This time I used the front door and thankfully no one woke up to see who was coming in at such a late hour. Feeling so tired and drugged from the medicine. I laid down on the bed not even bothering to cover up. I fell asleep fast without even realizing I had fallen asleep before laying my head on the bed, Max had taken my pillow to sleep on. Again, I hadn't heard anyone come or go even though I was surprised to find my blanket no longer underneath me but covering me snug up around my chest with my hand propped up on a pillow. Max was sound asleep still at the foot of the bed as usual. I felt so comfortable I let myself sleep a few more hours.

This time when I woke up, I noticed a bit more in the room which I hadn't seen before. I wondered if mom put my things away while I was sleeping. All my clothes were hanging in the closet with the door open. All my undergarments were in the dresser with jewelry and a few pictures on top. The room hadn't looked like my bedroom at all; a few pictures were hanging on the wall of wolves. Even a small dark black rug was on the floor in front of the bed. There was a rather friendly note with a shower baggie next to it explaining how to place it around my wrist and arm so I wouldn't get the cast wet while I showered. It had felt good to stand under the hot water.

There was a change of clothes already folded and ready to be worn on the writing desk. Carefully drying off after getting out of the shower, trying not to touch my arm at all, I changed into the clothes not that I recognized them. I just hoped someone had not put them in here by mistake. It was a long sleeve black baggy sweater. It felt so soft almost like angora, but it didn't have quite the right look to it. A pair of black sweats with a silver line running down on either leg and even a pair of black knit socks were in the stack of clothing. The sleeves of the sweater covered my hand perfectly-being slightly too long for my arms. But then I guess it helped I wasn't that tall. I was only five foot two. There was another note left under all the clothing, and it read.

"I am very sorry about your wrist; it hurts to see you in so much pain. I promise to make it up to you. I hope I don't upset you with the gift of a new outfit and for cleaning up around in your room last night while you slept." The note hadn't been signed, and I didn't recognize the handwriting.

Both of my parents were home. It had been so quiet I had assumed they left. Getting a cup of instant coffee and dousing it with creamer. I had looked at both trying to figure out who would have come in and not woke me up after finding out I injured myself. Dad had looked up at me with an odd expression.

"Did you need something?" He seemed more curious than anything.

"No, I'm set. I just didn't remember covering up last night. It was chilly but I was so tired. I fell asleep before I had a chance to pull up the blanket." I figured that was enough to say in case either of my parents wanted to confess.

"I certainly wouldn't risk covering you up in that pigsty, now stand up straight or someone will think you were deprived of a proper nutrition, we don't need to be blamed for that and cut back on the creamer or you're going to end up fat." Not even looking at me she kept doing the dishes, so I threw in one more for them.

"Actually. All my clothes are hung up and the room is spotless. I figured you would probably like that." As soon as I had said it mom dropped the pan that was in her hand into the sink as both looked at me.

Not wanting to draw attention to myself I was about to walk out of the room when I heard my mother yell,

"Don't forget to find that leash. I don't want you losing that dog of yours again. I'm tired of paying for replacement leashes."

"Don't worry, I've always bought his leashes. I wouldn't expect you to. That's what I'm heading out to get now." Not that I wanted to risk it again but with the note, I had found I was just hoping not to walk into a worse trap.

My wrist was still hurting from being grabbed. At least I could guess it wasn't my parents in my room even though I wondered who would have gone into my bedroom and that Max allowed them to, he always alerts me even if someone is at the front door. It did give me the creeps the idea of whoever had grabbed me might have been in my room. Maybe during the day, I'll find out who it was. Not that daylight outside would help. It would still be dark inside the castle. Besides, who would have moved into Daniel's place? Taking an extra piece of rope and tying it to Max's collar. I had brought him along just in case. At least I felt safer with him. Not sure why but the walk to the castle seemed to take so much longer this time. But then last time I was trying to keep up with Max. He was in such a rush to get wherever he wanted to go. Hopefully, I will be able to take the books I had left on the ground after running away. I was curious what the person was going to be like and how he or she could have had so much strength to do that kind of damage to my wrist.

Soon enough I had seen the castle in the distance. There were no windows down below but on the second floor, there were two on either side of the very small towers. The one on the left could be looked out from the library and the one on the right was from the hallway just before the first bedroom. Someone was looking out from the library window not that I could make out who it was. The figure was too dark to recognize. I know I had hesitated before going any closer, and I think Max was picking up on how I was feeling. He hadn't seemed to want to go either or have a repeat of what happened the day before. Forcing myself to finish walking towards the castle. I wished Daniel had been here, his home was always safe with him but now there was this other person. I had no idea what to expect.

At the front door, there was a vase filled with red tiger lilies. My favorite flower was surrounded by baby's breath to fill in around them. Picking up the large clump of flowers, there was a note attached with my name in large bold writing. Opening it up and reading the inside it was another note of apology asking me to forgive the horrible mistake. What I had been hoping for had been some sign of who it was from or at least a name. Putting my hand out to push open the door, it already started to open. I was expecting to see someone standing there in front of me but instead, there was no one there. I didn't even have to search the entrance for a torch this time either. All the torches were lit on either side of the hallway along with several mini candles on the floor and petals lining the middle of the hallway leading into the main larger chamber room. Now I was beginning to wonder if the person was ever going to show themselves, or if they were trying to figure out how much damage they had done and if I was still angry at them? Or perhaps they were wondering how to finish me off? I wasn't sure what to think right now. Feeling braver than I should have been at this moment, it helped having Max with me. I had followed the petals and candles back into the library again.

Chapter Six

Not Really Gone

At least my path would be lit up as we both slowly walked up the stairs, I wasn't sure what to expect. A new little table sitting not far into the library had a bunch of books wrapped with a red ribbon that was set on it with a bunch of roses on the sitting chair. Looking around I hadn't seen or heard anyone, neither had I seen any footprints but then it looked as if someone spent some time dusting. Where the hand came through the bookcase was already fixed. I couldn't find a hole anywhere to explain how it came out from the other side. The note left on the books was rather interesting. It looked familiar just like one of the hand signatures in one of the books I had read. The books I picked out were all stacked and wrapped in the ribbon with two extra books. Picking up the letter with beautiful handwriting it said.

"*I am truly sorry for hurting you, for reasons I cannot explain. I couldn't exactly see you very well and thought you were someone else. I am a friend of Daniel's and was looking for him. Sorry, I couldn't apologize in person, but I need to be off. I wish you the best and the same. I saved the books you seemed to be here for,*

AFTER DARK

and I added two more I thought you might be interested in. It should keep you busy for your summer vacation. Sincerely Gerry"

The first thing I thought about had been how did he know I would be here just for the summer? I don't ever remember a friend named Gerry visiting Daniel before, not that I necessarily knew all his friends. Taking the books, I wanted to check out a couple of things before I left. Heading back downstairs I went up the other side of the stairs leading up, separated from the other side. I walked down the long hallway. There were a few bedrooms up here. I had never been in any of them even when I thought Daniel was gone. Now I was wondering if his supposed friend stayed in one of the rooms. I had to admit I was always curious about what they looked like. Not that it ever seemed like a regular home.

I was curious where his kitchen or living room was unless he spent all his time in the library or bedroom? I hadn't even stepped foot into his place until I was thirteen and that had only been for one simple reason, he had found out I loved to read, and he had a large library. Most of the time we spent time talking out in the garden, walking, or doing some other project. I was curious why my parents never wondered what I was doing or where I was, I think they were happy that I was out of their sight and not causing any problems. Probably just assumed I spent all my time at the playground while growing up on vacation. At least it was where they would eventually pick me up.

After he had disappeared, I checked several of the rooms out of curiosity, I had felt guilty for invading his personal space, but I wanted to find out if he planned on coming back at all. It was when I found every room was empty not that I would have known what was missing. Opening every door, each one had been empty, even the dust hinted no one had been in them. The last room is at the end of the hallway. I opened even slower than the rest of the rooms. I couldn't help but hope to finally find something. Stepping in I let out a rather deep sigh. I knew I shouldn't get my hopes up. At least there hadn't been any signs of anyone being in here. The last room had been his bedroom. The only thing I couldn't get off my mind had been how the person had grabbed my wrist from behind the bookcase. Looking out of the window, I could see the garden. The garden we spent a lot of time in was directly below. Looking at the swing he had put up for me when I was little brought back a few memories. It was the first time I had a crush on him or started to look at him differently, and then it would figure he would disappear. Sometimes I wondered if I had made him leave, but then it would have been rather drastic since I was only here for the summers.

I leaned against the wall for a moment, scanning the room. A sudden whoosh of air brushed past me and before I could react, the wall shifted behind me. It slid back, and I stumbled through, hitting the ground with a thud. For a second, I just sat there, stunned. The wall hadn't been real or at least not solid. I stared at the hidden space now revealed behind it. I hadn't expected a room back here, though clearly someone had found it before me. There had to be a better way in.

Pushing myself to my feet, I stepped into the narrow passage. It was surprisingly clean. No dust and no cobwebs. As if it had been used recently. I followed the corridor until I found a stairwell leading down, likely behind the main staircase in the living room. The darkness below was absolute. I couldn't see a thing. I reminded myself that Daniel never had trouble in the dark. I used to joke he was a vampire. He'd always laugh but never deny it.

Not wanting to stumble blindly, I retraced my steps to the main hall and grabbed two candles. Even with their light, the descent was uneasy. The flame barely cut through the gloom. I had to feel my way forward with each step, occasionally testing the ground ahead with my foot.

Somewhere off to the side, I heard a faint slosh. I knelt, holding the candle low. A thin layer of water covered the floor. I stood slowly, wondering if this was part of a cave system beneath the castle. It wouldn't be surprising. Most of the structure had been built into the mountainside, all the way to the water beyond. There was even a balcony that overlooked the lake. I'd always thought it strange. A castle this deep with so few rooms. They were large, yes, with towering ceilings, but it never seemed like enough space. Now I knew there was more. I'd found it.

So far, the hidden passage held nothing remarkable, only its secrecy. Still, I had to keep going. Something had to be waiting at the end. After a while there was a bit of a strange scent, I wasn't sure right away what scent; I kept taking in deep breaths before figuring out what exactly it was. Something I wasn't expecting since I hadn't seen any person or animal. the smell was moldy and sweaty. It was something that hadn't taken a bath or showered in a while. I could barely make out the movement ahead of me.

"Who are you" I hoped whoever was hiding might respond to me.

"You shouldn't be down here; you need to leave." I still couldn't see who it was, but I would know the voice anywhere.

"How long have you been down here?" I had to kneel to see him since he was lying against the wall on the floor.

"I've been here for a while but it's not good that you know I'm here, you need to leave." His voice sounded weak as he spoke.

As I was getting closer, I could see he wasn't in the best of shape.

"What happened to you? Let me take you to the hospital." I tried to hide my reaction of him.

He had looked as if he was run over by a freight train. Just looking at him, his arm and legs were broken; his eyes were swollen shut along with half of his face so badly bruised. His chest even looked sunken as if his ribs were broken. I wasn't sure if I would be able to move him without him dying. How could he have lived down here for so long in this condition? Maybe it's why he hasn't been able to get out, but then what would have hurt him down here unless it was the same person who had injured my wrist?

"You can't take me to the hospital. I'll be fine. I'm already healing. I need a little more time. I can't have them find me. How did you find a way down here? If you found it, then they will. I need to find a new place to hide." Not able to see at all, Daniel was struggling to stand up.

In the condition he was in he struggled trying to get up but was only able to move barely an inch.

"Don't try to move. I think it's only going to make it worse. What did this to you? Who are you hiding from? There was a man here earlier, but I think he already knew about this place since he was able to hide behind the bookcase." I felt sick seeing him like this.

I couldn't begin to imagine what kind of pain he must have been in let alone the fact he tried to stand on two broken legs. He hadn't resembled the former physical self that I had known. From the first time I had met him until he had disappeared, if it hadn't been for his voice, I never would have recognized him. I could hear footsteps coming from behind me. Standing up quickly in front of Daniel I didn't want anyone getting to him in the condition he was in, especially if he was hiding from someone.

"Do you honestly think you can guard him against me if he couldn't protect himself?" The voice had let out a slight laugh.

This was the first time I had seen this person. I was going to guess this was the person who had injured my wrist.

"I would rather try than not at all." I hope I will be convincing enough.

"I can see why you kept her around for so long, again sorry for the wrist. I admit I wasn't the one who did it but can't lay the blame right now. I'll show you the way out, so you don't break another wall. After all, we do need to keep him safe. For now, if anyone asks you if you have seen him, he is still not corresponding with you and all you know is that he took off." As he tried to grab my arm to take me out, I pulled it away.

"Who are you? I can't leave him down here. Besides, how do I know you didn't do this to him?" I wasn't leaving him until I knew what was going on.

"I happen to be his brother. The one who is keeping him alive for now and if you keep poking your nose around, then you're going to get him killed and he's probably going to feel guilty if you die. So, it's best for all of us for now until things blow over and he's better that you not come back here or talk about him." I couldn't believe what I was hearing.

I had no idea he had a brother. He never spoke about him.

"Trust him. I'll be fine but it's not safe for you to be here. There are things I can't explain right now. I will if I'm able to later. I promise. But for now, you need to leave. When you hit the age of twenty, I never thought you would still be coming here on vacation. I never should have been involved with you, and you would never be around a dangerous person. I admit it was my mistake." As he spoke to me, I knelt next to him.

I wished I knew what was going on. Placing my hand on his shoulder. I hadn't known what to say other than the fact I didn't want to risk leaving him.

"There has to be something I can do." I couldn't stop the feeling of being helpless.

"There's nothing you can do; I can't do anything right now until I heal, and I just need more time. You need to trust me on this. When I'm able to I will find you no matter where you are, and I will let you know I'm safe. I have my brother for now protecting me. Now please trust me and go." I swear I could hear the pain in his voice.

Not wanting to make it harder on him, not that I wanted to leave. I leaned in and kissed him on the forehead, giving him the lightest hug hoping not to add to his pain. I then stood and followed his brother out. He had escorted me through the woods and back to the bridge that connected both sides of the town.

I watched as he walked away. I wasn't sure why I hadn't thought about this until this moment. He had told me he was sorry for my injured wrist and that he hadn't done it purposely. He promised me he would come looking for me when he was better. I wanted to make it as easy on him as I possibly could. I knew I wasn't going to stop obsessing over him and I would worry until I knew he was alright.

My parents had been out late this evening so thankfully no one was at the cabin. Leaving the books in my room. I took off for town to grab a newspaper. Even though it was a rather small town I hoped there might be a job available so that I could stay in the area. Thankfully I wound up getting a factory job in the town nearby. Not that anyone had questioned me over the next several weeks, my parents had been happy to have me out of their hair for a while. I had enrolled in the local college to finish the last few credits that I needed to graduate. At least with school and work it would keep my mind occupied. Otherwise, I had done nothing other than sit and worry about Daniel. I hated leaving him the way he had looked. I had to remember what he was like and know that if he made a promise to me, he would keep it. After all, he had told me once he never made a promise he couldn't keep. Which was true, every promise he ever made to me, he kept.

I had taken an entire day looking for an apartment. After a while, I found it was cheaper to rent a cabin all year long. It was cheap enough and the tourists dwindled enough. In the last month of summer, I had my cabin ready along with a few pieces of furniture. I just had to announce to my parents when they left that I wasn't going to be going back with them. I even managed to get a loan to buy a vehicle. I couldn't help it, but it was feeling good living on my own. I never would have imagined I would have wound up here or on my own. I knew Daniel was aware that I was here. I would find new books every so often left on my front steps or the ones I had already read, leaving them aside so they would be collected. I had kept my promise by staying away not that I could ever stop thinking about him. The day had come when I had to speak with my parents. Funny I had been sleeping at the new place, and they never once realized I wasn't with them anymore. Driving my car up the driveway. I was going to get it over with and thankfully this would be the last and only time.

I could see them both standing at the front door, I wasn't

looking forward to this. I hadn't done anything wrong, and I could see the angry look on their face as I now walked toward them. The instant look of disproval probably wondering whose car I borrowed and where I went with it. Walking in I had gone straight for the living room. I knew in this room they would follow me into.

"Whose car is that? It better not belong to a boy; I won't put up with you sleeping with boys under my roof. You have disgraced this family far too often, when we get home, you are seeing a psychologist." At least by now I was no longer surprised by their comments.

"Actually. There's a bit of a correction to that, I won't be seeing a psychologist, and I won't be going home with you. I have a job and a place that I'm renting. I haven't been here for the last month. Besides, I am twenty-five years old. If I want to sleep with someone that's my choice but I have never once attempted to do anything under your roof you wouldn't approve of. I'm tired of feeling as if I should do something to finally give you a reason for treating me like crap. Thanks for giving birth to me and handling your obligation as a parent but I'm taking over now, honestly I should have done this a long time ago and I don't know why I didn't. I blame low self-esteem, either way, its time. I'm moving out, I have my own life starting now so you won't have to bother with me anymore. I'm only here to let you know." I didn't have anything else to say.

I highly doubted they had either. Not bothering to sit down or go anywhere else in the cabin. I had already moved my things out and made one long road trip home to pick up what I had left there. I had entered my room through the window. Sad to know it was so easy to open from the outside. Not bothering to say another word I walked out. I didn't want to argue and at least I had kept my voice calm and surprisingly I felt calm. They hadn't even said a word to me as I went back to my car. No need to tell them I was going back to college or that the car was mine. I doubted they wanted to know or if it would have made a difference. Not bothering to look back I drove home.

I started playing either the radio or the television more often just so I could hear another voice. I took Max for so many walks even though I was sure he wasn't complaining. I had visited the bookstore so often I almost felt as if I was working there. Not once did I feel lonely but then it was kind of nice to know Daniel's brother was checking on me. Not that I saw him. He didn't have to show himself. I knew he was around. The factory job I had was only going to be a part-time job except before I had paid attention, I was working full time. More hours kept getting added on except the distraction was helping until this evening. Not that my job was difficult at all. Once the mail had been delivered to the company. All I had to do was sort out the mail and deliver it to each of the offices. Then after I would do light filing and other computer entries for the company, I expected to have another boring day. One thing I missed had been the friendlier groups. Everyone here pretty much stuck to themselves, not a very social place at all. Sitting down at my desk getting ready to read through the papers that needed to be entered into the computer, there was a rather strange note lying on top of the pile. I couldn't even tell which manager it had been from. The letter had been written on a strange-looking piece of parchment, no one that I knew of had office supplies of this kind of paper. Unfolding the paper, it read;

"There is a problem regarding the proofing you handled for us a few days back and they are left on the desk to be analyzed again. Please make the appropriate changes that are requested before the end of this business day. Office 23A in the basement is in ill repair after you left, if you would explain your conduct."

As far as I knew there were no offices in the basement other than a few storage rooms and a large filing room. Whoever wrote this was accusing me of messing up an office let alone doing proofreading which hasn't been on my schedule for the past several weeks. Looking all over the paper, it hadn't been signed except the writing which reminded me of the calligraphy from the books I had been reading from Daniel's home, only there was a slight change in the writing. Instead, many of the loops were a bit more exaggerated and not as tightly written as the ones in the book. Curious to find out what was going on. I worked my way down to the basement. I would have asked my manager except she had already left early for her lunch break. Not wanting to wait for the elevator I took the stairs down. Not that it was that many stairs since I was already on the first floor. I never had any reason to go to the other two floors since all my work was on the first floor.

Opening the door to the basement I couldn't see a thing the lights had been turned off, which didn't give me a good feeling about this. Reaching around to the sidewall at least there was a panel of switches there. I kept flipping them all up until every light was on in the basement. Looking around still not able to shake that creepy feeling I walked in slowly not sure what to expect. Work so far has been normal and if it hadn't been for the styling of the handwriting, I wouldn't have thought anything strange about it in the first place. There hadn't been very much in the basement. Only a few small storage rooms along the hallway, then at the far end a large open room with the larger items the company had stored down here. Even the holiday decorations were stored down here. Checking each door as I passed it, I came to the one I was looking for at the furthest down the hallway. No lights were on inside the room as I opened the door. No one standing inside either as I looked around, the room had been pretty much empty other than the desk, a single chair behind it, and one filing cabinet.

There wasn't anything on the desk, I hoped for a name plate or something to show whose office it might have been. All I could think was this had to be some practical joke to waste my time. Maybe someone was trying to get me away from my desk for a surprise or something. After all, my birthday was in three days. Turning around to leave, the door behind me slammed shut. There was a slight shadow that disappeared behind the frosted window of the door. I couldn't make out who it was, either way the door was not opening. I was locked inside and now I could smell something rather foul almost a rotten egg smell from the far corner hidden by the filing cabinet. Not knowing what to do I did the only thing I could think of. I wanted out so I grabbed the chair from behind the desk and started smashing it against the window as hard as I could. I might not have been able to get the door to move, but I was determined to break the window next to it. The first couple of times it did nothing but then there were a few cracks. I kept striking the chair against it as hard as I could, trying to break it until I broke enough of the glass window. Setting the chair down, I stood on it stepping on one part of the frame in the door window and then jumping out to the other side. I couldn't smell that awful smell out here, but I was already feeling dizzy. Whoever had locked the door had turned off all the lights. I couldn't see my hand in front of my face and feeling dizzy. I wasn't sure what direction I was facing. I could only guess by feeling my way even though I was hoping not to run into whoever lured me down here.

I could hear footsteps coming toward me, trying to be as quiet as I could I started moving in the opposite direction. I didn't want to run into anyone down here. Passing the room with the awful smell. It seemed as though it was getting worse in the room. I kept moving until the hallway had stopped and opened into our large storage area. I tried to picture what the room had looked like in my mind; everything was stored in the same places every time they were brought down here, and the machinery was all on the left side. The emergency door was also on that side. I did my best with my hands out in front of me as I walked straight ahead or at least I hoped I was still walking straight. I could hear a couple more footsteps behind me a bit fainter than before and now some whispering. I wanted to get as far away from whoever it was. I could see a small flash of light from what I guessed was a flashlight looking around probably looking to see where I was at. Now standing behind a large shelving unit that held several spare fax machines and copiers, it had been right in front of the emergency exit. Ducking down as the flash of light went overhead, I held my breath not that it helped. I just hoped they wouldn't figure out I was already over here.

As soon as the light shifted away, I felt my way to the corner, I knew there were stairs over there that should lead to the outside. I crept up the steps, trying not to make a sound. I felt around for the door at the top; cold metal met my fingertips. Locked. I pushed against it with everything I had, but it didn't move. An emergency door? Locked? Since when does that happen?

At the far other end, I could see the light from the main stairwell as three people left the basement. From the distance I could barely make them out other than the fact there were three people. As the door closed the last available light disappeared with it. Carefully heading back down the steps to the ground floor again. I sat against the storage cabinet when I felt something strange. The ground started to shake. I could hear several strange sounds. At one point. I thought I heard my name being called not that I ever heard footsteps or seen the door at the far end open again. I could hear my name being called both from behind and in front of me, but never once could find anyone that might have been there. I didn't want to move too far away from the emergency door not that I could get out from it. The ground started to tremble even more as I heard what sounded like explosions. Something small but hard hit me on the head as I realized the ceiling was caving in. Pulling out two of the extra printers from their little cubby under the stairs, I climbed in, better they get squished by what's falling than me.

I could see what was falling overhead. Huge pieces of the ceiling were collapsing down into the basement. I tried to tuck myself back as far as I could even though my leg still was grazed by a large piece of cement. Everything started happening so fast. The basement no longer looked like one as the other floors caved in. Oddly enough I still hadn't seen anyone. Not that I wanted to see anyone, but it was strange I was the only one down here now. I waited until the shaking from the building stopped. It took quite a while for the debris to stop floating down. Some of it stung my throat as I tried to breathe in air. My leg was burning and there was quite a bit of blood on the ground. I kept hearing my name being called by someone except I didn't recognize the voice. I tried looking in the direction it was coming from. I still couldn't see anything. Strange how one voice could shift so much. There was a huge slab of concrete blocking my way. I could crawl underneath it. I just didn't know if I would be able to go further, besides that, I was still worried the slab would end up shifting and falling on me.

I knew I couldn't stay here forever so I had to try something. Other than someone calling my name. I couldn't hear anything else. Not sure what possessed me not to call out. I felt I had lost my voice not that I wanted to let anyone know where I was. Something at the back of my mind kept telling me to keep silent, that nagging persistent self-intuition that always seemed to pop up at times. Sliding out from my somewhat safe spot. I squeezed myself through the small hole. Looking up I was going to have to climb over a few things, but I could see sunlight not far from where I was at. Moving carefully across the pieces there were wires and other sharp metal pieces sticking out of the concrete. It felt like forever, but I made it to the sidewall that still stood. Working my way out through the small crack. Once outside, I looked back at the building that once stood over me, I was almost in shock. All three floors had caved in on top of me. I was extremely fortunate to be at the end I had been, otherwise I doubted I would have made it out alive. Looking around I hadn't seen anyone and neither had I heard the person who had been calling my name anymore.

Where was everyone? I looked around seeing that the parking lot was empty. Other than my car and three others. I wondered if they were still in the building but then I hadn't heard anything. Walking around the outside to see if I could notice anything. Any kind of possible sign there might still be someone inside. I couldn't hear or see anything. It had been the weekend with fewer workers, but it still seemed a bit strange with no one around let alone anyone noticing that an entire office building just collapsed. Four other buildings could be seen from this site and those seemed rather strangely silent.

I was sure I was alright as I rested my hand on my forehead the way I normally would when I was thinking except this time the touch of it stung. Placing my hand out in front of me. I could see the blood, not just a little. My hand was completely covered with it running down my arm. I hadn't even been aware that I was injured but I also think I was still in shock any of this happened. Looking down at my shirt I could see where the blood had already dripped staining it. I started thinking I must have been numb since I hadn't felt much of anything at all. Walking over to my car. I was going to drive to the local police station except I noticed the door was unlocked and left slightly ajar. Not sure what possessed me to do this. I picked up a small brick piece of the building while standing back a little. I threw it at the car door. It might have been out of insanity, but I kept getting that nagging feeling something else was wrong. As soon as the piece hit the door, bright red and orange embers exploded from inside of the car billowing outward and kicking up a strong wind current. It had not only knocked me off my feet but also blew me backward several feet. Someone wanted to make sure I was dead. Laying on the ground everything had turned completely white before I blacked out.

When I had woke up, it was dark out. I could only guess I had been here for several hours, and everything looked the same except my car was now smoldering rather than having an intense flame. The other two cars were gone however the building itself was not roped off with police tape and still, no one was around. How could everyone disappear like this? Why hadn't anyone been by to either work or realize what happened? Did I lose my mind and imagine all of this? Then I realized if I had imagined it all, then I wouldn't be dealing with the physical part of it. My headache was very convincing. Wiping my forehead, I had blood dried all over as my arms and hands were now bloody from being thrown back and a few pieces of stone from the ground embedded into my skin. Already in enough pain. I pulled out the foreign pieces not that I felt anything. I was either in shock, numb or in enough pain that it hadn't registered mentally or physically yet. I felt so weak and dizzy I wasn't thinking about where I was going. All I knew was that I wanted to get as far away from this place as I could. I had lived fifteen miles away. I knew I could walk it except the idea of walking even one mile wasn't exactly what I wanted to do either especially with the way that I was feeling. I had walked rather slowly through the back acreage. I knew as soon as I was at the end of the property I would be walking through the woods in the dark. I could barely see with all the trees blocking out the moonlight. I could barely make anything out even after my eyes had adjusted slightly. At this point I had nowhere to go, I couldn't go see Daniel. They said they were going to hide somewhere else until he was better, and my parent's home was two states over not that it was an option. I wasn't even sure if going back to my apartment was going to be safe. After walking for a while, I barely had the energy to hold myself up as I tripped over the slightest tree root. Falling to the ground I didn't even bother getting up. At least I was fortunate it was a warm evening, it's either that or from feeling numb, my brain was going to let me believe I was any temperature I had convinced myself it was.

Chapter Seven

Not What I Would Assume

Not wanting to move I lay still not that I thought I could move. The energy just wasn't there. I was only aware of the hours ticking away when I would occasionally look at my blood-covered wristwatch to check the time. This last time after sleeping a while I was woken by footsteps. I wasn't sure who it was at first but at least when they spoke, I could figure out who they were, and this was the last situation I had wanted to be in. Laying still I had hoped they would assume I was dead and leave me alone not wanting to get caught with me. Unfortunately, it wasn't what they were planning.

"Think she's dead? She's covered with blood." The one voice was slightly above a whisper.

"If she's not dead we need to kill her. She can't live and be allowed to talk to Lucian or anyone else about this. Check to see if she's alive." The other had not sounded to certain himself.

"How do I know if she's alive? She's human... she is... human, isn't she?" I could hear the one slap the one who had just spoken.

"Yes, she's human, she would have a beating heart if she's

alive, hurry up and check I have a weird feeling we're not alone. Check her neck also, see if she's wearing the pendant." I could feel a rather cold hand reaching down to touch my throat as it recoiled back rather fast with a rush of air running over the top of me causing a huge cracking sound. I panicked thinking they had broken my bones except I hadn't felt any more pain. Was I already dead? Why did they want the pendant? The last time a coworker was trying to look at it and pulled too hard on it as he stepped back, I had only saved the pendant before it hit the floor. I now wore it on my ankle bracelet because the necklace was too destroyed to have it fixed. Looking up to see what was delaying my death, all I could see was a pure white arctic wolf standing between me and my attackers. Struggling to get up. I hadn't wanted to get in the middle of it except I couldn't help but silently thank the wolf for slowing them down. Still feeling dizzy I leaned against a tree. Unfortunately, I wasn't going to get very far as I watched the one come running at the wolf at such a fast speed. All I had seen were the leaves below his feet picked up into the air as he charged the wolf in front of him. I wasn't sure if it was my eyes playing tricks on me from losing so much blood or if they were moving so fast.

Standing up while leaning against the tree. I could hear the wolf howl as the one standing over it. Grabbing a rock, I threw it as hard as I could at the man standing over it. As I threw the stone just a small bit of momentum pushed me against the tree, and I lost my balance again falling to the ground. Looking rather amused the man looked over at me smiling as he left the injured wolf on the ground, he moved towards me.

"I think a mosquito licked me." Never once taking his eyes off me.

"Don't you mean a mosquito bit you?" Stopping for a second, he broke his gaze to look at his partner.

"Are mosquito's a special creature?" The other guy just shook his head in disgust.

"She's stalling. Just kill her while I finish with Lewis." Starting to make a move towards the wolf. I wondered if he knew the named wolf. Did he know his owner? Just like before I felt more wind rush past me not being able to see them until they had come to a stop. There were at least four other wolves now. Then I had seen something I hadn't expected to see, and I wished I hadn't. The two had taken after the one in front of me as one protected the injured wolf. The second man had left his partner to deal with the wolves alone while he fled at an alarming speed while his partner was getting ripped to shreds. It was so gruesome I had wondered if I had done the right thing trying to protect the wolves even though they were the ones keeping me alive right now. Were they going to come after me once they were done with him? Almost as if they could hear me, the one had walked over to me not that I could have outrun it the way I was feeling. I stood still hoping they were not going to destroy me as they had with him. At least it will be over quickly. Now leaning into me I thought this must be it, it's all over. After a minute or two, the wolf simply leaned against me as the other two seemed to be caring for the injured one.

Moving over slowly to him I kneeled. Neither of the others seemed to be upset that I was approaching him. Not that he was too heavy. I looked him over seeing that most of the blood was coming from where the flesh had been torn away from his front shoulder blade, and along the side he was damaged rather badly, his rib was sticking out through his skin. Carefully placing my arm under his head and good shoulder, then I lifted his back end. I was determined to help him. I had planned to take him to the vet. I wasn't sure where the energy had come from other than sheer stubbornness. The other wolves were making noises making it look as though they wanted me to follow them. Maybe they wanted to show him to their owner? Deciding to follow them, it wasn't as if I even knew where I was right now, they had at least gone slow enough I could follow. We had walked for quite a distance. I was hoping we were going to end up somewhere when I had seen smoke in the distance coming from a little cabin. Walking up to the front door a young woman walked out with a worried look on her face.

"What happened to you Lewis?" Holding the door open as I entered, she said, "set him on the table. I'll take care of it. You can sit in the living room, Kara, Mia, and Kenneth will take you there." As soon as she had said this, I expected to be escorted by the other wolves except a young man was wearing gray sweatpants and a very tight t-shirt revealing a rather muscular form.

The two young girls standing there were wearing all white sundresses and no shoes. Not saying a word, they waved their hand toward the other room. Walking out in the direction they pointed. I sat on the couch not that I wanted to get the couch dirty even though I was sure by now the blood was well dried. I was curious how this woman had wild-looking wolves with her let alone why she was living way out here where there seemed to be no roads to her cabin. Maybe she wanted privacy? Not talking the girls had left me sitting in the living alone as they all had left. Not long after they went outside, I heard wolves howling. How many were there in this area? Not having to wait for very long. The young woman who was taking care of the injured wolf came into the room.

"I have a change of clothes you can wear if you want to get out of your bloody ones. I'm sure you're about my size." Before waiting for my answer, she handed me a towel with some clothes, "the shower is at the end of the hallway." Standing up I had taken the clothes from her.

I didn't know who she was, but I did want to get out of my clothes, even my skin felt like it itched from being so dirty. Walking down the hallway I noticed the other doors were open, one, in particular, had a very little girl sitting on her bed engrossed in reading a book. Then I realized what book it was. In bold letters, it read, 'principles of psychology,' not exactly a book I would have assumed a child, maybe around eight or nine years old to be reading. It had looked like it might be at least six hundred pages for being a thick textbook. Closing the bathroom door behind me. I was beginning to wonder what kind of household this was. Even though everyone seemed nice enough my attention was on the hot water that was now running over me. It felt so good to be rinsing off. I could have slept in here I was so tired, sad it hadn't hit me until now that I was eventually needing to head home to see what condition it was going to be in. After all, those guys seemed rather intent on killing me and who knows what the guy that got away was going to do. He knew I was still alive and temporarily protected by those wolves, not that I knew where they had gone to? I still couldn't believe what I had seen, while I was in the shower though I heard a rather distinct male voice.

"I wonder what those guys were after her for? She's only human and doesn't seem to with it. Might be because she lost so much blood, not sure if they had already done that to her but it would be hard to believe she would have made it that far, they would have killed her before that. I just don't know if it's safe to let her leave if they wanted to kill her, they won't stop until they do, after all, they work for Katherine." The man seemed rather sure of his opinion.

They were speaking low enough that I had to strain over the water not that I wanted to turn it off. I wanted to keep hearing what they were saying, they might not speak about it if they knew I was listening.

"Should we be keeping an eye on her?" The woman seemed concerned but also had a bit of a quiver in her voice.

"Not sure if they showed up again, they could have Katherine with them even though it might give us an idea if it has anything to do with Lucian and Jacob? I'll keep an eye on her for a while; it might have been a fluke that they ran into her out in the woods." The woman hadn't seemed convinced enough.

"Even if they had just run into her in the woods then why was she covered in blood? The girls said there was some activity up north. A large group of vampires clashing; they weren't sure if it was just with themselves or if they were destroying something? Whatever it was she might be from that?" Not wanting to hear another word I wanted to leave.

Vampires? Did they exist? Is that what I had seen

standing over me almost ready to kill me in the woods or were these people crazy and how could he have found me. I was found by wolves, not a human. Great, now they have me thinking that way and I haven't even talked to them yet. Shutting off the water and drying quickly. I put on the clothes she had given to me. Stepping out of the bathroom I could see the young couple at the end of the hallway waiting for me.

"Hi, I'm Lewis, do you live in town? I don't remember seeing you before?" He seemed rather curious, at least it was an answer I didn't mind giving.

"My name's Teddy. I moved here a couple of months ago, but I haven't seen much of anyone since. It's strange. Back where I was, people vanished at night. Here, it feels like the whole town disappears during the day. Streets empty, houses quiet, like the place is holding its breath. There's no one around to talk to let alone befriend. I was still up north when... everything changed."

I wasn't sure I was ready to tell them more, not yet. Even if they did seem like the kind you could trust.

"I'm Evangeline, Lewis is going to get Wolfie, and he will lead you to town, don't worry about returning the clothes. I have a lot of them. If you don't want to head back, you're welcome to stay here for the night, and we can bring you into town in the morning." As soon as she had said this, I felt a small cold hand take hold of mine.

I looked down and saw the little girl that had been reading a rather impressive book was now standing next to me smiling.

"I'm Amanda. If you stay it will be like a slumber party, we haven't had anyone stay over in a long time. At least not since my cousin used to sleep over but she's moved away. You can be my new friend now." Not waiting to hear my answer she was already leading me back down the hallway.

"I guess I'm staying the night?" Both Evangeline and Lewis seemed rather relieved not having to send me off into the night.

Even I was glad I didn't have to decide. My nerves were

too shot to think straight. I left the choice to the little girl. My body ached with exhaustion, and the thought of wandering through the dark again made my stomach twist. Knowing my luck, I'd trip over a rock and knock myself out cold. Amanda led me into a strange, almost eerie room. The carpet was a deep forest green, and the walls had been hand-painted to look like a thick, shadowy rainforest. It felt like the trees might start whispering if I listened too closely.

At the center stood a canopy bed, draped in hunter-green lace, shredded and worn as if it had survived decades of storms. The tattered fabric hung low, brushing the floor like ghost fingers reaching out. A dark green comforter covered the bed, with crisp white sheets tucked beneath it. I ran my hand across it, puzzled—it wasn't goose down. The texture was unfamiliar, almost too still, like it was holding its breath.

Then Amanda stepped in front of me and pulled out a narrow trundle bed from underneath the main one. It was already made up. My heart gave a small, anxious flutter. Did she expect me to sleep down there? And if so... why?

"You get the bed. I get the pull-out. It's only polite. Besides, I like the pull-out. If you snore, I can slide it back under and sleep in my room." She was already pulling back the covers as I went to the other side of the bed to climb in leaving my shoes on the floor.

Covering up at least I knew I was going to be warm. The blanket was already generating so much heat. I was worried if the little girl was going to be too cold.

"Just in case you're wondering, the comforter is filled with lama wool. We have our lamas, and we use their wool for pillows, blankets, and making clothes. My thin blanket is made from the same and just as warm. Goodnight, I'll see you in the morning." As she said her last few words, it hadn't taken her long to fall asleep as soon as she had turned, I could hear small hums from her breathing.

Laying back I was wondering what I was going to do if they were right, did I have vampires who wanted to kill me, and if so, why? The men had mentioned Lucian but then so had Evangeline. Who was this person?

"So why were you covered in blood earlier? I figure your thinking loud enough I might as well ask." The little girl propped herself up waiting for an answer.

"I'm sorry I wasn't aware. I was talking out loud, sorry I woke you up." I hadn't even realized she had woken up until she spoke to me not that I was sure her parents would be happy if I told her and not them.

"You can trust me; you can't blame me for being curious and besides, if we are going to be friends it helps to know what trouble you're in or I can't help you." She seemed so sweet as she offered her potential help even though she was a child.

"I doubt your parents want me talking to you about this, I appreciate your offer to help but trust me you don't want anything to do with this. One thing I wish I knew right now is where everyone disappears during the day. I've been around for a few months already and your family is the first ones I've met." Lying back staring at the ceiling.

I had just realized it was also painted with a night scene with shiny stars. It was amazing. I would love to have my room look like this.

"Mom's hand-painted this room, there are lots of people around, but you have to be out at night since they sleep during the day." A town that sleeps during the day instead of at night, possibly a lot of night shift workers.

I guess that would explain why not many worked the hours I had.

"So why were you so bloody, is it the same ones that attacked Lewis?" She seemed to be rather curious about who attacked their pet.

I guess I would have been also.

"You mean the wolf? Isn't your dad named Lewis also? Your pet saved my life from those men. I'm glad your wolf is safe. At least I'm assuming he is. Let's just say I had a bad night and fell a lot." I hadn't wanted to tell her and upset her parents by scaring their daughter.

"Why did you move here?" Basic enough question I guess I could answer that.

"I found a job here right away and close to the town that I am familiar with." Still leaving out the information I was sure she was too young for.

"Any boyfriends?" Not a question I expected to be asked.

Her expressions hadn't changed much from each question. She would have made a great poker player.

"Not exactly." Keep it simple.

"How can someone not exactly be your boyfriend. They either are or they are not?" I couldn't help but smile.

"Life gets complicated as you get older. It's someone I care very much for except we have never gone that far. It's just complicated." I haven't talked to a kid in a while so I was wondering when the questions about movies, television shows, school, or even makeup would be brought up.

"So, was it your blood on you or someone else's? I'm assuming yours since you have cuts on your forehead, my aunt Rose is a klutz, but she never looked as awful as you did." She seemed to be eyeing me over.

"Yes, it's my blood. I would have to say this is a first and hopefully a last for me." Sitting up further from her bed she let out a deep sigh.

"Alright, if you're not going to trust me, I'm going to my room to sleep. You're too boring. We can still be friends though. Goodnight." Standing up she walked out of the room leaving me there surprised by what she said.

Definitely an interesting little kid. Laying back down watching the stars on the ceiling I fell asleep myself.

Waking up in the morning I felt bad taking advantage of the hospitality of the couple when I had found I slept in till three in the afternoon. I was surprised they hadn't tried to wake me as I woke to light music being played in the background. Standing up I put my socks and shoes back on going out into the living room. There in the corner, I could see Evangeline playing the upright piano rather lightly.

"I'm sorry if I woke you." She seemed rather sweet that she would have let me sleep in even longer.

"I probably should have woken up several hours earlier. Sorry if I delayed your plans today. I should be getting home." Lewis had joined us from the kitchen smiling.

"I'm heading to town right now so I can take you if you don't mind; Amanda has a dance class to attend. Where in town are you heading to? If your home isn't too far, I could probably drop you off at home instead." Most would have avoided me after the way I had shown up with their pet injured.

My not talking too much about the night before. They went out of their way to help me out.

"I live right in town by the little park; it's the white cabin." It had been a rather large white Victorian house turned into four apartments rented out as a cabin in the summers.

I had the upstairs with a small balcony that wasn't likely to support a bird if it stood on it. I was looking forward to getting home, even though they've been extremely nice it would be nice to have some privacy so I could plan on what to do. I knew it wasn't safe to go back to work but then I also wondered if anyone had called. Lewis lifted Amanda to get her into the old pickup truck. As she sat in the middle, I sat on the far side looking out the window as we took off for town. Stopping right in front of the house I got out thanking Lewis for the ride home.

"If you need anything our phone number is on the card, we don't mind helping out especially since you're new to town." Smiling both waved to me as they left.

Turning to walk in I checked the mailbox to see if any of my mail had been forwarded here yet. It was still empty. Closing the lid, I went to the back of the house and walked up the steps that were not covered up to my door. I guess I shouldn't have been too surprised to find my place a mess not that anything had looked like it was missing. What was I supposed to do, call the police and tell them what happened? I had a hard time believing it myself. Sadly, not one message had been left. There were only two old ones left by two of my friends who seemed shocked that I had picked this place to live. It had taken me the next several hours to clean up my bedroom. There wasn't anything they had left untouched. What could they have been after? I didn't have very much to begin with, and certainly nothing of value. Picking up my phone I called work to see if anyone would answer or what recording might pick up. All I had heard was 'this service is temporarily unavailable, no alternative numbers are available at this time the voice had stated, not one I even recognized. Turning on the little television set that I had there was nothing on the news about it, just old programs and I had yet to find a local weather or news station. I wished I could have seen Daniel; I was wondering how he was doing unless whoever was doing all of this was after him? Maybe they found out I knew him and were trying to find him? They had told me they were leaving his home for a while until he was stronger, and it was safe, so I didn't know how long it was going to be. Was I crazy for waiting around, after all, I had to admit that Amanda, she was right how could we not exactly be dating?

I had put a single nail just above each window to make sure they couldn't be opened while I slept. Tonight, came way too fast, not that I was tired since I had slept in so late, much later than I was used to. I had felt bad since Max had been left out in the backyard for so long, not that he seemed to mind it. His auto feeder and water dish were outside. He loved being outside especially when the weather was cooler. At least having him with me, I felt a little safer except being a husky he was more likely to lick strangers to death than to protect me from them. I did want to see how alive this little town would get at night but then the factory had been the first place I had heard of. I was beginning to wonder if this place was a ghost town since the grocery store was closed during the day. I was getting tired of heading to the town next to it to buy food. I would have lived somewhere near our old summer cabin except it had been rather expensive there. Just out of my price range. Replacing the jogging clothes with a pair of my dark blue jeans and black blousy shirt. I would have worn a necklace with it except apparently the intruders hadn't wanted my jewelry, but then they also didn't want me wearing any of it. The chains were either broken, or the necklace pieces were smashed to pieces. The only jewelry that was intact had been the ankle bracelet that I still wore. Stepping out of my apartment. I walked along the sidewalk since the town was close enough, I didn't need a car not that it mattered anymore. It was blown to bits. I highly doubted my insurance company covered a car that was blown up and having to give them an explanation it would have been easier to get a used one.

Amanda had been correct; every store had its lights on and even the bar was alive with music. Walking into the bar there were neon lights on the walls. It looked like a very typical dance club and bar; the only thing is I had seen this in larger cities and not in such a small town like this. The music had a rather reggae and salsa sound to it, a very fast upbeat tempo. Walking over to the bar I ordered a basic coke; I didn't want to risk drinking anything. I wanted to stay alert and aware of everything around me. There was a live band that I hadn't heard of except they sounded good. Sitting down I watched as everyone danced wondering where most of them lived and since there were so many people here, where did they all disappear to during the day? Even if the majority of them worked or were up at night it seemed that some would be up during the day. Before I could even think of anything else I was being tapped on the shoulder.

"Dance?" Not saying much as I looked up into his eyes I wondered if I should.

"I don't know how to dance." Smiling I had thought it would be fun except I felt guilty not that I should, I wasn't dating anyone I was just hoping.

"Then tonight's your night. I'll teach you to dance." Not waiting for a response, he reached for my hand, he was now leading me out to the dance floor.

Turning me rather quickly to face him, he held me close

as he led me around the dance floor moving rather quickly, he would tell me to either move my left or right foot a little, and with his hip movement, he naturally moved my body right along with him and the music. For a moment I had forgotten that I didn't know how to dance. I fell right into step with him. Without doing any of the added flairs several of the other dancers were doing. I never would have assumed I didn't know how to dance. Moving around from one end of the dance floor to the other. I was relaxing and getting into it. I wished I had known about this before. I was having fun. Besides the two men trying to kill me, maybe this place might finally have some potential after all. This was what I needed to take my mind off everything. After spending several hours here, the place was starting to dwindle. I had never stayed at a dance club this long before. The place was already closing; looking out the door when a couple had left there was a hint of daylight already. I knew I was preoccupied and wound-up dancing with a few different people. I hadn't realized just how much time I enjoyed myself here. I was planning on coming back again.

A few of my new friends had given me their phone numbers hoping I would call to either hang out or let them know when I was coming back to the club again. On my way out, the bartender had handed me a small piece of paper. Opening it up it was a job offer. I had never worked in a bar before, but I was sure I didn't want to go back to work at my old place, that is if it was ever rebuilt. Filling out the application necessary, the lady handed me a schedule for work and the great part had been the clothing requirement. Absolutely no uniforms. I could wear anything I wanted. Happy that I had a job I headed for home. On the way home I felt like I was being followed, which I was right. I was. One of the wolves from Lewis and Evangeline's home came standing next to me walking me to the door of my apartment. As soon as I was there it had taken off. Closing my door, I almost expected to find everything destroyed again, but at least it stayed cleaned up. I hoped they wouldn't come back here, if they had I didn't know where to go. Making sure the deadbolt was locked along with the three other little locks on the door. I took Max to my bedroom. Taking a quick shower, I climbed into my bed almost wishing I had the comforter from Amanda's house, it was so warm. At least it didn't take long to warm up. Max had laid next to me sharing his heat, so I fell asleep.

The next night I was ready to go to work, even though I was still curious about my last job and why no one had called to see if I was safe, unless my boss was in on it? There was still no news about the building falling apart the way it had. There hadn't been any storms or earthquakes to start it so I wasn't sure it would be strange if someone had gone to that length to kill me. If they had, then why not a second attempt? Not that I wanted one. I just couldn't figure it out. As I walked to work, I was followed by the wolf again. It seemed as though I was going to have an escort for a while. Maybe this is what Evangeline and Lewis meant by keeping an eye on me? Learning how to mix drinks and taking orders took a while to get used to. The place hadn't served too many food items, the drinks were more popular with only a few ordering food. Then I felt a tap on my shoulder, as I looked up it was the gentleman who I had danced with the first night I came into the club.

"I never did catch your name last night." As he asked it occurred to me, that I hadn't introduced myself.

But then we hadn't talked much last night. We spent the whole-time dancing being occupied with the music and fun of last night.

"My name is Teddy. And yours?" He had a familiar smile cross his face as he heard my name.

"A rather unusual name for an unusual lady, my name is Erick. Are you enjoying working here?" As he asked, he sat down on the barstool.

"I still need to memorize many of the drinks, other than that, I love it. I get to listen to music all night and it's great it changes every night." I had to admit this was a great job.

I could help myself to any drink if I was able to keep up with the customers and I loved the music.

120

"Dance with me again?" As he held out his hand at least this time he waited before trying to whisk me off onto the dance floor.

"I would love to, but I'm working right now. I don't think they would like it too much." Smiling I was hoping he wouldn't feel rejected, but I didn't want to upset my boss and lose my job.

"I know for a fact the owner won't mind, he's my brother, I was hoping if you accepted the job, I would keep seeing you. Besides, there are more people working tonight than are needed." Taking the bottle I was pouring, he set it on the counter now taking my hand, he led me around the side of the bar.

I looked back at my boss as he watched his brother take me away from the counter. Waving at me to go have fun at least I felt comfortable heading out onto the dance floor with Erick. This was a very relaxed place. As we danced, he tried talking to me this time. It had helped the music wasn't such a fast tempo as it was the night before.

"I don't remember seeing you here before in town, how long did you say you've been here?" Holding me closer as we moved to another area on the dance floor.

"I've only been here a few months. My family used to stay in the bigger town next to here every summer. It's how I found out about this place. How long have you been here?" I was curious if he had been here long enough that he might know who Lucian was, but then I wasn't sure if I wanted to risk it in case he wasn't a liked person.

"My family has been here for almost as long as the town has been. You're getting much better at dancing." As he tried to compliment me, I knew my dancing hadn't improved.

"If I'm better it's only because I have a great lead." Smiling back at him he seemed rather happy with my response.

"Is the wolf outside a friend of yours?" I hadn't seen him when I walked in but apparently, he noticed the wolf.

"Actually. I met his owners for the first time a couple of nights ago. I had gotten lost in the woods." Nodding as he listened.

"He seems rather intent on following you. I thought you might have been a family member of theirs. They have a large clan but not too many stick around here for too long. If you don't have plans tomorrow on your night off, I was thinking we might watch a movie?" Thinking for a second, I knew I hadn't made any plans, but I hadn't seen a theater either.

"Is there a theater here?" Smiling back at me a bit more he seemed rather amused.

"No, we would have to go to the town over and catch a midnight showing; we could catch one around ten or eleven if you wanted to go to one earlier in the evening?" A movie could be fun even though I wasn't sure if I wanted to risk taking off in a vehicle with someone I didn't know too well.

I guess I already broke that when I got into the truck with Lewis and Amanda, but then that situation I felt safer since they had their kid with me.

"My sisters will probably come. They usually look for any excuse to meet new people. I'll meet you here tomorrow night. I should probably go see what my brother wants." Placing his hand on my back he pulled me along with him making a path through the crowd.

As he left to talk with his brother, I stood at the counter again making drinks for the last of the customers who had stayed for the last of the evening. By the end of the shift, I had been ready to leave for home I was so tired. Working nights took much more out of me than I thought it would. As I was stepping out of the club, Erick had come to say goodbye to me. The wolf was already waiting for me, and he didn't seem to like Erick too much as he growled lightly at him.

"I guess I'll need to talk to his owners about his following me around." I wondered why he didn't like Erick.

I was used to trusting the instincts of an animal, they were a rather good judge of character.

"His owners? You don't know them very well, do you?" The way he had asked the question seemed strange.

"What do you mean?" I wanted to find out what he had

meant.

"Nothing, I can't wait until tomorrow night. We'll have fun. Goodnight." As he said goodbye he leaned in and kissed me on the forehead before he had gone back into the club.

The wolf had come to stand between us not allowing him to stand too close for too long. While walking home the wolf still stuck rather close to me, I almost thought it was going to enter my apartment with me except as soon as I opened the door, it took off in a shot. This time I wasn't as tired as I had been the night before when I left work, that second burst of energy kicked in.

I still felt wide awake. As I was leaving the apartment, I hadn't seen the wolf waiting so I made my way to the grocery store while it was still open for another two hours. This town certainly kept strange hours. I was beginning to wonder if everyone knew each other and knew I was the new person. Not just in the club but also in the grocery store. I had several people stare at me. At least people were friendly saying hello to me, it still felt strange having everyone watching me. They also seemed rather eager to meet me. I had been either introduced to or had people come straight up to me asking me for my name and how I liked living here. Even though the popular question had been why did I pick this town to live in. Getting a few new numbers from people offering help finding places or getting around had been offered. I was beginning to think I had moved to one of the friendliest towns on earth. I couldn't shake this unsettling feeling, like there was something important I wasn't being told. Maybe it was my tendency to doubt people, or maybe it was because of what happened a few days ago... I just didn't know, and that uncertainty was eating at me.

Chapter Eight

Being Watched

Making my way home there was another couple who waved to me as I waved back, I made my way home a little quicker, I could see the wolf across the street watching me. Closing the door, I hurried over to each of the drapes, usually during the day even if I was sleeping, I still had the drapes open to let in the sunshine except I had a strange feeling I was being watched. Was it paranoia to think a wolf was watching me? Picking out my clothes for the next evening I didn't have anything else to do but sleep. Slipping a movie into the player. I watched it until I had fallen asleep. My days seemed to go much faster working nights. I started wondering where the time was going, I had to admit I did miss working days. It seemed like there was more time during the day. Later when I did wake, I made sure I had taken Max for a walk, and as before everyone was very friendly waving to me and even asking if Max was a special creature. Not sure what they had meant by that. I had simply responded by saying, 'no he's just a friendly husky,' which was true, after all he would be friendly to anyone no matter who they were. I had seen Amanda playing at the playground, so I walked over to say hello to her.

"Are your parents around?" I had hoped they would be.

I wanted to ask them about their wolf. At least it looked like he healed quite well.

"Lewis is close by." I wasn't used to a little girl calling her dad by his name.

"I don't see him, why do you call your dad by his name?" I was hoping to learn more about her family.

"It's his name just like you want to be called Teddy. Just a name, so what's your real name?" Tipping her head to the side a little as she looked at me.

"That is my name. My parents wanted a boy, so they named me Theodore anyway. My middle name is Francis Raynn; you can call me Francy. My grandmother used to." Amanda seemed as though she was concentrating for a second.

"What's your last name?" She seemed rather curious.

"Allen." The strange expression that was now showing on her face as she scrunched her face up showed she hadn't cared for any of the names.

"You were screwed over with the names; I must get going. School starts soon." Hopping off the swing she seemed serious.

"School this late in the evening? When you see your parents let them know I need to ask them a question about their wolf. He seems to be following me to and from home quite a bit." I was hoping she would remember to tell them except I couldn't get over her saying she had school this late in the evening.

I still had quite a few hours until I was to meet the others at the bar. It seemed strange the kids would be on the same work schedule. I had never heard of a school operating this late at night or at least colleges you could take night classes but not for elementary children.

"Everything here is different, and my parents already know." She didn't give me a chance to ask how they knew.

I hadn't asked them anything, yet she was already on her way to the school in the distance. Going back home I hadn't seen the wolf until I was almost through the door, I had looked back feeling something was watching me and there he was. Closing the door, I decided to get dressed early. Not wearing too much makeup. I had decided not to wear any perfume. I didn't want to give him the wrong idea except I did like the idea of getting to know him. I just couldn't help but get this nagging feeling like I was betraying Daniel. We were just friends. Leaving a few minutes earlier than I needed to I had wanted to hurry up and get to the bar. I had left Max outside since he seemed rather happy not wanting to be cooped up in the apartment on his own. Who knows maybe the wolf would play nice? I could see Erick standing outside of the bar before I was there. I wasn't sure how many people would be going with us. There seemed to be at least ten people waiting there and of course, as I had expected the wolf was off on the other side of the street keeping a rather close eye on us. It could have just been the timing. I stopped suddenly the second everyone in the group looked at me at the same time. I was beginning to think I had just walked into something much worse. I might be wrong but now that nagging feeling was starting to kick in. After this, I needed to be careful and try to back off a bit and hopefully survive through this.

"Good. You're here early we can get going. We'll be taking three cars, it will be just you and I in my car and the others will divide up with the other two cars. We had a pretty good turnout." Everyone kept giving me a strange look.

I couldn't help but look back at the wolf and notice he had let out the slightest whimper and now I felt scared. I had that desperate desire to run but where would I go? Was I overreacting or should I rely on my gut feeling? Not sure what to do I decided to go along with it for now. I felt I was simply being hesitant from the trauma of the building being destroyed somehow and people trying to kill me, it wasn't easy to turn that fear off.

Getting into his car I was hoping I wasn't going to regret this. It had taken us an hour to go to the next town over. I had watched out the rear window or side mirror, every so often to see if the wolf had followed us except I hadn't seen him once. Pulling up to the movie theater Erick had dropped me off in the front while he went and parked the car. Most of the others had waited with me to get tickets for everyone. Erick and his two sisters had parked their cars rather quickly. We didn't have to wait very long for them. Catching the earlier show for the night, the others had been eager to get inside. They had looked rather uncomfortable until they were inside. The sun wasn't out that strong. It was very chilly and overcast. Even Erick had gone inside rather quickly. I had the feeling if he had the choice, he would have picked me up and carried me in to get me moving faster.

"I'm grabbing some popcorn for us, what do you drink?" As I told him I saw someone I knew.

It felt good not to be too alone. He was standing over by the men's restrooms.

"I'm going to use the restroom real quick. I'll find you at the seats if you get there before me." Excusing myself I had worked my way over; I was going to say hello and find out what he was doing at the movie theater.

I wanted to know how Daniel was except he kept staring at the woman's restroom. Even though I could tell the others were watching me as I made my way to the restroom, I had walked past him in case he did not want it acknowledged that I knew him. I didn't know what to do other than to stand in here for a few minutes so it would look as if I did need to go in here. If they were watching him, he might not try to contact me, especially here. Standing in front of the mirror I tried to fill time except I decided I wasn't going to wait in here any longer. There wasn't any point. Stepping towards the door. A woman had walked in closing it behind her. She hadn't said a word to me other than to put her finger to her mouth and slip a piece of paper into my purse. Nodding I went out into the main hall. I guess I would read the paper after the movie when I was at home.

Two of Erick's friends were still waiting in line at the

snack bar. Heading in to see where he chose to sit, I could hardly see with all the lights off. Following the lights down the center aisle looking from side to side hoping to spot him. No one was waving or trying to get my attention. Heading back to the far back part of the theater. I had stood there hoping he might come back to get me. I watched the entire credits and the movie started. Even his friends who had been waiting at the snack bar never came in. The usher had told me that I needed to find a seat. I was supposedly disrupting the movie for others. I highly doubted anyone had even known I was back here. Picking a chair at the far back in case he walked back here, at least this way I wouldn't miss him. Settling in I watched, yet another rendition of Shakespeare's Romeo and Juliet played on the big screen. After the movie let out, I watched as everyone filtered past my seat, and not once had I seen anyone that was in the group. I started thinking maybe they changed their minds and went into the other movie; it seems strange they didn't tell me if they had. Walking around in the lobby area I watched as the last few had filtered out of our movie. Even outside no one had waited around for me.

I took the note out of my purse and decided I might as well read it now. It read, 'do not ride with them they are dangerous' folding up the note and quickly put it back into my purse. I had looked around and still hadn't seen anyone. I knew I had numbers of a few people that I had just met, not that I felt comfortable calling them asking for them to drive over here but then most I had met at the bar. I wasn't too sure I wanted to. Standing out at the curb I had looked both ways, not seeing anything. I just started walking. Either way, I had to get home somehow, and right now this was my only choice. Even though this town had been a bit larger there were no taxis around here. At least I had enough main roads to follow, and they were lit rather well until I would be out of the town. I would have to settle for concentrating on the main road to get home.

I wished things had been cheaper here or I would have lived in this area, it would have been closer to where I needed to be, and I would almost be home by now. I was thankful I had decided to leave food and water out for Max in case we had stayed out late. This just wasn't the way I had pictured it. The stores were already closed and nowhere to sit. I had walked quite a distance until I was almost out of town. The small little road that led to the cabins we rented for the summer could be seen from the road. I wasn't in a hurry to get home. I had walked over to our old cabin. Peeking into the windows it looked strange to see it empty. I had almost expected to see my parents there. I doubted I would ever be here on vacation again. Opening the door since none of them was ever locked. I walked through and looked around. It looked so different. I was used to seeing my parent's things here.

This was the first time I had seen it without them. Mom had always come before our vacation and would get the cabin ready for us even though we always waited for our sheets. Walking upstairs to my old room the door had been left open. I had left some things that belonged to my parents apparently, they hadn't wanted them either and left them. The bedspread and sheets were still on the bed. Apparently, the owners weren't too worried about them being left either. The vase with the wilted lily of the valley sitting on the windowsill along with the crescent moon I had hung in the window was still there. Taking down the moon I looked at it. I liked the way the light in the morning used to shine through it casting a light blue moon shape on my wall. Putting it in my pocket I decided I would keep it after all.

I knew I would never leave a book behind especially not one from Daniel's place except when I had looked over at my dresser there sat one. Picking it up there were several hand-drawn pictures inside only a few had descriptions or names to them. There was no theme to this one other than the fact each had been hand-drawn with what looked like colored pencils. There were groups of people, mountains, buildings, homes, castles, lakes, streams, and a few animals. One picture that stood out had been the one with Lewis and Daniel. I didn't know they were familiar with each other. There was even a picture of my anklet only it had been drawn on what I could assume had been the original chain. Opening my purse, I set the book inside. I could only guess this had been put in the room shortly after I moved out. Sitting down on the rocking chair in the corner. I could watch the entire room. I wasn't in the mood to start walking again except I knew it had to be done. I just wished the sun was up. I kept getting that feeling I was being watched. At least when it was the wolf, he made himself visible. After being ditched I couldn't help but wonder what was going on, did they go after Gerry, was he alright?

Sitting there for a little longer than I had planned on I was jolted back to reality when I realized I had fallen asleep hearing a crash that woke me. It sounded like a window being broken. No one would need to break in here since none of the doors were ever locked. It sounded as if someone was tearing apart the furniture down below it was so loud. Opening the bedroom door, I was greeted by a cloud of black smoke curling up the stairs. I couldn't see what was downstairs other than bright red and orange flames making their way upward. Closing the door behind me quickly I raced over to the bedroom window opening it up. Thankfully I had been used to climbing out. I just wished there had been a tree that was closer. The one I used before was gone. The cabin had been made rather rustic with large tree logs and white putty of some sort holding them together. At least it was enough. I could hold the bottom ledge of my window and lower myself down a little before I had to jump to the ground. Looking in the lower kitchen window I could see someone in there spreading the fire. Why would they burn the place down on purpose unless they knew I was in there? Carefully walking away until I felt I was far enough. I started to run as fast as I could, I knew I couldn't keep this up. I just wanted to get as far away as I could. Not sure where he had shown up from, I ran right into him not even knocking him over. It felt like I ran right into a metal pole. Getting knocked back as soon as I had run into him, I hit the ground with a rather painful thud.

"What happened at the theater. I tried to find you. I even waited until the movie was over and I never saw you or any of your friends." I was so shocked to see him here.

I wasn't sure what else to say. Holding onto my purse closely making sure the book or any other contents hadn't fallen out when I hit the ground.

"What did Jacob say to you?" Not even bothering to answer my question.

"Who is Jacob? No one spoke to me at the movie theater other than the usher telling me I needed to find a seat." I was confused; no one had spoken to me, not even Gerry.

Taking a few minutes before he responded it looked like he was trying to figure out if I was lying to him or not.

"Why are you at this cabin?" Each time he asked me a different question I kept trying to find a way of getting away from him sadly there wasn't anywhere I could go.

I felt as if I was protecting Gerry and Daniel by not acknowledging that I knew them or where they had been, but then who was there to protect me if someone wanted to come after me because I was possibly seen with them?

"I used to stay here with my family for the summer, it's a nostalgic feeling and gave me a break from having to walk so far. Before I answer any more of your questions, I want to know why you ditched me at the theater?" As I was asking him the person from inside the cabin came over.

Erick hadn't seemed surprised by him, so he was part of the fire also. I think they had planned on killing me in there. Taking a step back, not that I knew where to run. I was hoping they were preoccupied enough with each other that I might be able to get away. That wasn't going to happen as he grabbed my wrist twisting it, I felt such a sharp pain I didn't want to risk moving making it worse.

"You're not going anywhere until I'm done with you. Where is the man you spoke to at the theater?" He was refusing to accept I hadn't talked to anyone.

"I already told you I hadn't talked to anyone other than

the usher and I have no idea who he is or where he went after his shift was done. I came back here to the cabin because I was tired of walking." Not letting up on my wrist I wasn't sure what he planned on doing with me.

He spoke to the other man in a language that didn't sound human. Too fast, too sharp, like it was slicing through the air. I didn't have time to make sense of it. He turned. Or —no. Whipped around faster than anyone should be able to move. A second later, I was airborne. Some invisible force hit me square in the chest and flung me across the room like I weighed nothing. My back slammed into the log wall of the cabin with a brutal crack, and I crumpled to the floor, every nerve in my body screaming. For a moment, I just lay there, stunned. What the hell was that? No one moves like that. No one does that. Something was seriously, seriously wrong.

Standing up slowly. I was in so much pain. I hadn't even seen him move. He was already standing right in front of me. I kept feeling these sharp stabbing pain feelings all over my legs, arms, and face. I had blood dripping from everywhere I had felt the pain. There were cuts everywhere almost as if I had taken a knife to my skin. Then I realized he wasn't cutting me with a knife he was doing this with his fingernails. I was trapped in the burning cabin. I could feel the burning heat coming through the cracks in the log.

"I have something that might get them to come to save their precious little meat bag." Not that I wanted to find out what they had in mind let alone the fact they just called me a meat bag?

I didn't think the sting from the slashes on my skin could get any worse, but they did as he poured something over the top of me. I had kept my eyes closed hoping it wouldn't impair my vision. It had felt as if he poured rubbing alcohol over my wounds causing them to burn and reopen to bleed again. If it had been that at least I wasn't going to get infected.

"Why isn't she screaming for him. You said she would break easily?" Who did they expect me to scream for?

There was no one around to scream for help. Its why my parents loved this place. There was so much privacy but still close enough to town.

"You will learn to scream for mercy, now call him. Don't pretend that you don't know who he is." His tone of voice had deepened as even his stance became more threatening.

"I don't know who you expect me to scream for." I was getting just as frustrated.

I doubted it would have mattered what I said there was nothing I could do to get him to leave me alone.

"Scream for him to save your life." As he raised his hand, I could only assume he was going to slice me again or something worse, I had no idea what he was able to do.

"I scream for no one." That was all I was going to say.

There was no way out of this. I was not going to cower no matter how impossible it was. Grabbing ahold of me by the shoulders he threw me again sailing through the air and out the door until I hit a tree, again landing on the ground in a rather painful thump. There was no way that I was going to get up this time. I laid there figuring they were going to kill me, not that I wanted to give up. I just didn't know what else to do. Broken branches on the ground had already caught flame while the outside of the cabin was now on fire. Grabbing the stick on the ground slightly burning my skin. I threw the branch at him as he came at me. I wasn't sure what I had planned on happening with it except it did at least slow him down.

Erick wasn't afraid of the fire he just hadn't planned on how flammable his clothing had been as I watched him go up in flames. When his attention was off of me, he was trying to smolder the fire from his clothing. I had a sudden surge of energy to pull myself up. I took off as fast as I could running through the woods past a couple more cabins. I wasn't going to risk looking back to see if he was following me, I was sure he would be. I was just hoping I might outlast him, if he was some kind of creature, I was hoping the sun would come out soon. I had a few hours before it would start peeking through the sky.

I wasn't sure if he could track me or not and I hoped his senses would be like that of a dog if I ran across the water, he would lose what direction I had gone. Heading for the creek. I ran along the muddy side of the water. My footprints would fill in immediately with mud and water and I knew it slowed me down a little, but I hoped if I ran down far enough if I crossed, they would take a while still to find me.

There was a cave over here I used to like hiding in except I had stopped when Daniel had convinced me how dangerous it was and that I should never go in alone. I was little when I wanted to go in here. There were so many areas you had to crawl on your belly to get around with several very deep pits in areas you could fall into and not be known you were down there. I had hoped they wouldn't be familiar with this place. It would be so easy to get lost in here if you didn't know which tunnels to take to get out. I had been through so many of them with Daniel as he taught me how to tell which ones to take. I had always wondered where he went when I didn't see him. He had told me once about his family and how close he was to them that most of the time he was with them. Then when he wanted something different or just privacy, he came out here to be alone. I guess I kind of changed that when he found me when I was little. Crawling back into the furthest part of the cave I had hoped I would hear them coming as it would echo a far-off distance, I knew they were fast at running. I hoped they would be slow at crawling if they weren't used to it. The sound of nothing but silence had been the best sound I had heard in a long time.

I sat down waiting for the sun to come up before I could make my way home, I mainly wanted to go to get Max. After that, I wasn't sure where I was going to go other than feeling tempted to stay in the caves for a while. It was safe enough to take Max in, at least I knew what areas to stay clear of. I just knew I couldn't stay in here forever. With no car and not feeling safe enough to stay in either the apartment or go to work. I now had no job or home. When I had thought about living on my own, I had never thought of anything like this but then I had never imagined what has happened in the last few days could exist. If I had spoken to anyone about it, they would have just thought I lost my sanity. Not that I wanted to know what I had looked like. My skin was covered in bruises and blood again. No matter how cold the floor had been it felt good as I slept for a while. I was never this tired before but then I was never this stressed out or fighting just to survive. I was beginning to think living with my parents hadn't been that bad.

Feeling a little groggy I figured they hadn't found me even though I wanted to be careful leaving the caves in case they were waiting outside for me. I hadn't seen anyone, not that I wanted to stay in the woods for too long and at least the sun had come out. Walking out to the road. I had chosen the only option there was, I walked along the familiar road leading outward and towards the much smaller town where no one was around or in sight even this time. I could have sworn the curtains of a few houses had swayed as I passed by. Heading for home I could see Max outside playing around blissfully unaware of the night that I had. He was excited at least to see me. Leaving him outside I went into the apartment very carefully in case anyone was inside. I wanted to be able to step back into the sunlight. I wasn't sure if it would protect me or not except if they had wanted to come after me still, I doubted it would have stopped them. Taking a quick shower and putting on a fresh pair of clothes. I made sure I was comfortable.

Packing up food in one container while I put the rest of the things I owned in my backpack. I was ready to leave. I hadn't owned very much so it wasn't as if I was leaving much behind. Grabbing the leash for Max we were already heading off down the road on our way out of town when I heard the beep of a vehicle. That sick feeling kicked in as I hoped it wasn't anyone who planned on running me over or was a secret friend of Erick's trying to get me to trust them.

"You look like you could use a lift? What have you gotten yourself into this time?" As he spoke, I hadn't needed to see who it was.

I couldn't help but feel relief the one person I highly doubted would harm me or they could have already if they wanted. At that moment I had wondered if they were aware of how dangerous their town was?

"Actually. I was heading out of town nowhere in particular just anywhere else that happens to be safer for me." I wasn't going to say much but I just felt the words pouring out.

"You're always welcome to stay with us until you figure out where you want to go." It was a nice enough offer I just felt strange taking advantage of a nice family especially if it might put them in danger.

"I doubt you want to risk having me around. Lately it seems like I attract the worst kind." Not acting put off he pushed the door open as he gestured for me to come in.

I hadn't noticed Amanda sitting next to him since she was leaning against him sleeping.

"She's been rather tired lately, come home and have lunch with us and if you still want to leave, I can help you get a place to stay for a while until you're on your feet." Not really wanting to turn it down I wasn't looking forward to sleeping in the cave alone.

I might have felt temporarily safe there but even the cave felt creepy and knowing what was after me it felt worse, not that I felt any safer staying in this town any longer than I had to. Stopping at their home he had left both Amanda and me off for a while. He had work to finish and explained Evangeline would be home soon. He had appreciated my being willing to watch Amanda while he was at work. Even though I hadn't voiced it I felt more worried for Amanda than myself if Erick had decided to come after me again while I was here. I was just hoping he wouldn't know I was here. I still worried for Amanda since she felt so cold, I was hoping she hadn't picked up something and became sick. She wasn't as limp as a child normally would be when they were sleeping. I carried her in the house and into her room, covering her up. She looked so sweet when she slept. I had left Max outside to enjoy the fresh air. He was always happier outside unless it was nighttime. Not that I felt it was right to have him inside while I was in their place. Leaving my bags in my room I walked around their living room taking the time to look at the pictures they had on the walls. Several family portraits of them at different places and even what I could guess the rest of their extended family. There were so many, and each one looked so much like the other. Then I noticed something again. There he was. Gerry and Daniel were standing in the row behind Lewis and his family.

Was this the family he had spent time with? He made it sound as if they were a long distance away and that he spent quite a bit of time getting to them unless he had a few here. Why hadn't I heard of this family before? There were a lot of other faces I hadn't recognized. At least I wasn't finding any of Erick or his supposed sisters or friends. Picking up a small photo album I took my time looking through it. There were so many of the family. I wondered just how often they traveled. Maybe that's how they might not have known the strange town they lived in? I wasn't normally invasive of others' privacy except I found myself searching around a bit. The photo book had laid out on top, so I opened the drawers below finding even more photo albums even some that looked very old. Many are in black and white photography wearing period clothing. It looked almost as if they had covered every era here. I had never seen a family this obsessed over fitting in with the image for the photograph, even the background of the pictures fit the whole theme. Daniel looked like he could have blended in with every generation. I was surprised to see just how many he was in. If I ever saw Daniel again, I would have to ask him about these pictures. I noticed the family always seemed to have wolves around them except when they were in the photo, Lewis was not in it and neither had four others who were in other pictures. Going from the hand-painted pictures to the flash photos they must have spent a lot on these.

I placed all the pictures back carefully to keep them in order. I had heard Amanda stirring guessing she was done with her nap. Walking down the hallway. She was rubbing her eyes as she was waking up, not too surprised that I was here. She sat down on the couch pulling out a book to read.

"I hope I didn't wake you up." I was hoping to look around a little more.

This family had been rather interesting but then I guess if I was careful, I could ask Amanda a few questions. She might think I'm a little crazy but then safer to ask a child than to have it confirmed by another adult.

"I was only a little bit tired. My body needed rest. I always read a book when I wake up, there's more in case you want to pick one." She had pointed at a stack of books.

None of which I would have chosen. They looked like a wide range of medical books to various gardening books. An interesting choice. Apparently, they wanted her to be well educated in every field.

"What do your parents do for jobs?" I figured that question would be a good one to start with before I started asking about the pictures on the wall.

"Normally dad is a teacher but right now he's a substitute teacher. He'll probably get another regular teaching job next year. Mom is a photographer, and painter and into sculpting. Depending on where we are she focuses on different things." At least that explained why there were so many pictures all over the place.

"I noticed the pictures on the walls. I wondered how she was able to get some of those to look so authentic. The clothing and background in each are amazing. You would think they were pictures of ancestors except they are the same people in almost all of them. It's difficult to tell which are old and which ones are not." As I spoke, I looked at the pictures on the wall again.

Standing up. Amanda had come over to me now pointing out some of the relatives which I had hoped she would do. At least I didn't need to prompt her.

"Some of these are very old." As she pointed out each person none of the names sounded familiar and I noticed that she skipped over two people almost as if they were not there.

She did the same in another picture. I wondered when the last time they had posed for a picture or if they even knew how he looked now. At least from the last time I had seen him.

"Who are these two in the picture. I noticed you missed them, or do you not know them?" Amanda seemed hesitant to answer.

I could tell she was trying to figure out what to say.

"I'm not supposed to lie but I'm also not supposed to say. We haven't seen either in a very long time. They went missing. My parents thought they might have been here, especially the way some things are, so we moved back here. My cousin used to come here to be alone except the town sort of grew up around his place. It happens everywhere now. I don't think we are staying too much longer. We were going to move back out a bit further." She had hesitated a few times not that I wanted to get her into trouble for telling me something she wasn't supposed to, but it was helping me understand a few things better.

"I don't want to get you into trouble, so you don't have to answer any questions you're not comfortable with. Has your family always raised wolves, kind of an interesting pet to have?" As soon as I had started talking about the wolves the worried look that had been there was replaced with a smirk.

"We don't raise wolves. They are part of our family just like I am." Strange comment but if she wanted to see herself as a wolf, I guess there's nothing wrong with that.

At least the kid has a good imagination.

"So, you consider yourself to be a wolf?" As I said this, she shook her head no, at least she knew the difference between make-believe and reality.

"I'm not a wolf...they are. I'm a vampire." Smiling she seemed rather pleased with herself.

She certainly hadn't looked the way I would assume a vampire would resemble but if she wanted to believe she was a vampire, that was just fine. Even though I would have called Erick one with no problem. He just didn't have what I was used to reading about when it came to myths of vampires.

Looking out the window. I had seen two of the wolves sitting down next to Max. He didn't seem worried about it, and they were friendly to him. At least I wouldn't have to worry about how they would interact with each other even though I knew Max was friendly with everyone. As I was watching them, I heard another car pull up close to the house. Looking carefully out the window, I noticed no one had come out of the car. The car just sat there. Staying out of the sight of the window. I tried to stay close enough to see if it was Evangeline or Lewis even though Lewis had driven the truck, I assumed he might be picking his wife up.

"Do your parents ever get visitors during the day?" I didn't want her coming to the window and looking out letting them know anyone was in the house.

It was so private out here. If you hadn't known where to drive. A person would not know how to get back here. There was barely a two-track to follow. Watching the car, no one tried to get out, which was making me worry. I was hoping they were staying in the car waiting for her parents to get home assuming no one was there.

"Do you have any relatives nearby?" I was hoping if she had we might be able to call them.

Maybe whoever was in the car wouldn't try anything if others showed up. So far, I had only been attacked when I was alone.

"We don't have any relatives here. The only ones close by are six hours away. Dad should be home soon. They should be in mom's art studio. She wanted to produce more before she goes on the road with them again. It's only fifteen minutes into town." Now she seemed to be curious why I was still looking out the window and asking those questions.

I was trying to think of a safe way to get her out of here if they were dangerous. At least it looked like only one person was in the car. I could keep the person busy while she ran for it. Not that I was looking forward to getting beaten up again. I still had bruises from before, all the scratches from the building caving in on me along with an incredibly sore back. The stitches I have I can't have removed for a few weeks still. I was beginning to wonder if the person wasn't getting out of the car because of the wolves outside. They were no longer laying down they were upright and ready to attack.

"Do your parents have a cell phone they can be called on?" Trying to think of any way of getting Amanda out of this place safely even if the wolves did keep the stranger busy.

I wished instead of coming back here I had just left town the way I had planned but then who's to say this person wouldn't have run me over on the road. It was hard to tell who it was they were. The person was covered from head to toe with clothing almost as if they were bracing for a very harsh winter.

The stranger finally stepped out of the car as the wolves started to close in growling at him ready to lunge. I had a feeling this wasn't going to be good. I hoped if this person was meant to be here the wolves would know the difference but then from the way this person had dressed, I doubted they were here for any positive reason. Staying between the house and the stranger. I wasn't sure what was going to happen. I had heard another vehicle except it had stayed out of distance. I was just hoping we were not getting outnumbered.

"We need to go to the back of the house." Setting her book down Amanda stood and motioned for me to follow.

I simply followed for now since it had seemed like a good idea, at least that way we might be able to sneak out the back while the others were distracted.

"If we need to take off, I'll distract them if needed but you are to make a run for your mom's art studio." I was hoping it would be a safe enough plan after what Erick could do last night, I didn't want to risk her staying around here and getting hurt.

"Mom says to stay here until Jessica is here to get us." She seemed very determined and definite about what she heard that I had not.

"I never heard the phone ring; how did you hear from your mom?" I hadn't heard anything.

Did she hear her voice? Maybe they were the ones waiting in the other car but then who was Jessica that we were supposed to wait for? Maybe it wasn't someone we should be listening to pretending to be her mother.

"She speaks to me. I can hear her. I was talking to her letting her know about the stranger outside and she said my aunts will slow him down until Jessica comes to get us, my uncle isn't too far away so he will also join them slowing them down. But we must wait in the safe room which is this one. Jessica has been here before so she can transport herself here." Now I was wondering if she was creating these stories to make herself handle the situation.

If it helped her that would be fine, I just had to make sure I had some kind of plan in case there were more out there that might be after us. Feeling a rush of air behind me. I felt that sickening feeling kick in as I turned, I was thankful I had a healthy heart, or it would have stopped just from shock. A woman stood right behind me taking a step back as she smiled at Amanda.

"Not to worry. I'm here to take both of you out of here. The vampires in this area are not safe, apparently, you have something they want." Amanda had come over to stand near her.

They seemed to know each other even though I wasn't sure I wanted to risk her leaving with this woman, she looked much younger than myself.

"I need you to hold onto my hand and not let go. You might feel a little dizzy or feel pressure around you however that's normal. It won't last long. We will be out of here very quickly." Amanda was already holding onto her hand.

I wasn't sure what she had planned on doing. Not that I knew how she was able to get into the house without my hearing anything. I guess I was distracted enough not to hear her. I wasn't sure if I was supposed to take her seriously or not.

"Take her hand. This is Jessica, she won't hurt us, she's going to take us to grandma and grandpa's place. It's safe and far enough away from here." As soon as she had said safe, I had to admit the idea sounded good but then how was she going to whisk us away from here unless the hidden car outside was hers?

We didn't need to hold onto hands for that. Jessica reached out her hand expecting me to take it. To humor them for a while and to find out what she had planned. I reached my hand out taking hers.

Before I knew it the space around us was white, I couldn't see anything other than Amanda and Jessica. There was so much wind swirling around us along with the pressure she had described. I wasn't sure what had possessed me to do the next thing. It almost felt as if it was a natural reaction. Just as quickly the white had been replaced with something else, I wasn't familiar with except I could no longer see either Jessica or Amanda.

"I thought you were bringing another person with Amanda?" Charlie looked around surprised.

Even Jessica whirled around to see I was no longer on her right side. Amanda was still holding onto her hand waiting for her to say when it was safe.

"Go find Larissa. She's around here somewhere. She will be excited to see you." Charlie tried taking her attention off the fact I was no longer with them.

"Where do you think she went. Is she back at the house?" Sophie was now standing next to them curious about what had happened.

Making a quick check back at the house and coming back to Charlie and Sophie she shook her head no.

"She's not there. I don't know where she is. I've never had anyone let go before." She seemed rather shocked.

She knew it could be a little scary if you were not familiar with traveling this way but then when it had been her first time, she was too afraid to let go. She had never known what would happen if she let go but then neither had Sophie. It just had not been done as far as she knew.

Chapter Nine

Lost

"Jessica, can you sense her?" Sophie started pacing worrying where she might be.

She had never experienced this problem before and now they were trying to figure out how to find the new girl, they had no name and no address to find her at, she only had a dog that was left behind. Careful not to leave it to die from no food or water being available, Lewis and Evangeline took it with them as soon as it was safe to leave.

"I just don't understand why she let go. I can usually find anyone even if I don't know them as long as there's something I can focus on. I always find them, it's almost as if she doesn't want to be found." Jessica told Charlie as he stood there quietly thinking.

"If she does know Lucian, he might have taught her to be guarded to keep them both protected, but then I don't understand why she's out there on her own. Even he wouldn't have left her unguarded unless he can't protect her himself?" No one could deny the look of worry on Rose's face.

"I wish Lewis could have found out more about the

rumors. The other vampires seemed to want her bad enough and they were convinced she knew where Lucian and Jacob were. She's doing a good job at keeping it a secret if she's trying to protect them; I wonder if she lived in the Vailville summer spot for the summers only, do you think it's the same little kid Lucian brought home with him once? Maybe he thought he was safe with her after all the rumors of them being around came once this summer started and that's when she came again." Rose had been trying to project herself to Jacob for a while now.

Jessica and Sophie were growing desperate. Depending on where Teddy ended up, she could be in danger, they had little time to find her, Jessica tried everything she had been taught and still...no sign of Teddy. Not even a flicker of her energy. Lucian had used cloaking enchantments, meant to shield them from Katherine's hunters. But the magic had worked too well. Now no one could find them—not even Lucian's own family. If something had gone wrong, no help would ever come. Jessica couldn't stop replaying that final moment. Teddy's hand in hers. The rush of magic twisting the air. And then—nothing. A slip. A breath. A void. She was just gone. She was supposed to be safe.

If Teddy was alive, if she were okay, she would have been located by now. The silence was too long. Too final. It didn't feel like hiding. It felt like something had swallowed her whole.

"I'm sure Jacob and Lucian are alright as long as they stay together. At least we know now what we are looking for. We just have to find the boys and hopefully, this girl will be able to lead us to them. There must be a reason they moved from the first spot. Didn't anyone know or remember anything about her?" Charlie seemed surprised there was no information available about her.

Other than who her parents had been. They spent every summer at a certain cabin that was found to be burned to the ground now. She seemed to have no idea about special creatures which means if she did know Lucian, she didn't know the truth about him either.

"I guess we have to wait until she either makes herself

available for help or try and guess where she might go, I don't like the idea of heading back to the vampire town. It's crawling with Katherine's people, it's not safe for any of us." Far enough in the distance, the family could hear the truck coming not needing to see who it was. Lewis and Evangeline were there.

Charlie had been eager to ask them questions to find out anything they knew about this new girl. Looking across the field everyone could see both Larissa and Amanda race to greet Evangeline and Lewis. At one time both of the girls had been the same age being close friends. It hadn't stopped them from being close, however if someone had not known them, they would have assumed one was a much older sister since Amanda had barely grown. After twenty years Amanda finally grew a full inch. By the time Larissa was a full-grown adult, Amanda would still look around the age of thirteen if she was lucky. Her mind grew sadly her body hadn't.

After listening to the adults talking to each other for a while. Trying to find information about her which they were coming up empty. What puzzled them the most was something incredibly basic, something most people do when they first meet someone. They hadn't even thought to ask her name; they introduced themselves to her. They even trusted her as a stranger to leave Amanda with even though she could have protected herself against a human easily. All they could find had been her parents' names and possibly that she liked teddy bears. Sitting patiently not interrupting until the adults had given up. Larissa kept jabbing Amanda catching everyone's attention and wondering what was going on between the two.

"I know what her name is, she might like teddy bears, that I didn't ask. But her nickname is Teddy. Her parents wanted a boy, so they named her Theodore Francis Raynn. She was asking questions about our family pictures, especially about Lucian and Jacob but for some reason, she kept referring to them as Gerry and Daniel." Amanda didn't seem to understand if she was supposed to know them and if she did why did she have the wrong names?

"Both Jacob and Lucian use their middle names sometimes when they deal with humans. Helps them recognize some later if they come into contact with them again, to know if they were once human and changed later or simply for privacy to keep them unassociated with other things. Right now, they would be using them from those who are not familiar enough with them. I think it might be the little girl he found. We still don't know much about her other than she was the only one he's allowed in his castle. He goes there for solitude usually to forget life, hard to do that when you have a human capable of dying around you as much as he had." No one could figure out why he had connected to her.

At first it was almost as if he was her proud older brother, he started protecting her the same way he had with Rose. In a way, it gave him a feeling of purpose again. Now that Rose had Jacob to keep her safe. He had stopped bringing her around when she hit her preteens.

Lorah had been off helping Valafar with something confidential even though Charlie now wondered if it had anything to do with Drezin? Lorah seemed surprised when she heard they didn't have the medallion yet. Not that she would answer, she just mentioned she was busy and had to get going quickly. Hopefully, she wasn't getting caught up in Drezin's world. Keeping his mind focused thinking over the last several weeks he wished Lucian and Jacob would at least give them a call. If anything, to leave a message to let them know if they were alright.

Lewis and Evangeline felt it would be easier if only two of them searched the girl's apartment in case something happened; they could get away easier. They had left the others while they searched the girl's old apartment that she moved into while she was here. Even this had been a mystery, why would a human choose to live around creatures, especially those that would kill her if given the chance? Unless she was just a very unfortunate mortal talented at attracting harm to herself. It left so many questions unanswered. Apparently, someone else had the same idea; it had been destroyed with leftover belongings all over the ground. Furniture broke into pieces along with several pieces of paper shredded laying on the floor. Flipping through some of the papers there was a picture left intact on the floor. Picking it up there was a name on the back. Theodore Francis Raynn Johnson. At least now we had a full name to go on in case she used it at all. We had to be careful how we treated her when we found her, after all, Lucian seemed just as protective of her as he had his sister. Lewis felt a slight vibrating in his pocket as he pulled out his cell phone. Amanda was calling, usually, she texted which meant she wanted to speak.

"Amanda, we are a little busy right now, can it wait? We should be home soon." Lewis had kept looking through the piles on the floor barely listening to the phone.

"Alright, I'll talk to you when you get home, and I'll tell you then where Raynn is." Hanging up the phone that last little bit had caught his attention except it had been too late.

He knew he had a tendency of putting her off and usually, her response had always been like this making him wish he had taken the time to listen. Calling back her phone was busy.

"I think we need to get going, I don't think we are going to find anything here and Amanda seems to have found something." Nodding in agreement Evangeline left the mess on the floor, leaving with Lewis getting home as quickly as they could.

None of the family would have come back here except after talking it over, we certainly were not going to find anything elsewhere without starting here. We had decided to take our chances with the other creatures in the area; thankfully we haven't had any problems with them yet. Charlie was already at the house standing outside with Larissa and Rose. Amanda had been waiting inside for everyone as she opened the door letting us in, curious how she had found out where the girl would be. She had her hands behind her back smiling since she had figured it out. We should have guessed she would, Amanda was always good with mysteries.

"I thought I should let you know that her dog is gone, she came back for it and left a note saying she appreciated our help, except she was taking off for a safe place for a while until all of this blows over." In one hand she pulled out a piece of paper.

"Is that all you have?" Evangeline seemed a bit surprised.

"No that's not all, there's more." Taking her other hand, she held onto a large blue backpack. We knew it wasn't hers so we could only assume it had belonged to Teddy.

"She is human, isn't she? She can't get that far even if she did manage to get a ride somewhere. It's a matter of figuring out where she would go." Evangeline Looked over at Amanda, she shook her head as if she still couldn't believe we were not waiting until she was finished.

"Is there more?" Lewis prompted not that he had to.

"Yes, impatient people. There is, at least just this last little bit." Pulling a poetry book out from the backpack, and opening the inside page there was handwriting inside with two addresses. One had 'grandma' listed next to it and the other was basic with no extra notes next to it.

"She might not be at either place; we can check them out however it would be hard to explain why we are looking for her if she's not there?" Lewis was still somewhat lost in his thoughts.

"I know when I want a safe place and I'm not at our home. I go to grandma and grandpa's house. I doubt she would think differently, I'm positive from the way she talks that is where she would go." Evangeline and Rose went to check out her grandparent's home while Lewis and Charlie went to check out the other address.

Amanda and Larissa went back to Charlie and Sophie's home, no one felt safe leaving the girls behind at the house here. At least here we never had to pretend to have a babysitter for Amanda, because there were only vampires and other creatures living around us. At least the kids would be protected with Sophie. The kids had made the trip several times even though now we had to be careful; it wasn't worth risking them in case someone thought they could use them to get to us or the girl.

After everyone else had left the girls took off watching as they went making sure not to be caught; only occasionally walking when they were close to a town where they might be spotted.

"I think someone is following us; he's been behind us from your neighborhood. He's been able to keep up with us so he's not human." As she had said this, he made his presence known making a quick dash for us.

We both took off as fast as we could, racing across no longer worried if anyone were to see us. If they noticed something moving fast, we would hopefully be gone from sight before they could figure out what we were, otherwise we would be another rumor like Bigfoot or Loch Ness monster. Moving quickly, we made our way not directly for home which might surprise the one following us, we had gone straight for a particular town that knew our family rather well. We were within a few miles of the town when a few people had come out to help when they recognized us. We knew where they would be hiding as we ran past them. There was so much brush we were familiar with hiding spots and made our presence clear so no one would ambush us. Panic had set in as we were almost there; he was so close to us. I hoped Amanda and I would make it. Thankfully she was a fast runner like I was. We passed one of our parent's friends who was hiding in the bushes, once we went passed, we heard the man chasing us yelp out loud in pain. He had been tackled to the ground. Stopping when we realized he had been caught. Neither of us recognized him other than the symbol he wore on his shirt, a definite mark of one who worked for Katherine.

"Are you one of the seven?" He demanded as the two men who had ambushed him held him.

They had looked at us wondering what he was saying.

"Seven what?" I couldn't think what that would have been.

We only knew there were ones who wanted three pieces of jewelry that could make serious problems if they landed in the wrong hands, but then they could also help Amanda. We never heard anything about seven of anything?

The men held him not that they had him for too long. Nothing we were aware a vampire could do; he must have been something else. He turned into a cloud of black dust that simply blew away, as we watched wondering if it would even be safe to make the rest of the journey without the family around. We decided it would be much safer to stay at Karie's house which was closer, until our family was able to collect us. We called Sophie letting her know what had just happened. She was as surprised as we were.

"Sophie, do you know anything about the number seven? The man who chased us asked us if we were part of the seven?" We could hear her sigh wondering just how big this thing was going to get.

"No, we are not familiar with it, there are Wiccan, pagan, Christian, and other cultural significance to the number seven. However, if he was asking you if you were a part of it. I can only guess he was searching for someone that is part of a particular group or something else I can't quite figure out. I'll call Charlie to let him know. Stay with Karie and we will get you soon." Flipping the phone shut we made our way to Karie's hoping even though he turned to dust fleeing that he wouldn't risk coming after us again.

Making our way to Karie's house we noticed no one else had been out, rather strange for creatures, the two men we had run into hadn't said anything. The moonlight had lit our way, I was feeling anxious to get to her house. Not that we were too far from it. I always loved the way she had her house painted. Instead of the traditional white or beige, she had painted it dark purple with black trim. Knocking on the door no one had answered. Feeling above the door trim the spare key had either been picked up or not replaced. It wasn't under the greeting mat on the front step, and it wasn't in her light fixture either. Walking around to the back there was a large statue of kids playing in a fountain. In the one kid's hand, she held a bucket. Reaching into the cold water as it poured out, I grabbed the little box at the bottom pulling it out. It had been waterproofed to keep the extra key from rusting. Opening it up at least the key was still there.

Opening the door there was a mess in the kitchen, looking straight ahead the living room hadn't looked any better. Pillows slashed with feathers all over the floor, furniture torn to pieces, even plates broken on the floor with each cupboard left open. It had looked the same as Teddy's apartment. I kept my hand on the cell phone in my pocket in case I needed to dial Sophie's number. Looking around the rest of the house none of it had looked any better except the study had looked worse. I dialed the number as Amanda shouted to run. Turning I dropped the phone on the ground. There was the man again in the house; apparently, he followed us after all. Shutting the door, not that we were sure if it would keep him out; we guessed they might have been the ones who had destroyed the house. There was blood all over the walls, ceiling, and carpet. Opening the window to make it look as if we went out that way, I even lifted my foot to leave a footprint of blood on the window ledge. The blood was fresh so it couldn't have been too long ago that they killed her. Both of us stepped into the closet as they broke down the door.

Amanda had leaned against the wall making it slide back a bit. Not really having much of a choice as they looked out the window, we made our way through the crack of the wall. It had been her secret ritual room which was protected with enchantments. She made sure only certain creatures could make it in here, if they were evil, they were not allowed in. We had been here the day she made it except now that she was killed, we didn't know if her invitation would still allow us in. The wall slid shut behind us thankfully quietly. There was a red light glowing in the corner lighting the room. The table in the center had been set up for the next time she had planned on using it. All her herbs and potions had been on the left side, and her books or handwritten grimoires were to the far back with symbols all over the wall. On the floor, there was a huge pentagram in the center of the cement floor. On the right-side wall had been several robes and various clothing hanging up. Even her wands, staff, and other items she used were on the right-side wall. The only thing we had noticed had been when one of the robes had moved. We expected to see Karie come out except it wasn't her. It was another girl standing there looking confused and terrified. We could hear loud slamming on the other side of the wall. With the protection symbols in place along either side of the wall, they were not going to get in without us letting them in. This is why we had wondered why it opened to us; it usually hadn't unless Karie let us in with her. Even though it had not viewed us as evil we had her blood on the bottom of our shoes. Generally, in the locked position you must be invited in, and then we thought maybe the girl had invited us in.

"Do you know what happened to Karie?" Larissa spoke softly trying to relax and reassure the girl we were not going to hurt her.

"Those men killed her, she told me to hide in here until it was safe, but I don't know if it will ever be safe." She was barely able to get her words out.

"I'm Larissa and this is my cousin Amanda, how did you know Karie?" I was curious why she would be here let alone what trouble she would be in.

"Karie is my protector, and I found that out this summer. I was spending the night at a friend's house; we were both going to summer camp and my sister had something else she was doing back at home, so she didn't come with me. She doesn't like camping; her idea of camping is a cheap hotel with bad room service. I just found out my parents are not my biological parents, that there are people who want to kill me, and Karie was protecting me because of a promise she had made to a friend, but she died and now I don't know who that was. She was going to introduce me to my real parents; she told me that I had a gift of some kind. I don't know if my sister is safe." Clenching her hands together she was incredibly nervous.

"Our grandmother will know something is wrong. I dropped my cell phone out there and it was already dialing her number, when we don't answer, they will come looking for us. Just before we got here there was a man who asked if we were one of the seven, have you ever heard that before?" I was curious by any chance if she was part of it?

"Karie mentioned part of it to me except she never had the chance to finish telling me about it. My sister and I supposedly have five other sisters. I'm Taylor and my sister's name is Piper. I don't know the other girls who we are supposed to be related. We've always been able to do things that are unexplained except our parents always told us it was evil to use those gifts; they called them curses and said we would put ourselves in danger if we used them. We were accused by them of using witchcraft or something worse. I never admitted it, but I practiced it myself in secret." I had looked at Amanda, I was sure she might be thinking the same thing I had been.

"Do you know what ritual Karie was using before she was killed?" There were a few herbs and other items on the alter she used, however, the ritual had yet to be finished.

If the girl knew what she was working on we might be able to finish it, perhaps it would help us figure out how we were supposed to help her. Especially if such dangerous things were after her, there had to be some way of protecting her after we were gone from here.

"She was doing a conjuring or location spell of some sort; I think that's what she was working on. The plate with the dark water was supposed to show her where the person she was looking for was hiding." Not that we were familiar with her craft, we looked over the ingredients, each had already been separated in their small amounts laid out.

Unfortunately, there were no notes to explain the steps she was using.

"How familiar are you with doing this? Maybe you could figure it out better than we could?" Amanda was hoping she was educated enough in the craft that she would be able to take it over and finish it.

"I know the mixing of the items would be fine. I just

don't know how they fit in with the scrying of the water bowl," Picking up a few of the pieces she started putting them in the little cauldron on the table, mixing each being careful until there was a small amount of smoke coming from it.

When she was finished putting in the different ingredients she had thrown in a match, all of it had gone up in flames, not that it had lasted very long, using the burnt mixture she poured it into the bowl with dark water. As she did there was a white smoke swirling around inside then it settled as it started to show an image of a man standing there. We were all watching the man walking around; he looked as though he was concentrating on the piles of papers on his desk. I had never seen scrying like this before even though I knew it existed; Grandma Sophie talked about it. But she hadn't taught us about it yet. As we watched, he looked directly at us as if he could see us. All of us had stepped back from the scrying bowl at the same time. Smoked started billowing out from the scrying bowl, something Taylor had never seen while she had practiced.

Karie had been teaching her for quite a while. She hated lying to her parents and sister about where she was going. She had gone along for the ride with her friend to stay at the camp except she had never registered. Once she was there, she found a ride that took her to Karie's. She was giving her lessons when they had been attacked, she had witnessed her murder when she was behind the wall, and it had closed before the men could get in. The smoke started filling the room to the point none of us could see each other. Amanda had grabbed my hand wanting to make sure we did not lose each other. I had held onto Taylor's hand also.

The room had filled so thick we could almost touch the substance in the air. My eyes burned so I kept them closed. There was no option of leaving the room with the men still banging away on the outside. There had been no way out and no explanation for the thick smoke unless we had caused a gas of some sort not that it hurt to breathe it in. My whole body felt extremely hot almost as if I was burning up from a fever, something I hadn't felt in a long time was natural heat. Then before we knew it, something strange felt as if it was squeezing us. We were still holding hands not moving from our spot however the air we breathed felt so clear and then we were gone leaving the room empty.

Not long after I dropped the phone. Sophie had answered knowing it was coming from me. She had heard the screams; she called Rose and Charlie letting them know about the situation. They were already on their way with Lewis and Evangeline. Lorah had listened to the message that was left on her phone that the girls were in danger, and she had taken off with Valafar and Jessica. Goseck and Dinah had worked their way back home after their research had finished. Stopping by the house with Sophie they were told to wait until the others found out what the situation was and if they needed help, they would call for them. Charlie was the first to inspect the house. They had found the same disastrous room. Hearing the banging upstairs he worked his way towards it, as the men had seen him coming, they had done what the man did earlier. They shifted to black dust and then blew out the window rather quickly before Charlie could grab either of them. Looking around there was blood covering every inch of the room. There was a small footprint on the window ledge however it was only a single print. Not sure if the girls had been able to get out, he wondered what the men were banging against. Looking at the wall he noticed the smallest blood smudge right next to the wall. Rose was the first to touch the wall looking for a way to move it. As she did, the wall started to slide to the side, and a huge billow of white smoke came out of the room showing an alter room with no one in it other than the usual ritual items or stored items that Karie kept private.

Evangeline looked at the small vials that were now empty lying on the table, smelling each one, she distinguished what they were. Looking down in front of the ritual table there were small footprints in blood except she hadn't found any bodies or anyone hiding. Then looking over at Rose she knew how she felt, after all, her daughter was missing also. Then she realized the scrying bowl was glowing. There was a man not looking in the direction where she could see his face however, she recognized the girls. She could only guess somehow; they worked a spell of some sort calling themselves to someone or they were called by that person. As far as he had known, neither Larissa or Amanda knew how and there was a third girl with them around Larissa's age, at least it's how she appeared.

"Rose, at least the girls are alive, their footprints were in here, they might have just walked through the blood when they came in here. They are somewhere I just don't know where they are right now, however they are with each other." Looking at the scrying bowl the glow started to leave as the image of the three girls as well as the man disappeared.

Now not only were Jacob and Lucian missing along with Teddy. Larissa and Amanda were now missing however they looked safe for now; at least we hoped they were. Before anyone else went missing everyone made sure to show up at the house with Sophie. With everyone in the living room completely confused and frustrated. Lorah had let out a bit of a sigh. She still wasn't sure if she had trusted Drezin too soon or not. She was sure if the girls were with anyone, it would have been with him from the description Evangeline had given about the man standing in the scrying bowl.

"Let me get this straight, we no longer know where either Jacob or Lucian is, there's some girl out there that's mortal running around with vampires after her. Larissa and Amanda are now missing except they happen to be with a mysterious girl and man. There was another mortal girl who now is at her own home finishing her vacation however she handed over a medallion to someone we are related to but barely know, Drezin. Lorah thought Charlie should have been given it by this other mysterious person by now and Karie is dead? There's something to do with the number seven, most likely people and not an object. I take it I'm caught up now?" Goseck had such a puzzled look on his face.

"That's all of it. I just feel like I'm losing control, for

centuries it was the life stone but that was controlled, then it was the forbidden cities Jewelry that belonged to this other world where the life stone came from and now they want to throw certain people into the mix." Charlie was rather frustrated pacing the floor as Sophie sat worried on the couch about the girls.

"I don't mean to be rude, but your family has been chaotic since I met you. This almost seems normal." Goseck shook his head in disbelief, Dinah still hadn't said anything she simply sat next to Sophie.

"So far, we have no leads to go on. The one girl named Teddy has no paper trail and both Jacob and Lucian are good at hiding themselves, we have no clue who the girls are with, and we haven't heard from Drezin either." As soon as his name was used Lorah had a rather sad look on her face.

Jessica had been outside trying to focus on the girls not being able to pick up on them either, it was as if they had a protective barrier on them. Which is what Lorah had thought was most likely on the boys as well.

"Does anyone know if Drezin met Amanda?" Lorah was trying to figure out if he was getting all the pieces himself.

The main reason no one had bothered Amanda all this time had been the simple fact that Drezin kept the council away from her and the rest of the family. Felt a bit guilty she was judging him before he had a chance to prove himself.

"Not to worry if he had the girls or even the pieces we would hear from him, if they are with him, they would be safest, he knows how to hide or protect himself better than anyone. Besides if he is with them and has the pieces, I'm sure he has a reason. I've worked with him long enough to trust him and so do you." Valafar had been directing his comment to Lorah and no one else.

The rest of the family had been curious about what she had meant by her question.

"Lorah. Come outside with me." Dinah stood near the door however now stepping outside; Lorah went along not looking at anyone.

"I don't know that much more than anyone else, if I knew where the girls were I would say something." Lorah felt nervous about holding back so much from the others.

"You're usually the only one who does know what's going on. Goseck and I have been gone for a while, and I know for a fact you've had regular correspondence with Drezin. I hadn't said anything about him since he hadn't contacted Charlie or the rest of the family. We felt he would when he was ready. I only found out he was alive because of Goseck filling me in on the life he's been living for the past century. Are you sure you don't know where the girls are?" Dinah had a way of telling Lorah was keeping things to herself but then out of all the siblings she had been closest to her.

"I might have an idea except I don't know if he has them. From the description, he might, and he has the medallion. Drezin was supposed to bring it to Charlie while Valafar and I brought Avani home safely. Valafar feels if he is doing something there must be a reason. He's always looked out for us when he could." Looking down at the ground for a moment Lorah felt bad for second-guessing him, after all, he had done so much without getting credit or letting anyone else know.

"How do you usually contact him?" Dinah was already making plans when she called Jessica and Lily over.

Aaron, Delaney, Alexandra, and Anwen came over to see if they could help. Charlie, Sophie, Valafar, Evangeline, Lewis, and Goseck all came outside to see what we were working on. Looking over at Charlie he had also been staring directly at Lorah wondering what she had been keeping to herself, knowing somehow Dinah must have found out. Forming a circle, we concentrated on the man that Lily had seen, she still had the protection spell over her that Drezin cast. With a few of us ready to go, Charlie stayed behind with Sophie, he had questioned how often Lorah had used transporting with the guardians as a way to find Drezin in the past. With a gust of wind and a bit of smoke, we all disappeared from our spot leaving nothing behind. As we had held on, I knew we could at least find out what happened to the medallion, Larissa, and Amanda. As soon as we were together, we would have to go in search of Jacob, Lucian, and his girl.

Chapter Ten

Back Again

Looking around the room as we all entered, none of us knew what we would be landing into or if Drezin would react first before he found out it had just been us. Normally he would be expecting Lily and Lorah before we came. Separating for a moment we looked around to see if there had been any signs of the girls being there. Beginning to wonder if Drezin had even been here for a while. Lily found something intentionally left behind for someone to find.

"Lorah is this from your niece?" Looking at the piece on the floor and picking it up slightly there was a purple letter 'L' on the band, a gift I had given to her.

Larissa had left a hair tie behind.

Not being able to pick it up. Lorah looked to see what the ribbon might have been caught on until she saw half of it was caught by the floorboard. Running her hand along the board feeling for anything that might give a clue where the door or opening was. As she slid her hand there was a small piece of chipped wood popped up to appear as if there was nothing special about it, other than a piece that had separated on its own. Just her finger could slide into the tiny hole it left as she gripped her finger on the other side, she carefully lifted the lid that covered the stairs going down. Heading down the steps Lorah took the lead as the others followed. There had been voices lightly speaking until we had come closer, then they ceased no doubt trying to figure out who had figured out the entrance. No one was expecting Lorah this time, so she needed to be careful this time.

"Drezin? Are you down here with the girls? It's me, Lorah, our sister Dinah and a couple of guardians." No response had come immediately.

Not wanting to risk it they waited a moment longer, and then they heard Larissa call out.

"We're back here Lorah." The only reason for a delay would have been if he wanted to hide something.

Walking forward there was a light in the distance with the girls waiting for us as well as Drezin. Dinah just shook her head. She hadn't seen Drezin since they were very little and he had left to play with his friends; this would finally be her second time in the last few weeks.

"It's still hard getting used to your being alive, don't get me wrong. I'm glad however, I'm still waiting for someone to say it's a cruel joke.

"I would be the same if things were in the reverse. Your nieces are perfectly fine we just had a chat. I guess I should introduce you to my daughter." As Drezin announced this he looked over at Lorah who looked rather confused.

"Your daughter? I took your daughter earlier and have her hiding with a friend. How is this your daughter?" Dinah looked from Drezin and Lorah rather puzzled since she hadn't known he had any children.

"You're right to be confused; yes, you did hide my youngest daughter except I haven't told you everything. I have three, she is my oldest daughter, apparently, they found her, and Karie was protecting her for me." With a twinge, Drezin had thought about the fact Karie had died protecting his daughter.

"Why are you leaving them to others to protect, why are you not protecting your daughters yourself?" Dinah still looked a bit confused.

"I have some problems with the council, we parted ways however there is a member who wants the power my daughters can wield, I can only guess he had found a way of taking it from them to use it or he intends on absorbing their power himself. If his idea is an experiment, it's not as if he would be worried about the girls surviving. That's why I needed to hide them, however because of this member coming after me the presidium have a wrong viewpoint of me, if I can change that or get a chance to prove my side, then I would be able to better protect my daughters myself. As long as they are divided, they stand a better chance of surviving. Gerard thinks I'm dead and I can cover trails and do other things until it's safe again." Drezin's problems had gone further than what he wanted to explain, if he did, the truth about the other daughters might come out.

"If you had let the rest of the family know. We would have helped; we understand protecting each other." Dinah almost seemed insulted he had left her out of this.

"I know the rest of the family would do anything for me; however, I didn't want to risk their lives with the council or the presidium. It's bad enough I have others involved or even Lorah. We had run into each other simply because of her connection with Valafar. If it had not been for that, we never would have seen each other again.

"Is there anything we can do to help you?" Dinah asked before Larissa and Amanda made their way over to us.

"Just pretend you have not seen me; most assume the family was convinced I was dead at a young age. I can handle the rest; I'm not risking the rest of the family. I shouldn't risk Lorah anymore than I already have. One thing you could do is make sure Jacob and Lucian are safe. Apparently, this girl is in a lot of danger if she stays out on her own." Reaching into his pocket he pulled out the medallion he was supposed to give to Charlie.

"I couldn't risk the family at the moment; it wasn't safe

with Charlie being watched so closely." Lorah was right that Drezin had a reason for withholding the medallion for so long.

"I guess we could look over Lucian's cabin again, maybe we missed something?" Dinah was already making plans about where to search.

"I can help." Amanda had chimed in rather excitedly.

"You should go back with your parents, Lorah and I can handle this. Lewis and Charlie will no doubt keep looking." Shaking her head Amanda looked frustrated however only Larissa and Drezin seemed to notice.

"We can drop the girls off with the guardians, Dinah will search the cabin, and I will take another with me, and we can search around the town and maybe the girl's apartment again." Even Drezin had thought searching these areas again would be a waste of time.

"You should reconsider your plans, if you haven't found any clues the first few times what makes you think you will this time? Besides, Lucian is rather smart and he's going to find a quiet private place to hide that is not far where he can get supplies, and this is going to be a place this girl frequents. No doubt it's where you will find her, after all, she wants to stay close so he can still find her." Drezin had made sense even though that left the town next to Lewis and Evangeline.

The summer place attracted several tourists every year.

"Can we be dropped off at grandma's house?" Larissa had hoped they might be able to instead of heading home since the rest of the family hadn't felt too comfortable in case they were to go after the kids again.

Lewis had his family members around except it had been better not to take any chances. Connecting the reason, she had moved one town over after the summer cabin her family used to rent would also be a bit confusing. After all, why would a human settle in a town of vampires, even if they were not aware of it, wouldn't she notice something odd about the town not being opened during the day and only at night. That the entire town came alive at night only? There had to be someone that had seen her. After leaving Drezin at his hideout with his daughter. Dinah had taken off with Aaron and Delaney while Lorah had taken Lily and Alexandra. Anwen stayed behind with Larissa and Amanda at the grandparent's home. Lewis and Evangeline had already left searching for the girl; they had been given a couple of tips from friends who thought they might have spotted the girl they were looking for. Charlie had left with Sophie, Valafar, and Goseck to look around the town again. Over the last several years Anwen had learned and known the girls far too well to assume they would not get involved again, which is why she had volunteered to stay at home with them.

"Alright, tell me what you two are planning?" As soon as she had asked the two girls looked at each other pretending not to know what she was talking about.

"We don't have any plans; we just wanted to be here." Amanda had been the one to speak since she was much better at hiding emotion or any change in her voice.

"Maybe that works on everyone else except it doesn't with me, now out with it, I know you're going to sneak off and it's much easier if I just come along to keep you safe. So let me know, I'm not stopping you." Standing there with her arms crossed determined neither of the girls was going to leave her out of their plans if she wasn't going to stop them.

"We plan on checking out Lucian's cabin. Not the one the family keeps checking. It's a different one, he had shown Amanda if she ever had to hide there, except it was only under certain dire need otherwise we are not supposed to be there, I'm positive that's where they are." Larissa had spoken giving the rest of the information.

"Even I knew I should listen to you Amanda when you said you could help. You only speak when there's something you know or if you're able to help." Smiling Amanda was rather proud of herself.

Even Larissa couldn't help but smile at her cousin. She always trusted her instincts or ideas.

"I need to know where I'm moving us to otherwise, I

might not even come close. I don't know what to focus on. Lucian is under some sort of protection spell that Drezin cast on him so I can't focus on him, or I would." Grabbing a piece of paper Amanda wrote down an address, she didn't have a picture of the place since she was expected to keep it a secret.

Concentrating on the address it hadn't taken long for the three to end up on the side of the road next to the mailbox with the address on it. Not having a name other than the numbers, it had a single note inside of the box from the post office stating the owner would have to come in and confirm they were living there before the mail would begin to be delivered again, the mail from before has been sent back to their original senders.

"Where is the cabin?" Anwen had looked around curious since she couldn't see any.

Even the other cabins in the area were spread apart from each other.

"It's further along the trail; we must cross the bridge into the woods. He's located closer to the water." Patting her pocket Anwen had made sure her cell phone was in there.

At least she could move them all out if she needed to. Following behind the girls she couldn't believe how much her life had changed when she was first kidnapped. She had been born an ordinary girl from a very ordinary family. One day when she was out with her friends discussing a date she was going on, after all, it was her first and she was so excited. At least she had been until she went out with him only to find he knocked her out. He brought her to this rather strange place where many more people like herself had been brought to dig. Not just basic tunnels for many different uses. They were searching for the possibility of some special stone. For some reason, it was believed there might be a stone to match the original's power. At the time she and the others had never heard of magic, let alone known a stone that could wield such powers. They had always thought it was a myth or that this woman had simply lost her mind. She had worked with the others for a long time exhausting themselves even to the point that some died.

That all changed when Jessica had come, she had the true power passed onto her and she learned how to pass and share that power with others. Her gifts had mimicked those of a shade with several more gifts along with them. There had even been witches who shared similar gifts however we held each one instead of only a few. I had guessed this was Drezin's reason for having his children, he might have wanted children however with the way he likes to experiment with magic, and his wife's background in witchcraft and Wicca, it wouldn't surprise me. From the sounds of it, he had been rather talented at summoning creatures, calling forth the dead, and several other dangerous methods. With the rest of us, we could protect each other much easier. We still had to be careful; there were still those who wished to exploit us however it was no more than those who wanted to use the gifts of a vampire or other creatures that existed.

As we followed the barely-there path, the shrubbery had filled in looking as though no one had been here in years. Except that could be the way he wanted it in case neither wanted company? Catching a rather strange scent Anwen grabbed both girls pulling them off the trail rather quickly and out of sight hiding behind the trees. Looking around there was something that wasn't quite right. It had been the same scent she used to smell in the caves, almost a looming of death in the area, something was dead except there was also the sound of something walking around, too heavy to be an animal and possibly a person. Whatever it was it certainly wasn't dead. Staying low to the ground they waited to see if it would pass by them, hoping not to get caught. The sound was getting louder while the scent was also getting stronger. It was almost nauseating, keeping alert in case this thing was to surprise attack us from behind. We each looked in another direction until Amanda shouted.

Turning to face this large black-looking monster towering over us from behind, his hair had been rather shaggy while his entire body had been covered with hair. A mortal would have thought they had seen Bigfoot on crack. His eyes were huge, he looked crazed but then maybe anyone would have been covered in blood, he had something else rather slimy and green dripping from the corner of his mouth, almost a thick foggy phlegm shot from his mouth as he looked at us. The girls grabbing a hold of Anwen. She quickly concentrated on a safe spot transporting them out immediately not waiting to see what the creature had intended on doing. As long as that thing was there, they wouldn't be able to go that route to Lucian's place. We had all hoped that creature hadn't found him either. We had dropped in near the cabins, thankfully it was near the end of the season, and most had already left for their year-round homes.

"Now what do we do? We can't go back if that thing is there except, I'm positive he must be there. I can just feel it." Amanda had been rather determined about her feelings on it.

"Then we just have to find another way of getting there and hopefully not run into whatever that thing was again." Anwen thought for a moment how exactly they would manage it.

It seemed a little strange a creature like that would be this close to mortals unless there was something or someone around controlling him. Most likely, someone we didn't want to run into.

Taking the girls, they walked along the road until they came close to town, in the distance the town had looked rather busy for being so dark. Leaving the road and heading over to the stream that had separated the other side of the island. There was a small bridge that looked as though it connected both sides at one time. Even in the far distance where they would have come from much higher, there was a bridge, the very one they would have crossed over if they had made it that far. Watching they had seen the same creature making his way over it, at least it wasn't looking in our direction. Getting closer to the bridge testing it out first before the girls were to walk across, even though it looked as if it was about to crash into the water, it was still solid enough to get across.

"Should we call mom and dad telling them about that thing?" Larissa had still been looking where we last saw the creature.

"If we do, they will demand that Anwen take us home." At least Amanda was right, agreeing with her we kept walking along the shore down lower.

It was interesting how the town had been built lower down the hill from all the homes and cabins. We could only walk so far along the coastline before the water had started overlapping it. Looking around for an area we might be able to climb up to. I couldn't find anything. Even the ledge up above us didn't look like it had a place we could land safely if I transported us up there. Then around the next bend, I could barely make it out as I could see the corner tip of a house. Hoping I wasn't making a mistake or miscalculation by doing this. I held onto the girls as they were curious about where I was moving us to, or if I had seen something. I concentrated on that area next to the small peak; we would end up in a flat area. As soon as we landed, I had to pull Larissa closer to me, we were so close to the end of the cliff, looking down below there were several rocks that emerged from the water. Taking a step back I couldn't help but take a deep breath of relief.

Even though I had practiced this skill with Jessica and the others. It was still difficult getting used to feeling air pressing tightly around me, white blurs all around me not being able to see anything until I was standing where I had been picturing. The first night I had fallen asleep after learning. I had dreamed so vividly about where I was that I caused my sleeping body to move to each place. I had only learned to stop doing that and control my dreams and thoughts better when Sophie gave me advice on how to better control myself. I also made sure to keep my emotions in control. Looking over at Amanda hoping we found it. I knew we had by the excited smile on her face.

"This is it." Amanda had exclaimed making her way carefully around the side of the cabin to the front. There were steps leading down quite a ways as if we had shown up on the backside three floors up.

Standing in front of the supposed cabin. There was no way this was a cabin; I was going to explain the definition of a castle compared to a cabin to Lucian when we found him. His view was rather distorted if he truly thought this was a cabin. The front door had been locked not that we hadn't expected it to be. I could barely see through a crack however it was enough to form a picture in my mind of the other side. Reached out holding the girls' hands again. I focused on the inside area. I could see hoping there wouldn't be any traps set. I moved us in rather quickly not wanting to stick around outside just in case that creature was to spot us here. The room we appeared in was extremely dark except as we walked. The old-fashioned torches along the wall would automatically light up until we passed them, and they would extinguish just as fast.

"This place looks like it has been empty for a long time." As we walked the dust swirled around our feet, cobwebs covering the walls and pictures that hung.

"If Lucian was injured so badly, why didn't he come home, why hide for so long?" I was trying to make sense of this.

I knew the family had been dealing with this for a while however this just seemed too strange, almost as if it was being made harder than it needed to be.

"If he's found he can be taken, he's protecting the human girl by hiding, he loves her. He doesn't like anyone to see he's weak. He's used to being the one to help everyone or protecting others. Lucian hates being used against his family so when he can he hides so no one can do that." Not thinking anything of it Amanda continued into the home looking around for clues that either of the boys might have been there.

"Anwen, can you locate them by vibrations? Maybe we are close enough you can pick up on them, hopefully, the magic spell won't cover them if we are this close?" I know the girls were hoping I would be able to find them except I just could not pick up on anything.

Whatever spell Drezin used was a very powerful one, he

certainly meant to keep them hidden. Then I noticed Larissa standing still concentrating rather hard. I was beginning to think she was trying to move, except even she knew she wouldn't be able to do that.

"What are you doing Larissa?" I was curious even though Amanda didn't seem to question it, maybe she had seen her do this before?

"It's a family connection; the older ones can do it except I have never been able to. I just wanted to try." As she stood there a while longer, I looked around more.

There were very few rooms to go into. Not going far from the girls, I peeked into one of the rooms. The kitchen had been in there except it like the rest of the place as though it hadn't been used in a very long time.

"Larissa?" The voice had been extremely faint.

Larissa had almost jumped when she heard it.

"Did you hear that? It sounded like Jacob." Not that she was directing her question towards me.

Amanda had told her no she hadn't heard it. Concentrating again Larissa was deep in thought.

"How did you find that place? Don't move. It's not safe, I'll come up for you." The voice had been extremely faint having to strain for it.

Larissa let us know exactly what was said. Apparently, Jacob was here and coming to get us. Although he no doubt assumed only Larissa was here, she hadn't told him the rest of us were with her, even though he must have known the rest of the family never would have left her alone.

Jacob had looked worn out; he looked surprised to see us waiting for him. Not talking I was beginning to wonder if Lucian wasn't the only one who had needed healing. On the side of Jacob's face down the side of his neck to the partially visible chest had been five bright scratches. We had followed him up the steps to the right of the room. I was curious where the other set went except, I hadn't wanted to lose everyone, so I kept up. Walking behind making sure everyone made it safely we followed Jacob. Moving a dresser away from the wall, there was a rather large piece of the wall that slid to the side that we walked through. Pulling the dresser back to cover where we walked in, we kept following Jacob walking down now a set of steps that were rather confining. We had walked down so many steps my legs were tired until we were at the end. Walking down the narrow pathway a distance there was a medium-sized square room with a bed in the corner. Walking in front of the girls. I made my way to the body that lay in the bed. Looking down at Lucian he was barely responding, he had looked worse than what was described. I doubted he was able to heal himself at all, even with time he wasn't getting better. Since it had been so long, I knew I was going to need help from the others.

"How long has he been this bad?" I was hoping I might be able to get Jacob to answer.

He was still barely whispering now that we were even closer to him. Sitting down on the floor before he was able to answer.

"I was attacked by the creature trying to keep it from killing Lucian. It's the one I was hoping it wouldn't find you out there. Lucian was healing until that thing attacked us." His voice trailed off except I could still make out what he was saying.

Larissa had sat down by her uncle holding him up since he looked as though he was about to slump forward on the ground. Neither had any strength barely to get better or move to get help. At least I knew a definite way to get the others here. It might scare the others since they won't be expecting me to call them to me right now, however it would let the rest of the family know something was up. As I was concentrating on the other guardians calling them to us. Amanda pulled out her cell phone texting the emergency code to her family. I just hoped no one else would pick up on the signal. As I concentrated Alexandra and Lily were the first two to arrive, then shortly followed by Aaron and Jessica. Delaney had been the last to appear; I still had to practice calling everyone at the same time. Jessica could without thinking about it however she had several teachers and much more practice, something I had to stop putting off and work on.

"How did you find them?" Jessica was impressed we were standing in front of them.

"Amanda found them, and Larissa was able to find Jacob mentally, he showed us directly to Lucian. They need healing. I just can't do it on my own." Nodding the others understood.

We all placed our hands first on Lucian concentrating. His body began to heat up momentarily and then went cold. He was bathed in a golden glow that surrounded him. As we healed him, we could see the cuts and broken limbs healing back where they should have been. Even though we could heal we had still been limited. We could repair skin, broken bones, and cuts almost to any depth. Except we were not able to heal someone back from death or cure major diseases, especially if the person had it for a while, we could only heal what we considered minor. As soon as Lucian was breathing normally, we now concentrated on Jacob even though he kept trying to tell us to concentrate on Lucian. After a while Jacob was looking much better than in the condition we had found him in, only the scar that had been on his side was not as visible as it had been before and was still barely noticeable. We couldn't completely get rid of it since it had been there for so long already. Larissa's cell phone started vibrating getting our attention. Even the phones that Lily, Aaron, and Amanda carried were going off. Different family members were calling us.

"They must be worried about where we disappeared to." Lily flipped open her phone, Lorah was calling her since she had found out the other guardians disappeared also.

"Tell them to meet us at Charlie and Sophie's home." At first, Aaron wanted to move both Jacob and Lucian there except both boys refused.

"We need to find Teddy, she's in danger. I'm well enough to find her." Standing up Lucian had looked much stronger and healthier except he still seemed to be in a bit of a fog.

"Let us help you, if we do find her and there's trouble,

we can move you out much faster and safer. We almost had her before except she let go of Jessica and we don't know where she is right now. She won't trust us unless your there." Alexandra was correct, we all had thought she might have let go because she hadn't trusted us, or she was trying to protect Lucian.

"I never should have been around her; I've done a horrible thing to a wonderful person that doesn't deserve any of this, and she must be so terrified. I tried to hide our world from her except I just couldn't stay away." Lucian was taking this rather hard blaming himself; at least he agreed to let us help him find her.

It helped he had a picture of her so that the rest of us knew who we were looking for. We let the family know the rest had been called to help heal Lucian and Jacob. Lily dropped Amanda and Larissa off at their grandparent's home, at least now they knew Lucian and Jacob were safe. That we were helping them find the girl. The rest of the family had agreed to stay at the house waiting for us to come back. We hadn't wanted to scare her even more by having a large group coming after her even if Lucian was with us, we broke down into two groups. At least she would recognize Jacob also. He had gone where he last remembered seeing her curious if she would try showing up again, even though we had hoped she wouldn't try to come into the woods with that creature walking around. I hadn't mentioned the blood on creature; I was just hoping it wasn't hers.

Anwen had left with Lucian; he was hoping to find some clue where Teddy might have gone after checking out the cabin her family used to rent. Only the foundation was left, apparently, they had already cleared it after the mystery fire. Jacob had kept the fire a secret not wanting to risk him looking for her while he was still not well enough. Then I took him to the last spot she was known to be before she had let go. Standing at the house, looking around where her dog had been. The factory she had worked at that was now completely cleared out. Trying to think the way she might, there was one safe place she might try to travel to, even if her grandparents had died when she was little it might still be enough safety for her, she might risk it. Only occasionally we had stopped asking people if they had seen this girl, then showing them the picture most responded they hadn't seen her. There had been a few creatures around except wanting to be careful and not let anyone know she wasn't with us; we had only asked mortals if they had seen her.

Jacob and his group searched her parent's home carefully finding nothing. They hadn't even kept her room; they had changed it into an office and as for her grandparent's home it had been torn down making way for an apartment building. They had been worth checking out except each led to a dead end. Heading back to where the former area where the cabin had burned down Lucian had simply stared at the foundation for over an hour wondering where she would have gone. He had always told her he would be able to find her and now that he needed to, he couldn't. Sitting on the ground feeling frustrated trying to keep his thoughts clear hoping not to lose his control or composure, he knew she wouldn't go very far, she wanted to make sure he found her, which is why she settled down in the town next to this one. She had no clue it was filled with so many creatures. Then it hit him. Moving quickly, we raced after him wondering if he knew where she might be.

There had been one creature she had met she liked, even for working for Katherine this one had been rather kind to the rest of the family, she even explained once she had only worked for the woman out of necessity not because she had wanted to. Making his way to her home, coming up from behind hoping no one would see us there; Lucian hadn't wanted to cause any problems for her. Almost up to her door it opened as the lady stood there motioning for us to come in. It was almost dark enough outside for the other vampires in the area to be out and possibly see us.

"Have you seen Teddy?" Lucian wasted no time getting to the point.

"Actually. I had, she was here a few weeks ago except she

was worried staying around here, she was safe enough except she wanted to take off for another place, she was positive you would be able to find her there." Walking over to her cabinet that was displaying old dishes, Ericka opened the frail-looking door removing a dish.

Not sure why at first, she turned it revealing an envelope. Placing the plate back and closing the door she handed the envelope over to Lucian. Opening the envelope reading what was inside Lucian suddenly smiled.

"Why didn't I think of this place, I can't believe I forgot it?" Shaking his head, he couldn't believe he hadn't thought of this place first.

It was a place he brought her when she was little. She was getting rides there so hopefully, she was on her way safely and not getting rides from other creatures.

Chapter Eleven

Teddy Raynn

After letting go of Jessica and Amanda it was a rather painful landing. I had at least been eight feet in the air when I dropped straight down, the last several weeks I slept in the cave with my dog while demons were searching for me. The longer I was hiding the worse the creatures started to look. I just hoped Lucian was right when he said he would be alright, to heal and eventually find me. Even this small, once-peaceful town held no refuge anymore. After staying with Ericka for a while. I found it was much better to take off for a place that Lucian would assume I would go. At first, I thought I would be able to hitchhike to where I needed to go, except I found I was much more paranoid now than I used to be, but then I also knew there were dangerous creatures out there now, it wasn't bad enough I had to be careful of everyday mortals who were dangerous. I had a whole new group of creatures to worry about that I had no clue who to trust anymore.

Walking along the road there had been a woman who was off on vacation for a while, a very sweet lady. I think from the way I looked, she took pity on me and was willing to drive out of her way slightly to help me get home, at least that's where I told her I was going. She drove at least eight hours before her route went an entirely separate direction than the way I had needed to go. I still had to walk but it saved me a lot of time. I wasn't sure if vampires could track down when a credit card had been used so I was careful only to use cash which was starting to run low. I did withdraw more money from my bank before I went up any further north. I didn't want to risk getting cash from a bank too close to where I wanted to stay. There had been old copper and iron mines up here along with plenty of freshwater lakes around and most important enough, places to hide. Lucian's family had an old house up here that I hadn't been to since I was extremely little. I only stopped at a few hotels along the way. One night I had heard so much clashing and screaming only to find out it was a couple arguing and throwing things around catching everyone's attention. I had listened through my door not wanting to come out. I was careful not to let anyone see me. After all of this, I was going to do everything I possibly could, not to walk for a very long time. There were a couple of new buildings in the town and a few more houses up here. As I walked through the town there had been a couple of people standing outside talking to each other and just enjoying the weather. No one seemed to be in a hurry, and no one looked surprised to see a stranger walking through.

I did start to feel as if I was never going to get there. I had a hard time remembering exactly where it was, I could only remember slightly the memories I had as a small child. I was just thankful not too much had changed, or I never would have found it at all. Counting down the turns, the hills, and certain mines. I finally found the place when it started getting extremely dark. After living in that one town, I had done everything I could to avoid being out in the dark and did most of my traveling during the daytime and in the sunlight. Fortunately, I was almost there, and I hadn't seen any hotel, even if I had been only fifteen minutes from where I needed to be. I would have stayed at a hotel just to avoid being in the dark. Not that I wanted to attract attention to myself. I kept every light on that I possibly could.

Not that far ahead of me had been the house, excited to finally see it, nothing had changed other than the siding fading a little. The porch had a few loose boards, and the front door hadn't been locked. Taking the spare key from above the door. I stepped inside being careful looking around. Searching each room making sure no one was there. There had been sheets for the beds in plastic bags already cleaned and ready to use from the last time they were here. Each of the mattresses that were on the beds had also been wrapped in plastic to keep them clean and free from dust. Fixing up one of the rooms, taking the broom to it. I had cleaned out Rose's room. At least when I had spent the night here, I shared a room with Lucian's sister Rose. That usually was when my parents had left me with my aunt; she never noticed if I was there or not.

One thing I had done differently here had been to keep the lights off. If someone realized there were suddenly lights here when no one had been around, they might come to check it out. I had, however, kept all the doors locked even though after what I had been through and seen these vampires do, I highly doubted locking the doors would stop or slow them down. At least this way I would hear them if they were to come through. The crime must not have been an issue around here. Rose still had cash in her drawer. Not that I had taken out very much of my own money I felt guilty for borrowing her money without asking first. I just wanted all of this to be over soon, after all, I was going to completely run out of money, and I needed to get a job except I had to be careful. There were far too many looking for me and I wasn't sure why they wanted me so bad. I only assumed it had been because of Lucian, not that I knew why they were after him? I felt sick to my stomach when I thought about the way he looked. I hated leaving him like that, I kept thinking I should have refused to leave, at least that way I could have taken care of him. He always took care of me and protected me. I used to have the strangest dreams about him and most of them had been when I was young, we would be racing through the woods at such fast speeds, I knew it couldn't have been possible; I just had an active imagination. I felt so guilty being worried about myself when he was in so much pain. I just wanted to make sure I lived long enough to see him again. I hadn't made any plans after I saw him. I had no clue if he was only going to explain what was going on and where I was to move from there. At this point, I had no future planned at all other than waiting for Lucian and I was beginning to wonder if I had made a smart move. I cared about him, but it wasn't as if we were dating, he might still look at me as that little girl or simply a close friend he came to trust.

I had already stayed in the town for a few weeks when I had seen a sign at the local grocery store hiring part-time help. Applying, I wound up with the job, they had said there were not very many people around so the likely chance I wouldn't get the job was very slim. It was easy. I came in and unloaded the truck, took the items out of the boxes, priced them, and then set them out on the shelves, occasionally I would arrange the shelves to simply make them look more organized. At least the job kept me busy, I even hooked up the cable to the house and no one ever questioned why I was doing it. No one seemed to care, they all kept to themselves but then I think most lived up here to have privacy, as private as everyone was, at least when you did speak with them everyone had been extremely friendly and helpful. The weather started to get colder out and even the mornings started out now with a thick layer of frost. I had checked the snowmobile in the shed to make sure it still worked. Lucian used to tell me how much snow used to be up here, which is why he only took me up here when it was during the summer.

I was thankful Rose had left some of her clothes here. I started to wear her sweaters and use a couple of blankets that were stored away. After being here for a while I did begin to wonder if Lucian would find me here or not. Then it hit me. What if he's not going to get better? What if he pushed me away because he didn't want me to see him die? That thought—God, that thought—ripped right through me. He promised he'd always find me, no matter what. Always. But what if he can't this time? What if this is it? My legs gave out, and I just collapsed. I couldn't stop the tears. I couldn't even breathe. It felt like the world was ending right there. I couldn't handle it if I found out he had died, and I had left him like that alone. I knew he had Gerry to take care of him, I just wished I could see him again, I had always kept my promise to him, and he counted on it. I wished for once I had just told him it was a promise I couldn't make because I couldn't keep it. I missed him more than anything I had ever remembered missing before; I found it was very difficult to breathe.

One of the days I had gone to work, setting items out on the shelves, there was another new person that came in the store, not that anyone else had a reason for hiding. I made sure this person had not seen me. Keeping an eye on him he picked up a few items for camping, not the best time to go camping during the early frost or winter. He didn't stick around, one thing I had noticed was he was certainly looking around as if he was looking for something. Or in my case possibly looking for me? I wasn't sure however I made sure I went home during the daylight even though this stranger came to the store during the daylight hours. The house seemed perfectly normal. No signs of footprints in the very light snow on the ground. Pretty soon I wasn't going to be walking into town even though it was only a twenty-minute walk. Summers it would be fine except I wasn't looking forward to it during the winter even if I had planned on using the snowmobile. Then I had to remind myself, hopefully, I won't be here in the summer.

Laying down in bed that evening I stared at the ceiling. Rose had a fascination with the constellations, so she installed several shiny objects on the ceiling to intricately make up the formations of the stars. I had been so busy watching the ceiling I hadn't noticed until there was a hand placed firmly over my mouth and a man who moved very fast sitting on top of me pressing me downward. I couldn't move or scream, but then who would have been around to hear me?

"Who are you?" The voice was rather deep and direct.

Was he serious?

"Humph." Was all I could get out.

Did he honestly think I could answer him with his hand pressed so hard over my mouth?

"Sorry I forgot." Shaking his head as if it just hit him how foolish he was.

"Not sure if I want to tell you, after all, you just attacked me, I saw you in the general store earlier. I'll probably regret telling you this, but my name is Teddy. Am I allowed to ask yours?" Not sure what he had planned.

I just hoped he wasn't a vampire, at least for a human like me there might be hope but if he was a vampire I was doomed.

"I think you're the girl I'm looking for." As he said this, he was trying to get his phone out of his pocket without letting up on me.

He placed his hand over my mouth again. Taking a picture of me he sent it to someone. Taking his hand off my mouth for a moment I thought of the only thing I could think to say.

"I have one of those faces I look like a lot of people." Not that I expected him to buy my excuse.

He had started to smile. I just hoped it was from what I had said and not from what he was being told by the person he had just called.

"That's funny, I think I would have liked you, except I'm going to be killing you, and I need the bracelet first." He just sat there staring at me as he now was setting the cell phone down, raising his hand as if he was going to smack me to death.

"You want my bracelet? Seriously?" Of all the things I was going to die for. He asks for a bracelet.

"Don't act as if you don't know, it's been given to you as a gift, we want it back." Looking him over, he looked rather serious.

He wasn't going to give me his name, and I certainly hadn't recognized him. The only bracelet I had was the one given to me by Lucian unless he had been attacked because of it. If so, I didn't plan on handing it over, at least no one would recognize it since I no longer wore it on my wrist, right now it was in my right shoe.

"What are you going to do if I don't give it to you?" Trying to hide the quiver in my voice buying time to find a way out of this.

Not that I was seeing too many options other than hoping to get him off me so I could make a break for it.

"I'm going to kill you regardless. So, you can either save me time finding it or I can kill you mercifully and make it quick and slightly less painful if you just hand it over." He leaned in a bit, I could smell his breath, and it was so horrible smelling it could gag a maggot.

Leaning back, I think he saw my reaction as soon as he was breathing on me.

"Maybe I should just play around with you for a while, perhaps that would make your boyfriend come after me, after all, I don't seem to have any luck finding him." Closing my eyes, I didn't want to see him.

I didn't want to be the reason Lucian stopped protecting himself. I could feel his hand slide down the side of my face, slowly along my neck down to my chest. As he did, I could feel a sharp pain, he was leaving a thin slice along my skin as I bled a little.

I swear from all the times people keep trying to set me on fire, embed sharp objects into my skin causing me to bleed so much, if anyone ever asked me why I look so horrible I swear I'm going to lose it.

"If you get off from me, I'll go get the bracelet." I had to try something even if I were to give him one of Rose's bracelets.

Maybe while he was temporarily distracted, he might lose interest in me, or I might run far enough. Then I remembered there was a little snow out there, he could just follow my footsteps.

Shaking my head, a little I had to think of something, I

couldn't give up.

"I think I would rather have some fun, after all, it's been a while, I deserve it." As he leaned in, he went to kiss me on the cheek.

As he did, I felt a strong wind blow past me as I felt his body almost being thrown off me. Not sure what it was, it had broken the window knocking him outside. Standing up off the bed. I put my jeans on right away with the dark blue sweater. Trying to get my shoes on quickly. I made my way down the stairs. I don't know what managed to get him off from me except I was going to take the chance to get away and not wait around to find out why. Quickly half running down the stairs there were a few people in the living room, they had looked up at me but returned their gaze to the window as they watched the man being thrown through the window. Before they had the chance to talk to me, I ran back up the steps going into one of the other rooms. Locking the door and placing a chair behind it I heard someone knocking at the door trying to talk to me. They had my name also but then they could have heard me tell the other man. Sliding the window open. I stepped out onto the small roof that jutted out. I knew it would be a small drop. I was just being careful not to hurt my legs or ankle; it would suck to get a twisted ankle when I was trying to get away. Landing the best that I could, I ran for the shed, even though I couldn't run very fast I could get away with the snowmobile much faster. Just before I made it to the shed, I heard my name being called one last time. Turning I couldn't believe what I had just seen.

"Teddy, stop running." I stopped dead in my tracks.

Feeling lightheaded. I wondered if I imagined all of this, maybe that other man had managed to kill me, and I was bleeding out imagining he was finally here. The others from the living room had come out now standing behind him. The one girl I had recognized that tried to bring me somewhere once when I had let go. Walking over to me I couldn't get over how he had looked. Nothing like the way he looked when I had last seen him.

"You're here? There's a man here trying to kill me, I don't know what caused it, but he went through the window, I had my eyes closed." Placing his arms around me I suddenly felt safe.

Holding onto him I never wanted to let go.

"I know. I attacked him; I won't ever let anyone hurt you like that again. I never should have had you leave me, even if I was in a horrible condition. At least I would have known you were safe. I thought I was keeping you safe having you leave, I hoped no one would ever connect you to me. I'm sorry." Holding me still neither of us wanted to let go.

Giving us some privacy, the others went back into the house.

"There are some things I need to explain to you. I've known you since you were a very little girl, and I've hidden so much from you because I hoped to keep you safe from it all, except it's hard to when it's my world. Then I regretted staying in your life because being with me puts you in danger. I just can't seem to stay away from you. I tried for a while. We kept running into each other or at least other creatures kept finding you and I had that desire to keep you safe. I just don't think you will want to stick around once you find out the truth." For the first time, Lucian had leaned back a little looking at me in the face.

He looked so worried as if I would run away from him screaming.

"Whatever it is it can't be that bad. I trust you." I had hoped he would say he wasn't a vampire, the ones I had met so far wanted to kill me.

"I fell in love with you, I shouldn't have." The expression on his face turned rather serious.

"That doesn't exactly sound like a bad thing unless you are upset you fell in love with me?" I wasn't sure how to take it.

"Falling in love wasn't the bad thing, it's the fact that I did," looking at me I was sure he understood he had confused me, "I never thought about how I would break the news to you?" Now Lucian looked confused while he was trying to explain it.

"I don't know if I like the direction this is going, after the last few months I think I would rather hear you're a vampire." I wasn't aware of just how accurate I was.

After hearing the little he was saying. I started feeling sick to my stomach. I had worried so much about him except I never expected this. Even the look of shock showed on his face.

"You know what a vampire is?" More, asking out of curiosity Lucian kept staring at me.

"I've had a few try to kill me, this last one. I doubted would have been the last one if I had managed to get away and yes, vampires are very painful and scary except if you're going to tell me you think we shouldn't see or speak to each other anymore. I think those creatures are going to keep coming after me anyway, or at least until they know I gave over the bracelet you gave me or that I died." Waiting for his response he still seemed rather shocked.

"Sorry. I'm still surprised by your vampire comment." Still looking at me with curiosity wondering what involvement I had with them other than living in the same town with them.

"I had the crap beat out of me at the old cabin, then I found out people I was hanging out in the last town wanted to kill me, I had an entire building explode and collapse around me and had a few vampires try to kill me since then and some wolves found me. I've lost a lot of blood in the last month or so, not from a vampire but just as an aftereffect of things happening. Then I met a strange family who had this person who either did an impressive magic act or is capable of using magic, she's the one that went back into the house with the others." Not sure how Lucian would take this even though I was still under the impression his name was Daniel.

While I had described being beaten up and the others finding me out in the woods about to kill me, he had cringed.

"I never should have involved you in any of this. I promise I will keep you safe until you will be safe without me." As soon as he had said without him, I felt my heart drop into my stomach.

"After all of this. I'm still going to lose you?" None of this had sounded fair at all, if he truly wanted me to be safe on my own, I would rather just leave and deal with whatever happened.

"I don't know how else to keep you safe." I could hear the frustration in his voice.

"Daniel, stay with me. If you love me then stay with me." Holding me close again letting out a sigh I knew I was getting the point he was trying to make; I just didn't want to accept it.

"Then I need to be honest with you. To start with my name is Daniel Lucian Michael, my family calls me Lucian. I am a vampire." Almost as if he was holding his breath no doubt waiting for me to freak out from hearing him tell me what he was.

At least he was agreeing to stay with me, which was all I was concerned with.

"So, you agree you're staying with me?" Smiling at me I know I wasn't giving him the answer he was expecting except this was what I wanted to find out.

"Yes, I'm staying with you, does it bother you what I am?" Lucian was surprised by the way I had reacted.

"I've known you for so long, yes you did hide it from me, and I wish you would have known you didn't have to hide it from me. You have protected me for so long, I know I have yet to see you age; you look the same as when I first met you. I knew there was something about you I just never knew what to associate it with. If you were going to hurt me in any way you would have done it years ago. I take it I can't call you Daniel anymore?" It would feel strange at first calling him by a different name, except if he was happier with Lucian, I would call him that.

"You can call me anything you want." Smiling at me then the expression on his face changed.

I had only seen Lucian look at me this way twice before, once when he thought I wasn't paying attention while watching something else, the other time I had almost thought he was going to kiss me and hadn't.

Looking at me for a moment before he leaned in, I could feel his cool breath on my skin before he pressed his lips on mine. Cupping my chin with his hand while his other hand had been on my lower back as he pulled me towards him, closer and much firmer, his kiss had been much more urgent the longer he kissed me, almost as if he was savoring my lips. I could feel such a strong sensation running from my lips, through my neck to my feet as if I was warming up from the slight vibration running through my body. The world around me disappeared, I had even momentarily forgotten where we were or the fact a few minutes ago. I had a vampire trying to kill me, or a simple fact the man I fell in love with just told me he was a vampire as well. I let myself get completely absorbed at the moment. Actually. Lucian had also, and neither of us had heard the voices behind us right away calling for us. I wished this moment could have lasted much longer. I didn't know when the next time we would get the chance.

"Sorry to ruin your moment, but we have some unpleasant news." Judging the expression on Anwen's face, everyone could tell how serious it is.

Keeping his arm around Teddy's waist he asked.

"What's wrong?" He thought possibly Drezin was caught or someone else had run into the monster?

"We called Charlie to let him know that we found the girl except he couldn't speak long, it sounded as if he was running at the time. He said to meet at the family safe place; he said you would know where it was. Apparently, it's not safe to go home right now. The presidium has found out that Katherine is still alive. I don't know how that should affect us; however, she's getting much more desperate for the pieces she's looking for." Having a serious expression show on his face I wondered what could be happening?

I knew more about Lucian than any of his family. When I had last seen them, I was rather little and didn't remember very much.

"I take it you didn't get a chance to tell him we were already there. I wish I knew what was going on or I would send each of you out to bring the family here. It might not be safe enough to send just one in case you end up in the middle of something. It could make it worse for you and my family." Shaking his head confused Lucian felt stuck without knowing what was going on.

"I could always go myself and find out, it would be safer if just one showed up that way if I could help, I would at least be there. It's better than nothing right now." Everyone hated hearing her volunteer to take off on her own.

Except we knew it could be dangerous, she could get killed but then so could Charley if we don't do something. It was difficult to know what we were walking in the middle of.

"We can stop by the house and collect Larissa and Amanda, possibly Sophie if she's there or anyone else." Aaron had given a wink to the others that Lucian had noticed.

They'd worked something out between themselves— something quiet, something we weren't meant to hear. And as much as every instinct told us to shield them from the world, we knew we couldn't hold on forever. They were already learning how to speak to each other in ways we couldn't teach. So, we had to let them find their own way, even if it meant stepping back. Because one day, they'll be out there without us—and when that day comes, they'll need to know how to survive, not just with each other, but despite everything waiting beyond our reach.

Aaron was the first to disappear followed by Anwen. The rest hadn't taken very long to leave all with different destinations. Even though we were sure it was unsafe, we all would have risked our lives for Charley. We didn't know if the others were in dangerous situations either. Staying here with Teddy, we waited for the others to show making sure once they did get here it would be safe, not that I knew how long that would last if we were being hunted. After only a few hours Nichole and Anthony had been the first ones to show. Not that the cabin was that large it was going to be getting crowded rather quickly. Dinah and Goseck hadn't taken long either to join us; from the way they had looked when they arrived, we knew they dealt with problems on the way.

"Katherine is getting desperate; she's not messing around this time. She has old-time associates working with her now, it's not like dealing with unskilled vampires or her usual self-made creatures, these know exactly what they are after and if they don't get it, you're done for. She's no longer playing nice. She's willing to kill off everyone who gets in her way until she finds what she wants. I just don't know what she's looking for?" Goseck had always made a point to know where Katherine was and what she was working on.

More than the rest of us. He hadn't trusted her even when he hadn't been looking for us.

"Why come after us now? She had so many chances before to get whatever she is looking for, why can't she just charm an item to get what she wants out of it?" There were so many things she could do.

Why be so firmly decided on only these specific items?

"Other objects have not absorbed as much energy as these have over the last several centuries, also the materials they come from are rare and no longer obtainable. What linked their access before is long gone. She has tried to find them without drawing attention to herself, not that she doesn't have much of a choice so she's much more desperate to find them now." If that had been her reasoning, I could understand that except none of us were sure what we would do if she found us, especially Teddy.

We tried the best we could to hide it from her even though we were sure she was aware something dangerous was happening, especially after the attack earlier with her.

"I feel like I stepped in the middle of something that I should know. Why does she want jewelry from you so badly?" Teddy asked nervously.

"She had a vision of how powerful her sister was going to be and the object that had been created for her. We all thought Katherine killed her sister only to find out that Najee, a shade had hidden her in another world where she would never die. While she was there, she healed and was ready to come back. She had placed a protective spell for the life stone to go to various guardians' until she could eventually come back for it. This was to keep it away from her mother and sister Katherine. She did come back, and she killed Najee, then her mother, and tried to find the stone except by then, it wasn't coming to her anymore. She at some point wasn't recognized as human or a shade, a requirement she made with the protection spell. Katherine did end up killing her, but all this time she knew somehow the stone was connected to our family. We don't know why since she changed most of us into vampires to stop us from doing that. If she allowed anyone to live, it's because she found you useful for later. Once you're no longer needed, she kills you. The life stone was absorbed into Harmony, and she found a way of sharing this so that other guardians would have the same powers and protect each other better than leaving one alone and vulnerable. The stone can change a vampire to a mortal, heal, make it so vampires can walk during the day, it could kill instantly, shred the flesh off a vampire, kill thousands of vampires in a second of a flash, transport anywhere in this world or create portals to enter for other worlds. There's more, but that is all we know of it so far. The problem is it's in people and can't be taken out except with the three pieces. She believes it can reform the life stone again. It can stop a person from ever dying except she already has a curse on her that does that. Her physical form doesn't hold up for long, she has strong magic aiding her right now, without it she would have to take over another strong body or keep taking over creatures that happen to be around, the stone could fix that for her. The reason you haven't died yet from any injuries and I'm sorry I wasn't there to protect you. The medallion you ware around your ankle is enough to keep you alive. Imagine how much more powerful it is with the other two pieces, and there's something about the number seven. Somehow that factors into it and that we know involves Drezin and his daughters. Drezin and his wife could never have children, so we don't know how he managed to have biological daughters. We've only met two, one of our sisters helped him hide one, he hadn't told us about the other one until we met her recently. She didn't seem to know her father all that well, but we don't know the full situation. Drezin doesn't always feel the need to fill others in if he thinks it will keep them safe. All we know is he had the rest hidden. I'm positive knowing Drezin, there's a lot more to this that we don't know. You're caught up on the main parts, from what you've experienced you can get an idea how bad this is going to get." Lucian hugged Teddy close wishing he had never given her the medallion.

He never imagined anyone would suspect the girl was human. Much less that he'd fall in love with her. Most of those he tried to protect ended up worse off: marked from the start, dragged into danger, or dead. But something about her reminded him of his sister, and at first, his need to protect her was instinctive. Over time, that bond deepened into something far more complicated. He left, once, hoping distance would make her forget. But he never could.

None of the guardians had stayed around except to drop off a few family members and then quickly disappear without saying a word. The only one that hadn't come back was Anwen, leading us to wonder if something happened or if wherever she was, the others were now following her? Not that we were missing too many family members now, most were already here at the house. Jacob, Rose, and Larissa were all sitting on the couch while Sophie paced, Aiden holding onto Emma. After being with our family for a while she had been finding out that life with us was very different from the mortal life she had been used to. Lewis's family had joined us totaling forty family members.

"Have we heard from the rest of the family?" Sophie had been pacing no doubt wondering how Charley was doing.

"I'm sure Charley is alright, he's quite skilled and can take care of himself when he has to." As gentle and soft-spoken a person as Charley was, he still had a side of himself he chose to hide, which is why he understood the pull Drezin had when he joined the presidium.

Charlie has learned the hard truth: the only escape is

death or slipping so far down the council's ranks that they forget he was ever there

"We heard from Charley when we got here, so far, we are still waiting on the rest, and no one is answering their cell phones. That could mean a few things, not necessarily that they are in danger, but it might be safer just to have their phones off right now." The only family we hadn't heard from yet was from Aidelle, Anna, and faith or a current update from Charley.

Getting up from her seat Nichole walked over to Sophie to help relax her, we had no idea how long it would be before Charley joined us.

"Mom, maybe you would like to come outside and get some fresh air? I'm going to check on the girls, we have enough family here, and it's always safer with everyone together so we let the girls play outside for now." Not that there had been very much to be said. Nichole hoped to occupy Sophie for a while, even her pacing was making everyone nervous.

While we had waited. Anwen and Charley had their problems to deal with. She had gone after him which hadn't surprised any of us. With most of us here at the house all we could do was wait until we heard from the others. In the meantime, the house was overly filled even though Lewis's family spent most of their time outside in wolf form keeping an eye on the area. At least for the most part no one would assume a wolf was anything other than its physical form, with so many wolves naturally living in this area.

Chapter Twelve

Anwen

The moment Anwen stepped into the smoke-choked air, half-blinded by the strobe of firelight and shadow, she wondered if she'd stumbled into a war or something worse. For all she'd seen since gaining her powers, chaos like this still hit her like a punch to the chest. She hoped but started to feel she'd never grow numb to it. Maybe she wasn't meant to. And now, facing something she didn't fully understand to try and save a vampire far older—and far deadlier—than she could ever hope to be, she finally understood why the family lived in shadows. You stayed hidden because, when the world burned, being invisible was the only thing that kept you alive. And Charlie was in the middle of something he tried to protect them all from.

There were loud clashing sounds from all around and Anwen was not sure what was blowing up, the place had looked unfamiliar, not being able to see anything along with the fact it was so dark. Not that it should have been, it was still in the middle of the afternoon. For a split-second seeing Charley race in front of me not realizing I was the one there reaching out, grabbing him trying to transport him away from here it had failed. I had never experienced this before; the gift had always worked with no problems. At least they were no longer standing where they were before, as a bright flash of light had hit exactly where they had been standing. Did Charley prevent it from thinking I was someone else? There was still a dark fog surrounding us with lightning bolts being shot from everywhere. As quickly as we could, we ran for cover instead of hiding by the trees. There was a large rock to sit behind. Not that it was all that much safer either. Chunks of ground sprayed up and around us.

"I thought I was done for; you shouldn't have risked coming after me, don't get me wrong. I'm thankful but it was a dangerous choice for you." I knew he was right, but I had to come, he would have come for any one of us if we needed his help regardless of the danger.

"I just don't understand why I couldn't get you out of here; I wasn't planning on moving us far, just over to this spot." I was hoping Charley might have an idea.

"Katherine has this area closed off, she thought any of the guardians that might come to rescue me, she's trying to make a point by killing me in front of them. She's closed off this entire area, even the mortals won't be able to get in here. She's risking everything. She's so desperate she's risking exposing our world in a rather large way." Charlie let out a huge sigh.

"Until she gets stopped or we find a way out, we are stuck here?" Not that I wanted to hear it.

"Until we die or something else happens, yes, we are stuck here and hopefully the others won't follow you in, there isn't anything they can do about our situation or you. I wish there was some way I could at least get you out, I just haven't found it yet." Feeling a bit frustrated I kept thinking of something Charlie had told me when I was first learning.

If I had wanted something bad enough, I just had to work hard for it or find a way to get it done.

Looking around trying to see through the fog that I now noticed was just dirt being constantly stirred up almost as a constant sandstorm, hopefully, mortals will just assume it was a weather phenomenon. Trying to focus on the others. I couldn't even get a message out to them. I knew the longer we were in here eventually they would come looking for me. The last thing we needed was all of us trapped in here, it was already difficult hiding the two of us.

"Have you seen Katherine since you've been trapped or is she still looking for you?" Not that she would have let him go if she had.

"No, I haven't, she's still looking for me. I don't think she knows you're here yet." From the look on his face, I could tell he was figuring out a way to keep me safe even if he couldn't save himself.

"I don't think I like the way you're thinking. I'm sure we can figure something out for both of us to get out." As I looked directly at Charley.

"Sometimes things don't end the way we want them to, if she thinks she has me then she will drop the cover, and you can transport me out of here." That's when it hit me, not that I liked risking it.

"I have an idea; I just have to hope she doesn't hurt you for it to work. Do you think she will try to kill you right away or will she wait?" I was hoping if anything to buy some time.

"She wants something from me, and she hopes I will either know where it is or tell her where she needs to go to find it," Charley was wondering what I had planned, "you've risked your life enough; besides, I don't know how Katherine will react, I used to know her rather well but now that she's lost it and isn't thinking rationally at all, I don't know what to expect. Out of anger she could kill me right away or notice you escaping, we need to plan this carefully to get you out of here." He was still just thinking of me.

"You've risked your life plenty of times for the rest of us. If we can't figure something else out then I have an idea, I'll have to wait for her to drop the shield and then ill grab you and transport you out." From the looks of it, I doubted we would find our way out but then it also was less likely she would let either of us walk away.

I just hoped by handing Charley over she wouldn't hurt him.

"If you get the chance to take off, your to-do that and nothing else. I appreciate that you came to save me, but this isn't what you thought you would be walking into. Besides, it's much easier to take care of things if I don't have to worry about someone else. I've dealt with this long enough; you don't need to be dealing with this. You will have enough of your problems to deal with." Just looking at Charley he had appeared as though he was finally done with all of this.

Especially with the way he had said he dealt with this long enough.

"Your right. I will have problems later and I need to learn from you; I'm not leaving you. Besides, I don't want to be the one to tell the others I left you here to die." Anwen gave him a light smile.

I hoped to lighten the situation even with all the flashes of light going off around us, with the ground lightly shaking it wasn't that easy.

"If I tell you to take off, I need you to listen to me. The flashes are coming faster, I think she's figured out I'm not over in that area anymore. See that darker hill area over there, move us over there." Looking over at it holding Charley's hand we transported rather quickly since it wasn't that far away.

The dust wasn't as thick over here; we could see a few figures moving in the darkness to the area we had just been hiding behind the rock. Frustrated at not finding us there she blew up the rock. Still holding onto Charley, I knew if we stayed here, she would find us as easily as we had spotted it. Trying to move as far away from here I hit a wall with a painful force, at least Charley hadn't hit it. The wall was the only thing that had stopped me. Thick brush that was burning filled with smoke, even more, it hurt to breathe. Looking for any other place to move there was a shattered building at this end. Moving us inside quickly. I wasn't sure if the building would cave in on us or not. Except for now it was the best we could do. The smoke would clear up over here also if the brush around us would stop burning, but then it was also keeping us hidden. At least inside the building it helped cut off some of the smoke, holding part of our shirts over our nose and breathing through the fabric. Not that there was much space to move around in, but at least we could still get out if we needed to, hiding underneath a slab of concrete that had caved in when the ceiling gave way. No doubt thanks to Katherine. The shaking of the ground had yet to let up, apparently, Katherine wasn't worried about who found her here unless she thought she would be gone before then? Then it hit me, maybe she did know one or all of us would come after Charley, maybe she was hoping to be transported out also?

"I think she does know I'm here, at least she's figured it out. She can't explain you're moving around and hiding so quickly, she had you almost caught last time." Nodding his head, I think Charley had come to the same conclusion I had.

"I can't risk the council thinking you or any of the other guardians were a part of this. I've been trying for hours to find an escape, the best I can do is just hide for a while until she gets tired of searching for me, and either nukes the whole place with fire or as I hope starts making offers that might be possible to escape from. Even those I'm sure she's going to be extra careful of. She learns rather well from her mistakes." I could barely hear him as he spoke.

Apparently, Katherine had given up on the other side and started working her way back in our direction torching everything in sight.

"There's no use hiding from me. I will find you or destroy you, whichever comes first." Katherine's voice boomed over all the noise.

"I can't keep hiding from her, stay here until it's safe for you to leave. You need to trust me." Without saying anymore Charley stepped out from where we were hiding leaving the temporary safety of the building.

"Katherine, I'm over here." Standing too far away from the building hoping she hadn't seen where he had come out from.

I hated seeing him give himself in, I just hope I wouldn't see his death as well.

"Where is the guardian, you couldn't have moved out of the way that fast, I know there's one in here."

"I'm alone. There isn't anyone else here with me, I've been unusually fortunate. You have accused me of it before." Not changing his tone at all we both knew she wasn't falling for it.

"I found her." I had felt myself being dragged out of the building.

I never saw him come in; all I could guess had been that Langston must have been hiding watching our moves? Being dropped next to Charley, he helped me get back to my feet. Now the expression on his face turned to worry.

"Alone? I don't call that being alone. I have plans for them both. Langston. I want you to move them to the core. I have some people I need to lead in another direction first." As soon as she had said this, she took off leaving us with Langston and a few others who now stepped out from the dust storm.

"I know about you kid; try anything. We kill him or you. It doesn't matter which one. If you try to disappear with magic, we are holding onto you and going anywhere you do little lady, so don't even try it." Not bothering to look at Charley I had all four men staring at me.

Other situations scared me before but nothing like this. Lifting me off from the ground as if I had been light as a feather, it took no time for Langston to whisk me away. As the scenery sped by my feet dangled coming nowhere near touching the ground. Being held only in his one arm, he had me held rather securely even though he barely needed to hold onto me. Looking outward I had my hair constantly plastered against my face as the wind held it there. Looking back behind us I could see they had tied up Charley with one carrying him. The only things I could see had been those following along with us. Apparently, they hadn't seen me as much of a threat. My sides were starting to hurt from being held the way I was. His grip never once lightened and never tightened thankfully. Making our way between two mountains there was a rather old rickety-looking shack in the center of them with a waterfall off to the left side of it. Even the distance of the falls I could feel the mist spray towards us as we entered the shack. The room we entered was empty with a nasty old half-bug-eaten rug lying in the center of the floor. Sliding the rug aside with his foot, there was a black knob he stepped on as the planks on the floor raised revealing steps leading down. I couldn't see a thing as we walked down and through what I was guessing had been a tunnel. When some light was in the distance revealing a large room, we walked right past it and back into the dark, it had felt as if we were going even deeper underground until I could hear slight screeching. Not sure what it was, I felt myself get flung as I hit the wall with force. Temporarily knocking the air from my lungs, it had hurt trying to breathe again as I tried to listen for Charley. I hoped they would at least put him in the same room with me, not that I could see what kind of a room I was in, it was far too dark for my eyes to adjust to it.

There wasn't a sound as I felt my way around the floor, eventually, I could feel cold iron bars. The walls felt like cement, not that I could see them. After feeling around, I found the room I was in was rather small with no one else in the room. Sitting down on the floor against the wall I concentrated as much as I could to find Charley hoping to transport to him. Each time I had I would end up with a sharp pain in my head and come crash landing against the wall. Giving up after the fourth try. I could only guess they had this room specially made for ones like me. Not that I knew what they were planning. I just hoped Charley was safe. From where I was, I still couldn't contact the other guardians to warn them. I had no concept of time passing, so I was sure my anxiety of being trapped in the room made it feel like it was later then it truly was. Sitting there feeling like vulnerable prey. I wasn't sure what they were planning on doing with us.

Only one floor above me, Katherine had Charley taken with the other men. Tightly bound not able to move an inch or balance himself he collapsed to the floor as soon as the men threw him in. Closing the door behind him all he could see was a stark white and well-lit room. The lights from the room were brighter than they ever needed to be almost burning his skin a little from the intensity. One look at Katherine everyone knew she was wearing something protective on her skin; whatever it was gave her skin a strange green tint.

For as long as Charley could remember he had mainly seen her in the shadows or somehow in the dark, he had never laid his eyes on her under the light before. Growing up in the family estate, even if Katherine wasn't there, the place was always dark. She was amazingly beautiful. If a shadow could show beauty as it did in the light, that is what she was, it was how she was able to lure so many to their death. Lifting Charley from the ground and rather forcefully shoving him backward until there was a solid structure behind him, now tying him to the straps lining the wall. Making sure he couldn't break free. Katherine motioned for the others to leave until she called them back in later. Katherine always wore her signature outfit regardless of what century it had been. Black leather dressing gown covered with black lace, black riding boots with lace-covered hands. The way she looked she could have walked right into the future from fifteen hundred, except this time with a few new scars. Brushing her hand through his hair Charley tried to turn to look away.

"Did you ever understand why you were my favorite? Now here you are no longer a child, a full-grown man. I trained you for a reason; I've even kept you around for my selfish reasons. Unfortunately, you never followed; you just don't have it in you. I tried to corrupt you except you just didn't understand it." Shaking her head sighing as she walked away for a moment, standing with her back to him deciding something.

"Katherine, why do you insist that my family has what

you are looking for?" We knew what she wanted just not what she had desired it for which put us in a dilemma, do we give it to her if we found it, or do we protect it from her?

"Your family has a natural way of falling into the things you just shouldn't have. I knew Harmony would end up with the power. I never did see her passing it on. These other pieces I need to gain control. Life would be so much better if I were in charge, no one would ever step out of line, especially the council." Walking back over.

Katherine had a rather intent look on her face.

"I would never help you gain any control. Let the girl go, she has nothing to do with any of this." Trying to reason with Katherine was pointless but he had to try.

"The girl is only a bonus, at least when you dry up. Unlike you, as a child, she is still impressionable and might be swayed if convinced right. Amazing how right and wrong can be confusing when explained the correct way. Your family has been a thorn in my side ever since your father. He had what I wanted, and he lost it, all of this would be over if he had stayed out of my way. I would make Jamison pay for all these years of stress, but you will do just fine, after all, you're such a disappointment." Reaching into her pocket she pulled out a clear crystal the size of her hand.

Stroking the crystal as she looked it over, without warning she stabbed it directly into his thigh. Flinching, however, determined not to let out a yelp Charley kept the pain to himself.

"Such a brave little man, it's okay you can yell out in pain. I'm the only one who can hear you right now. If you had been a good boy, we would be torturing someone else right now, or better yet. I would already have what I want." Her voice raising a little as she pulled the crystal from his thigh with force, watching the blood she smiled to herself for a moment almost as if she was lost in her thoughts.

"Do you remember when Julie died? Such a terrible act a child could perform. Your poor mother stayed to protect the kids, if I had let her live, she would have made out like a saint. Your first murder and it's so sad you don't remember it. Your father covered it too well making it look as if she slipped by accident. There was the silly rumor that I pushed her. I had you play a little game with me, do you remember? It's what sent that poor woman to her death. Your pure evil. You need to learn to embrace it better, we could be a great team." Reached out scratching her nails down the length of his arm tearing away the clothing now spattered with blood stains.

"I would never work with you. What are you waiting for? I'll handle any death you have for me. Just leave my family alone, they don't have what you want." Trying as hard as he could to control the sound of his voice.

"So brave, you certainly didn't learn that from your father. However, you certainly hadn't learned it from me, you do know you're not my son." Smirking as she said it.

"I always knew Julie wasn't my mother, you are. What are you trying to get out of this? Not that I would mind finding out someone else other then you were my mother, except there wasn't anyone else." Why was she telling me this?

"I don't need anything from you. What could you possibly give me that I would want, or I would have had it by now? The rest of your family is another matter, not that you can protect them anymore. When I'm finished, all of you will be dead, I have no use for any of you anymore. Your birth mother was of no use to me either, your dear friend Goseck could have let you know about that, I had him kill her." Standing directly in front of Charley, Katherine was looking over the damage she had been inflicting.

Placing her hands over his chest she let out a sigh almost as if she was disappointed. Arching her fingernails digging into the cloth of his shirt tearing downward digging in as her nails scraped the top layer of his chest leaving long blood streaks. Closing her eyes as she listened carefully for any changes in his breathing as he slightly gasped, she dug her nails even deeper. Leaning in Katherine licked one of the blood-stained strips of skin up to the neck. Now leaning closer to his ear to whisper something to him, keeping his eyes closed not wanting to see her it was hard to suppress his sigh.

"You were always my favorite child to torture; you react the way I love. Such a waste, just think. You could have lived a very long time if you had done everything, I ordered you to." Moving away from Charley she turned walking towards the door that was now opened with two men standing there.

"Time yet?" Had come one simple gruff answer.

"I have other things to handle before I take off, feel free to torture him for a while and then drop him in the basement with Langston. I want to watch when he's put to death." As soon as she said this the two men wasted no time coming after Charley with blunt weapons or simply their own hands striking out at him.

Only taking a quick look back. Charley was showing no expression and looked directly into her eyes as Katherine closed the door behind her. After waiting for a while in the dark cell not able to see anything or anyone. Anwen heard footsteps getting louder as they came closer. Not that she could see them yet, she heard someone else hit the wall the same way she had, and the iron door closed behind. The breathing was barely there but she knew immediately who it was.

"Charley, can you hear me?" Feeling around the floor quickly trying to find where he was laying, all I could hear was a slight raise in his breathing, either way, I knew it wasn't a good sign.

As soon as I had found him, my hand felt wet until I realized it was blood. He seemed intact not that I could see if he was still bleeding. There was one area on his arm that felt constantly wet almost as if blood was still pouring out. The same feeling you have running your hand under a faucet only much slower. Ripping the sleeve off from my shirt. I tried to wrap it around his arm the best I could to add pressure to stop the blood.

"I'm so sorry." Charley could barely get the words out.

"You have nothing to be sorry about." I felt sick there

wasn't anything I could do.

"If I hadn't been caught, you wouldn't be stuck here with me now. They don't intend on letting us out. Once we die or they kill us, they plan on sending us piece by piece to the rest of the family hoping they will hand over what Katherine is looking for. You're only here because of me." I had never heard Charley give up before.

I could only guess our future was grim. Holding onto him I wasn't going to risk letting go. I kept racing thoughts through my mind trying to figure out what could be done. I had already tried a few things and the only ones I hadn't. I had no idea if they would only backfire and kill us. They were new tricks that the other guardians and I had been working on. I had tried creating an orb of light to illuminate the room except I couldn't get anything more than smoke. Katherine may not have had our gift except she seemed to know many of the ways to block me from using it. The iron gate prevented me from breaking it from either overheating or freezing. Pure strength hadn't worked either. Whatever other mineral was in the iron was preventing my gifts from destroying it.

"Your broken friend on the floor is right, you're never getting out. This place was made to keep guardians in, if they can't get out neither can anything else." The voice was rather gruff sounding.

"If there's a way in, there's always a way out. You're the one who brought us here." I had recognized the voice.

"Smart guess, however, your friend is wrong about one thing. He's the only one that is going to die, Katherine has plans for you." The sound of his voice never changed once.

"It doesn't matter if she has plans for me or not, I won't work for her. I'm not leaving him here to die." Not that I was sure I had an option.

I wanted him to know I wasn't afraid of him; it had helped I couldn't see him, at least until he temporarily lit up his area. Just looking at him he was intimidating. Charley had said nothing during the whole conversation. It felt as if all he could do was keep breathing for now. I tried to heal Charley the best I could except it was hard to heal what I couldn't see.

"Your right, there is always a way except I'm not sharing it. I'm sure you weren't expecting it; besides I'm only here for one thing and that's to get caught." For the first time, his voice lightened just a little.

"How can you get caught if you're hiding in the dark? Besides, get caught from what?" What would he want to get caught by?"

"I can see just fine, if you move your left hand up a little, you're missing a spot you haven't healed, always nice to die when you're healthy. Being caught is my issue." His voice became stern again.

Moving my hand up a little I started healing the new area. One of the things I learned when attacked, find the weakness, and exploit it. I had only heard stories from the family about Katherine, so I didn't know much about her, at least not enough to figure out her weakness. I decided to go on one of my own, I always second-guessed myself. There were a lot of things I couldn't do here, but if I couldn't see then why should anyone else? Holding Charley closer to me I concentrated very carefully. I had done this before when we played hide and seek with the kids. I could be standing right in front of them, and they would never see me, only the other guardians would. They were the only ones I could never completely conceal myself from. I wasn't sure what I was doing would work. I just knew I couldn't risk leaving Charley again. If I did, I was positive they would kill him. At least I could make it harder for them to see us. Acting as if he was shocked not to see us as other footsteps were approaching. The man had been acting more for the other guards who were there to watch us. Standing back, he let the one open the door.

"Are you sure it's a smart thing to open the door? Perhaps you should ask Katherine first?" Without raising his voice to exert authority he simply sounded as if he could care less.

"She's already gone. How did she disappear, you must have seen something." As he walked around inside, I heard two sets of footsteps moving around us hoping they wouldn't step on us finding we were still there.

Remembering where we were before I covered us. Langston tapped me on the leg and tried to give me a physical bump in the direction of the door. Concentrating now I could move Charley into the hallway. I heard the iron gate close behind us, wishing I could see. At least I could hear one of the men speak.

"I thought they couldn't see in the dark. How did she find the gate to close it, Katherine's going to kill us for letting them out." I hadn't heard another word from the other man.

I almost wished I could free him except I couldn't risk it. Not that we were going far, I still couldn't transport out of the building. Finding the best place I could hide. I created the smallest orb of light, with it guiding Charley. I used it to finish healing him. For the small amount I had already healed, he still looked like a mess. At least his breathing was becoming more regular. After staying hidden for a few hours, I could hear several footsteps coming down the stairs joining in the room. We were set back in the second room without a door looking right out at three iron cells. Katherine had blasted the iron gate from the wall illuminating the rest of the room so everyone could see. Bones were laying in one of the cells. Langston simply stood relaxed against the wall not looking afraid, or nervous. As a matter of fact, he displayed no emotion whatsoever. He wasn't scared of Katherine. Most who dealt with her usually were.

"The cell was empty and then she locked us in here." The rather timid man tried explaining not that Katherine waited for him to finish anymore of his words.

Langston stood there not saying a word as Katherine lost her temper with the guard, peeling the flesh from the timid man's bones eventually leaving nothing more than ash where he had once stood. Still not saying a word Langston moved away from the wall and made his way past Katherine. I wondered why she hadn't done anything to him.

"Finish searching and find her. Once you find her, bring

her to me. I don't need Charley; he can be killed." I watched as everyone had left.

Leaving the door open above. I moved us upward. At least three floors were heading upward unfortunately Katherine was blocking the top of the steps. For now, I had to find another place to hide until we could get out.

The second floor was quiet, lined with a few empty rooms. No cells like the one we'd escaped from. If I hadn't been made a guardian, I never could've carried Charley, maybe it was just the adrenaline, or maybe it was the fear. That sharp, electric kind that buzzes in your bones. The healing spell I'd cast had slowed the worst of his wounds, but he was still too weak. Now all I could do was wait for him to recover or gather enough strength to move us again. I crouched beside him, casting a shroud spell with the last of my focus, willing the magic to hold.

Outside, the world was breaking apart. Physically Katherine had created so much destruction it couldn't be overlooked which caught the councils attention, packs fracturing, humans whispering about disappearances they weren't supposed to notice. And Katherine, one of the Old Blood, was hunting us still. The wards. The hidden cities. The whole damn treaty of not letting the human world know we existed.

I wondered if Katherine knew we hadn't escaped. Maybe that's why she hadn't left or suspected what we did. I didn't dare risk the stairs. If she figured out where we were, or if the exits were sealed, we'd be trapped. So, we hid in the only room without a door, lights off, silent. Hours passed in that stillness before I finally heard them, Langston and Katherine. I held my breath and hoped my magic was enough. I'd never been more ready for something to be over.

I pressed a hand to the floor, ready to burn every ounce of magic I had left to protect him. If they found us, it wouldn't just be our lives on the line.

It'd be war.

Chapter Thirteen

Can't Wait

"We can't keep waiting here like this, they might need us." Staring out the window for the last couple of days hadn't helped bring them back either, not that Sophie was about to stop waiting.

"We understand you're frustrated, we all are, and we all miss Charley and hope he's safe, but we don't know what we would be walking into if we go looking after him. If the worst has happened then we need to figure out what to do, I'm sure we would be next." Goseck had been keeping everyone calm except when the last guardian had left without returning, we all feared the worst.

"I don't think we have to wonder too much where they might be. Look at this news program." Nichole and Anthony had been watching the television for the last few days for the weather which seems to be getting rather violent not far from here.

The storm on the screen looked like something torn out of a nightmare. Dust and smoke twisted together into unnatural shapes, pierced by lightning that flickered green and violet instead of white. Tornadoes spun like the limbs of some enormous creature, lashing out at the earth. But what really made my stomach drop were the voices. Low, whispering things that slithered through the static of the broadcast. We couldn't make out the words, but they crawled under the skin, full of warning... or a lure. The storm didn't drift like weather should. It hunted, and the ground beneath us jolted in sharp, rhythmic bursts, as if something buried deep was trying to rise. This wasn't nature. This was her. And we had to go before it found us.

Not that anyone had voiced it. We knew soon we wouldn't be running just from Katherine but the council as well. It would be hard to believe they would allow this and do nothing about it. Eliminating anything that had to do with it to prevent any mortals from finding out what was behind it. So far, they only assumed it was a very rare weather phenomenon causing this windstorm, severe lightning, tornadoes that looked like hurricanes and earthquakes all at once. After all, how often do you see something like this so far northeast of the United States? Taking our attention away to see who was walking in, one of Lewis's family members had slowly walked in looking extremely concerned as he made his way over to Lewis. No longer in wolf form changing to speak with Lewis, even Lewis had a look of warning that he couldn't hide.

"We can't wait for Charley any longer; we need to get moving and does Raynn have the item Katherine wants or not? It might be the only way we get out of this, or Katherine will keep hunting us down, especially if she's not afraid of dealing with the council, who knows what kind of crew she has working for her." Kenneth hadn't bothered mixing words as he watched for Lucian's expression.

"What are they talking about?" Everyone had watched Lucian's expression.

"I haven't had a chance to tell you yet; Katherine is looking for the gift I gave you when you were little. I never would have given it to you if I knew it was going to put you in any kind of danger." No one had even thought to check if she had it on her or not.

"You've given me so many gifts over the years, which one is it?" Without waiting for anyone to tell her she started taking her shoe off with everyone wondering why until she pulled out the little piece and held it out in her palm towards Lucian.

"What happened to the chain it used to be on?" Lucian asked very surprised to see it just lying there in her hand.

"It broke a long time ago; I haven't had it fixed yet, so I put it on an ankle bracelet that I had until Erick tried to take it from me. Gerry knows what he looks like. I had seen him inside the theater."

"That would be me; I was following him when I saw she was with the group. I knew she had no idea who she was with. I wanted to get them to leave her and follow me instead, that way Teddy would be safe, and I could lose them." The family had been familiar with Lucian and Jacob using their middle names to introduce themselves to others.

Even Sophie smiled at the thought of it. Charley had done this himself for many years, even Sophie had used a fake name at times to blend in.

"Sorry, I meant Jacob, it's hard to call him by that when I'm used to calling him by the other name." Lucian had picked up that she was feeling uncomfortable being the center of everyone's focus, pulling her closer to him as the slightest gesture to let her know she wasn't alone.

"Most of us could leave now and go further up north leaving only a few of us behind just in case Charley does show up, but if Katherine is behind this chaotic weather heading up this way, we will need another spot to take off to, that way we don't lead her to the others, we can possibly lead her away? Maybe by then, the council will grab a hold of her, and we won't have to deal with her ourselves." We all knew getting out of it wouldn't be that easy.

The council would want to know why she wanted us so badly. She was willing to take the risk of massive exposure. The way they are we could see them wanting the medallions also, anything to add more power to their group.

"Who gets to stay behind?" Mia was the first to voice it, more of Lewis's family had come inside by now.

"Kenneth and I can keep watch from a distance; it's easier for us to blend in with the wildlife than anyone else. We would prefer the kids to go with everyone along with the rest of my family; it will be easier if we don't have to worry about too many staying behind. I'll send Amanda with Nichole and Anthony; she will be safer with them." Before Lewis could finish deciding who was staying behind Sophie interrupted.

"I'll be staying behind." Very firmly not letting anyone else convince her otherwise, sitting down now waiting to see who else she would be waiting behind with.

Not having to wait for very long it was decided that only Lewis, Kenneth, Sophie, Kara, and Lucian were staying behind.

Lucian didn't move. He couldn't. The others were long gone, swallowed by the forest trail that led to safety, away from danger, away from him. Still, he kept staring, his eyes fixed on the place they had disappeared, as if the sheer force of his longing could pull them back. The silence they left behind was deafening, pressing against his chest like a weight he couldn't shake. They were safe now, or at least they would be. But knowing that didn't make it any easier to watch them leave. Every step they took away from him felt like a thread snapping loose from something he hadn't realized was holding him together. He knew the small group would catch up to them later, that everything would be fine. But as the last trace of their presence faded, Lucian wondered if the emptiness settling inside him would ever let him feel whole again.

"Teddy will be safe with family; she has Rose looking after her." Sophie spoke gently.

"I know Rose would protect her but who will protect Rose?" Trying to smile to lighten up the situation, Lucian was just as worried about her as Sophie was with Charley.

"She'll be safe, Lucian. Rose won't let anything happen to her, you know that better than anyone. I get it, you've always been the one looking out for her... but right now, she's the one out there, and your sister's the one doing the protecting. Trust her the way she's always trusted you. That's how we get through this."

Sophie's voice was rather soothing but still, it wasn't enough unless she was here where he could be sure she was safe next to him.

It was something difficult to describe unless you were separated from those you loved. Sophie had already been separated from Charley for a very long during their lives and the most crucial time after she had been changed. Katherine had been the first to know of Sophie's change leaving her with a band of gypsies knowing at some point. Sophie would have an important part in all of this. She only assumed she would be able to keep a better watch over Sophie if she had been entrusted with her gypsy friends. Learning from them and unknown to her, being sold off to a family looking for a daughter. Sophie was rather fortunate with her circumstances that they were not worse but then Maddie the woman who cared for her secretly had her reasons.

Sophie had stayed away from the family for so long hoping to keep them safe except everything Katherine had worked so hard for kept bringing us back together and putting her family further into danger many times, being severely harmed. Taking a glance over at Lucian. She knew he had already been through so much and lost a lot because of the midnight madam, just like the rest of us.

I knew there would be drawbacks to being a vampire, not that I had originally planned to become one, after all, I should still be dead in my grave right now if it had not been for Aiden and Lorah. I don't blame them, their heart was in the right place, but nothing could have ever prepared me or anyone for that matter for any of this. When you build a relationship that's so strong, so many memories, regardless of whether they were all good ones or bad, being in tune with your partner, best friends, and each other's passionate lovers that one day after so many years or even so few you have had all of this, and you suddenly realize how vulnerable and precious your relationship is. So, when it breaks no matter the distance, time, or even by death it's just like dying halfway. You didn't believe it was possible until then to feel so numb, so lost.

I knew there would be consequences to becoming a vampire, not that I ever planned to. I was supposed to be dead. I remember the darkness of the coffin, the weight of the earth pressing down on me like a final sentence. I had been buried alive. My heart barely beating, breath slowing to almost nothing. I don't know how long I was down there before the Midnight Madam dug me out. She saved me... if you could call it that.

I was still halfway between death and something else when she handed me off to the gypsies, told them to keep me safe until she came back for me. I was too weak mentally, too confused to ask the right questions. They fed me, sheltered me, and tried to pretend we were a family. But I wasn't theirs. I wasn't even myself.

And Charlie... I don't know where he is. I don't know if he's alive, or if I'll ever see him again. All I can do is hope and convince myself he was safe. We were everything to each other: partners, best friends, lovers. When you have that kind of bond, you think it's unbreakable. Eternal. But it turns out eternity doesn't come with promises.

When you're ripped away from someone like that with no goodbye, no way of knowing if they're safe or suffering, it's like dying halfway. Like your soul gets carved in two, and the world keeps spinning while you're frozen in place, trying to remember how to breathe. I didn't know it was possible to feel so numb. So, lost.

Lewis was the first to scout out the area again, at least things had been relatively calm. Lucian had kept in contact with the others by cellphone. We weren't sure just how long we would have to wait or if it would come, other than guessing the fact the torrential storm had come so far this way already then without warning it had disappeared altogether leaving us to wonder where it had gone? Kara had let herself in to give us an update on what they had seen, there wasn't a threat yet except they were still watching to see what it was they had wanted.

"Lewis thinks he recognizes one of them he just can't remember if he's neutral or one of Katherine's men. So far, they seem to be waiting for something. It's a man and a woman." Stopping for a moment Kara was hearing something we hadn't.

Leaving us standing there she left the house again no doubt to catch up to Lewis. We didn't have to wait very long to see who they were talking about. Not wanting to wait any longer to see if they were dangerous to us or not, Lewis had chosen to change shape speaking with the strangers with his family close by for added protection if he needed them. Walking up to the house Lucian recognized the couple. Stepping outside I followed Lucian not wanting to leave him alone with them or to get too close. No matter how much he has experienced or grown he will always be my grandson, I'll always feel overly protective of him, especially because he has been through so much. Walking up with the two. Someone else had come out from the shadows, when she had, the others came in quickly making sure she wasn't going to attack Lewis by surprise. This woman I knew myself and hadn't seen in a very long time. Before the life stone had been absorbed and eventually passed on to a few new guardians we used to protect the life stone until it was passed on to the next guardians. Each guardian now who inherited the gift reacted differently to it, only difference had to be one main requirement, they had to be human. The life stone itself was created by a very powerful sorceress. It has the power to make a vampire stronger, as if they needed any more strength. It possesses powers they might not have. It can even make a vampire mortal again. It could make it so that vampires could walk in the sun without consequences. Half-breeds and humans are the ones who rule the day. With the stone, a vampire could rule night and day without any effects. It could steal the life force from humans if the user wished. It can also kill other vampires and half-breeds without being in contact with them.

Hold it up in the sun and look into it and picture something it will show you what you want to see. It has the power to increase or eliminate a vampire's natural desires and powers. I can't go into the sun so if you want to test it this is the safest time to do it. It also transports its user anywhere

I still couldn't believe I was seeing Caoimhe again. Along with her, I watched as Lucian went to greet the gentleman who was with them. At least I knew they would be safe if she was traveling with them.

"You're looking much better than the last time I had seen you." Hugging each other, the two wasted no time talking about the past.

Lewis just stood there wondering how they knew each other.

Sophie stepped forward, her gaze shifting between Andrew and her family. "Everyone, this is Andrew," she began, her tone a mix of warmth and significance. "If Aunt Evangeline were here, she'd recognize him right away. They were close friends from before. He helped our family during the fight against the original Doc and Katherine."

She paused for a moment, her eyes briefly flicking to Andrew with a hint of gratitude. "He also saved Evangeline's life. The demon hunters had been after her, and if Andrew hadn't stepped in when he did… she might never have made it back to us. That was before she and Mom rejoined the family."

Then, turning slightly, she gestured to the woman beside her. "And this is Charlotte. She's Jacob's aunt. She's been with us through everything. "And of course, Caoimhe one of my closest friends and trusted associate, Caoimhe knew me as Dorina." As Sophie introduced everyone, she was curious to know which time Caoimhe was referencing that Lucian was injured.

"Last time you saw Lucian he hadn't looked too good? What happened?" Lewis was rather curious.

Shaking my head, I had to admit Lucian had a natural talent for getting himself into trouble, either that or it came looking for him and he never knew enough to walk or get out of the way.

"Last time I had seen the family we were helping find Lucian, Valafar was having some fun with it. Too long to explain but at least it looks like he's healed up nicely, odd you still have bruising unless you've gotten yourself into more trouble? Making a habit of it I see?" Caoimhe stated as Lucian's smile alone had given it away.

"Unfortunately, I've made it a habit, maybe I'll learn not to someday." As we spoke both Kenneth and Kara went back out scouting the area to make sure no one had followed them or was hiding watching us.

"We mainly came this way to see what was causing the dust storm; the council is investigating it also even though we're pretty sure they already know. As soon as we caught up with it the whole thing just vanished leaving nothing to prove it was ever there except for one area it was rather scorched. We found this." Pulling out a pocketknife with Charley's name carved on the side of it.

"Where did you find this?" I knew immediately it was the knife I had given him as a gift.

"We found it in the scorched area, figured Charley might need some help. Is he even here?" As a look of concern crossed Andrew's face, they finally realized there was something wrong.

"Katherine is after these pieces we have; she might have Charley. We haven't heard from him since he made the urgent call that we all meet up here, he wanted us to stay together feeling it would be safer for the family." Lucian had spoken rather quickly even though I knew he understood I was having a hard enough time just keeping myself together then to answer a simple question.

Pulling out the two charms there was a white static shock as the two touched each other. Andrew hadn't seemed very surprised when he had seen them.

"Before we worry about the pieces we need to find out where Charley is or who might have him. Keep those hidden until we need them. Where is the rest of the family?" Charlotte had still been looking at the pieces as she asked.

"Everyone went up north just in case Katherine was behind the unusual dust storm. We stayed behind hoping Charley might show up.

"Instead of waiting for her to show up, let's track her down for once. Lucian, I want you to find a safe place away from the rest of the family and hide those pieces, I want you to join us, I think I might know where she's hiding if she's in this area. Are we missing anyone else?" Looking at Lucian and me, we hadn't mentioned the guardians.

"We are missing the guardians; we were sure they went looking for Charley except we haven't heard from any of them." Not that any of us knew how to contact them either.

"I want to make a quick stop, Lewis if your family could watch over Lucian for now that would be the best. We should get going before we don't have a chance to do this. It's never a good idea to be the hunted unless you've already prepared for it. I prefer to do the hunting." Nodding in agreement, Lewis had taken off with Lucian along with his family following behind.

Charlotte and Caoimhe were out in the lead as Andrew, and I followed behind.

As Andrew had said he wanted to make a stop along the way. He walked in a row of little shops; he went into one as we waited outside. Taking whatever, he just purchased out of the bag and placing it into his pocket we took off again. Clearing the town and off to the far side of the forest where everything was filled in. It was getting harder to run very fast without tripping occasionally on the overgrown vines and the fact there was no longer a path with the trees growing much closer to each other. I couldn't get over just how close they were. Andrew had known Katherine during the time he had been taught by other demon hunters, she organized and controlled for Doc Denthre. One of the places she would live without anyone knowing had almost been in our backyard. Only slowing up before we reached there to see one of her guards outside patrolling the area, we had to be careful not to set off any of her alarms to alert that we were nearby. Keeping close attention as they came and went watching their habits and mannerisms, none of them were dressed in uniform or anything that might make them look different. Andrew decided he would try to enter on his own to blend in with the others. Using his gift, much like Katherine. Andrew could also blend in with the shadows around him. The only thing that slightly gave him away would be his wrist to his fingertips, the slightest red stretch mark that stretched from his wrist to the end of his fingertips. His special gift had been to control heat substances in the air, even at times making it look as though he could control the wind only if there had been heat in the air. Up north here it was a little more difficult for him to draw from the air as he had in other areas.

Keeping a distance as we watched him blend in with the shadows, we stayed nearby in case we needed to keep the path out here clear for him. I wished I could have gone in with him. Caoimhe had stayed outside with me while Charlotte had followed along to help inside. She was also able to blend in rather well with the darkness, which is how she had first met Andrew when he worked with the demon hunters. They had stalked her for so long. Closest friends, family, and partners never exactly come from where you would expect them but then the unexpected is exactly what makes life so special. Andrew and Charlotte were on the far side of the little shack showing out of the ground no doubt covering for something much larger that we couldn't see from the underground level. Katherine wasn't exactly known for being simple, the more extravagant was her style, as she had put it, if she's going to be around for who knows how long she might as well enjoy it to the fullest possibilities.

Strange not to see anyone guarding the outside of the door, pushing the door in just a bit there hadn't been any other choice for them to enter. With no windows and only a single door showing the choice was limited. Stepping in slow carefully in case there were others poised around the entrance for anyone or thing that might unluckily enter not knowing what they were getting themselves into. Still, nothing which made Andrew a little more nervous, either Katherine was being distracted lately causing her to be careless or there was a trap he wasn't prepared for. There had been a medium-sized room with stairs leading downward. Both leaned close against the wall making their way in the room watching every possible corner in case someone was hiding. There hadn't been any movements or sounds until they had gone to the second floor below. One loud voice had been enough to freeze them both in their tracks. Katherine was yelling at someone.

"How could you just stand there letting him open the cage, your fully aware of what the guardians can do, you did not fall for her trick, why are you working against me now?" Katherine almost seemed insulted someone would do anything against her wishes.

"He had to learn somehow. Besides he was already opening the cell door as he said it. I don't need to work for anyone; besides, you can only pay me what I'm after anyway. Why not just kill me now as you did him?" Smirking at her Langston knew he was angering Katherine

"I would if it hadn't been what you wanted. If you don't keep your end of this, I will kill you before the council gets their hands on you," walking over to Langston, she had placed her hands on either shoulder leaning closet to whisper to him, "find his body or yours will do just nicely." Pulling away she scratched her nails down his arms leaving marks deep enough for permanent scars.

Only the slightest twitch had been good enough to thrill Katherine for inflicting a little pain for her frustration.

"Why do you need this guy so bad? Since when do you need anything from anyone? I think you're stuck and run out of plans, if these pieces you're looking for are not on him why do you still need him?" Still leaning in the same spot ignoring the blood stain widening on his shirt.

"Having him as part of this will force the council to deal with the rest of his family, especially the vampire daughter Amanda. They should pay for frustrating me for so many centuries. The council will take care of it immediately taking their attention from me while I take over. Harmony slowed me down enough and I'm tired of Charley getting in the way by protecting her, her group dissolved once she died. But it's always him, he has a way of messing things up. I've been close far too many times that I don't need his family around. It's true, I am running out of options, but no one will be able to kill me anymore; this curse will be lifted. I'll have a very powerful council beneath me, unlike somewhere they wish to take them out and rule." Turning to leave Katherine had stopped with his last question.

"What will I get out of this? If I take the heat from the council, who's to say they will put me to death? I could always say this was all you, no one else had a choice. You forced them into it, after all, who would say no to you?" Looking back at him looking angrier by the second.

"For starters. I would spend my time killing everyone you know especially your friend Drezin. Besides, there is something to my advantage for being around for so long and no one gets the point. We, vampires, are a very special breed with gifts and skills we have developed or because of innate gifts we inherit. Maybe because we've had them for so long or some just have not been trained long enough to quit the old human habits that destroy us while the stronger vampires continue through life because we have learned." Quickly turning around racing to the side wall without any warning.

She had reached for what looked like empty air on the ground pulling away what now showed an arm until a body showed shortly after almost as if it had been pulled out from the air.

"How long did you know he was there?" Langston looked around almost expecting to see the girl; he had hoped they were the ones he heard on the steps up above.

"Long enough to hear the guardian breathing, she won't risk going anywhere without him, and neither will she risk trying to leave with him, after all, she would end up with me also. You might as well show yourself... little girl. I know you're not the only one in here. You two from the stairs come in here." Not raising her voice for a second Katherine was positive the others could hear her.

Making a point she grabbed a hold of Charley crushing him into the wall until he collapsed on the floor. Grabbing a hold of him again lifting him into the air and throwing him into the other wall now leaving a dent, Andrew and Charlotte couldn't do much as a few guards now stood behind them.

"She's right, you do stand out and seriously for being trained with the demon hunters you should have known better. No wonder why the council never accepted you Andrew." Langston seemed rather deflated to see Andrew shaking his head in disgust.

"Take them down to the cell, all of them, and no one opens the cell, I'll do that myself. As for Charley, you've outlived your usefulness." Pulling out a glaive from her side sheath, a weapon we hadn't seen in a very long time.

She shoved the glaive into Charley's stomach and twisted it before yanking it out. Her hand reached for his neck, ready to snap it. That's when Andrew stepped forward, drawing Katherine's attention but before he could do anything more, a few guards grabbed him and pulled him back.

"If you kill him, I will make sure you never get what you what. Even if I die keeping you from it." Andrew threatened.

Throwing Charley down as she made her way over to Andrew.

"You can't keep away what you don't have." With a threatening tone, Andrew knew she still questioned whether he could carry out his threat.

"Who says that I don't have it? Certainly not on me, or is it? Let everyone else go and I'll give it to you, simple as that." Charlotte had not changed her facial expression at all as Katherine tried to judge if she knew anything.

Katherine hadn't bothered to look around the rest of the room still glaring at Andrew.

"You can give it to me, and I'll do you a favor of killing everyone quickly." Running her hands along his sides to feel for anything he might be carrying.

Pulling out two objects from his pocket, Katherine seemed to get excited. Clenching her hands closed moving away from Andrew. No one had expected to see any of the other guardians show up, not that anyone had heard or known where they had gone to. Jessica, Aaron, Delaney, and Lily appeared in the room without warning standing near Katherine.

At least now we know which side we're really on," one of the guardians said, extending their hand. "We've already taken the two who were waiting outside."

They vanished instantly, no struggle, no hesitation, leaving with Katherine as if it had all been planned. She didn't flinch or question it. The others stood in stunned silence, watching what looked like a betrayal unfold before their eyes.

Anwen stayed kneeling next to Charley, confused by the situation, but the emotions she picked up from the others didn't shake her; they brought no panic, only a quiet calm, because she refused to believe her fellow guardians would ever betray them. They had been through so much with each other, she knew this wasn't the hill they were going to choose to die on.

"This is not good if they are helping her." Andrew stepped further into the room as he and Charlotte were pushed in further, not that Langston made any moves to either attack or leave the room himself.

The guards themselves went into full attack mode. Langston had been standing near Anwen and Charley not bothering to get involved. With all the fast movement in one small room, it was difficult to see what was going on. Charlotte was much more skilled than the guards were prepared for. She had been working in sync with Andrew as they cornered the guards between the two of them. The only problem had come when one of the guards came in the door coming up behind Andrew as he was already in full contact with another. As he swung out to deal a powerful blow the guard dropped to the ground with his head rolling, stopping just in front of Charley and Anwen, looking up everyone was a bit surprised to see the guard had been killed by his side, Langston had quickly moved as soon as he had seen him, wasting no time at all separating his head from his body. With no expression on his face, he hadn't bothered saying a word about leaving the room. Out in the hallway, Alexandra had been waiting there for Langston, leaving with him as the others had with Katherine. Charley stood up with help from Anwen looking at the others.

"Who was waiting outside, which two others?" We all knew he had wanted to know if Sophie had been one of those two waiting or if it had been family.

"Don't worry. I'm sure she's safe for now. She's with Caoimhe. She never would have been caught unless she spoke with one of the guardians; we were the only ones who knew they were out there. There must be a reason why she went with them or that Katherine knows. Anwen, have you sensed anything from them?" Andrew wanted to figure out a plan of attack, knowing what to expect would determine how he reacted with the other guardians.

"They have been in constant contact with me just before they showed up, I just couldn't risk saying anything or reacting. Trust me when I say don't judge the others. Andrew and Charlotte. I need you to lead the council to a particular place. I'll take Charley with me; I can heal him but not completely." Letting Andrew know where to lead the others, Anwen disappeared with Charley.

Hoping they could still trust her after seeing how the others reacted, not that either wanted to deal with the council.

Chapter Fourteen

The Presidium

Andrew and Charlotte took off without looking back, the shack shrinking behind him as he headed toward the hills where the council had last been seen. They rarely ventured beyond their own borders unless something truly urgent was unfolding and this time, the rumors were all too specific. Creatures in the area had reported glimpses of council members moving through the trees, silent and watchful, but no one knew exactly what they were after. The only thing Andrew was certain of was this: they were asking about Charley's family.

Gerard and Hattie from the council were already in the area looking around, not making clear their intentions except most could assume they were here because of the strange weather. Not wanting to deal with them we had to figure a way to get them to the location Anwen gave us without getting ourselves caught. Even if we had information that would help get them there faster, we could lose our lives just knowing and not reporting it to them earlier. Not much longer Emery and Sarah showed up. Apparently, not just the council was getting involved. The presidium was also curious about this one. We had let them see us as they watched Charlotte and I walk in and out of a few stores. We knew we couldn't outrace or deceive them, so we had to be very careful. Not getting very far. I felt a hand rest on my shoulder, being careful not to overreact since we were around mortals. I knew it was him the moment I caught his scent, sharp, unmistakable. But I turned all the same, just as his hand settled lightly on my shoulder, pretending it didn't make my stomach twist.

"We need to have a word with both of you, sort of interesting you happen to be up here right now." David was just as careful not to say anything unusual in front of the mortals either.

Nodding my head both Charlotte and I followed him around to the back of the store. No one had been in the alley way making it a good temporary place to talk.

"Why are you here?" Shannon asked in a rather defensive tone

"We were borrowing a friend's cabin up here when we were distracted by the weather, it stopped suddenly so there wasn't anything to find. We were going to pick up a few things we forgot to bring with us and head back to the cabin." Charlotte was always good at masking the tone of her voice.

She sounded so casual when she spoke.

"Is the McAllister family here also?" Shannon seemed to be asking all the questions this time as the others listened in.

Only one mortal stepped into the alleyway to throw away the trash, not paying attention to us had gone back in.

"It's their cabin we are borrowing, but they are not here right now. They were not using it which is why they loaned it to us." At this point, I still wasn't sure how we were going to manage this except all we knew is that we had their attention.

"We will be keeping an eye on both of you, for now, you may go." Ruby seemed to be getting very impatient as she watched someone else from a distance, not wasting any more time with us they took off leaving us standing there watching them leave.

Making sure we stayed near town for a while longer they were correct on keeping an eye on us as we had two following us around. Only making a few trips to the cabin to leave a few things behind, we knew they would search the place once we left. They were only sending a few members of the council, which was not unusual for them. We weren't sure how we wound up getting all of them but then we weren't sure why all of them had been needed in the first place. Not having time to find out what the plan was or why, we needed so many council members to watch us, we did what we could not to raise suspicion without being attacked ourselves as the culprits of the storm that was visible to the outsiders, they had to know somehow there was much more behind all of it. Leaving a bunch of strange items laying in the living room in an odd pattern. I knew all of this would look strange to Charley when they came back here to see it. Then to kick it off we left something even stranger. Finding a dead animal, we borrowed the skin slicing it into several pieces and setting it on top of the chair, making sure they would assume it was human we stole a bag of donated blood from the blood bank soaking the skin in it. Then we sprayed the blood around a little close to the chair to make it appear we had killed a person.

Not staying long, we started traveling up north even further. The weather wasn't giving us any better luck traveling through the thick snow. Only stopping a few times just long enough to make sure we were still followed. They had sent only two of them to follow even though we hoped to get the entire group up here, apparently the bloody skin left behind didn't prompt them to all follow us. Stopping in at a shop along the way we knew had been operated by another vampire, we spent a few minutes longer than we normally would have and left a message behind for him to hold onto. Letting him know it was alright for the others to take the note. As we left the other two had gone in to see what we had purchased. Leaving town after speaking to them made us look suspicious enough. Leaving the note behind we knew we had to take off rather quickly before they caught up to us. Leaving a fake note for Langston, we knew he wouldn't be here except we didn't want to associate the family with this if we could avoid it.

The snow was getting almost too deep to run in slowing us down to almost a slow walk. At times we were waist-deep in snow barely able to move, not that we had to go too much further. We were looking for a particular cave. Turning to face what noise we had heard behind us we hoped they hadn't caught up to us quite yet. At least now we know they would search the cave since we made it a point to get here, at least we would get them to the destination we needed them at. Turning around I wasn't sure I wanted to be thankful to see them or feel concerned. Aaron and Langston were standing behind us smiling rather confidently.

"Need a lift, Andrew? The council should be right behind you, good idea to use my name on the note." Langston wasn't the slightest upset with us that I had used his name, Aaron was ready to move us.

"Are you working for Katherine?" I hadn't wanted to make another move until I had some idea who the guardians were working with now.

"Sorry. I can't tell you that, you just need to trust us." Not waiting for a response from us Aaron grabbed me, and Langston took off.

Thinking at first, they had chosen to leave Charlotte behind but then Jessica came to take her with them. There wasn't anywhere to hide or run to if Katherine decided to attack us right away. She seemed rather busy staring at what had been in her hand. The guardians dropped us off with the rest of the family. In a rather large open cave, we could see everything as everyone could now see us. Katherine's recruits were all standing around us watching us as they were ready to take her orders. I had never seen so many of her recruits in one area before, many were vampires. Even though I had recognized a few as being other creatures, only a few were still in their other form.

If you stepped into the cave, the tension would hit

you like a wall. Our family stood to the left, close, alert, uncertain, watching the scene unfold across from us. To the right, Katherine loomed on a raised platform of raw stone, steam curling from a wide crack at its center like the cave itself was breathing. Her creations, twisted, unnatural monsters with vampire blood and something worse in their veins, formed a wall around her: front, middle, and back, as if we were already surrounded. And in front of the platform, framed by the rising steam, stood Sophie. The guardians, our guardians, stood around her, silent and still. They didn't look at us. They didn't speak. And in that moment, it felt like they'd chosen her side.

We knew something was happening when Katherine's recruits started getting anxious moving around. Even we knew the council had arrived outside as the guards were watching the only entrance to the cave. We guessed the council was waiting for the rest to either join or access the situation. Then we started hearing loud explosions from outside that shook the ground. Barely able to stand, a few of us lost our footing dropping to the ground. Katherine looked around to see what was causing the shaking. Apparently, it wasn't her doing. Looking over a large pool of water, Katherine started watching the outside which only the guardians next to her along with Sophie could see. Someone had started up a rather large storm mimicking the one she had done when she was attacking Charley earlier. Searching around trying to find where it was starting from, she still couldn't find who was creating the mess. Not until she found a further out area where someone had projected themselves to. She could see Nichole and Emma standing there at the far end with their hands projected out creating a disturbance, Anthony stood near to protect them from being attacked by any stray followers of Katherine. Making it far too difficult to get out of the cyclone they had created misting the entire area so thick with the snow around eliminating visibility. Andrew had been standing behind the rest of the family shielding him as he also projected himself outside of the cave rushing winds rather strongly from the town, they had left to head here, leading the rest of the council here. Not waiting very long many other members of the council and the presidium had also joined them. At least eighteen members were joining up ready to stop the very prominent display. Only Katherine now could see the true form since the weather and projections were not being hidden from her. The ones doing this had masked themselves to look like Katherine.

As soon as they were sure the members were there in place. Emma, Nichole and Andrew stopped what they were doing. They made the point they needed to, now the rest just had to wait and hope everything went to plan not that everyone was aware of what it had been. We could hear shouting from the tunnel of the cave. Sparks of light shot inward as the ground continued to shake except now it was being controlled by the council, our group stayed near the far back trying to stay as separate as we could hoping the council might not assume we were a part of this. But then they might decide to destroy us anyway just for being here. Sophie and the guardians were still surrounding the pool of water watching as the council broke their way in killing Katherine's recruits on the way. She hadn't flinched once even though many of her people were being killed protecting her, not that any of them could stop the council from making their way in. At the base of the cave, we could see several of the council along with the presidium right behind them. Katherine made no move to get out of their way or to hide standing up there rather boldly.

"Oh, I'd roll out the red carpet, but funny, I don't recall inviting any of you. Still, what perfect timing! I was just about to pay you a little visit. After all, you've been clinging to the rest of what's mine. Or... had been. Don't worry though. I've found something far more valuable. And now, you three get front-row seats." Katherine had Sophie standing there still conjuring the spells she set in front of her casting several projections on objects in front of them as the guardians simply stood there next to Katherine, we had only assumed if things went wrong, they would whisk her away.

"We are here to take care of business not to watch you make a fool of yourself Katherine. We should have known you were behind this." William was the first to speak for the group.

"Others may be afraid of you; however, I am not." Holding up a few pieces in her hands, she started her chant as Sophie now stopped.

Looking back at us, not sure what was going to happen. Black smoke rose from the pool of water. Not one of the council seemed the slightest bit concerned, over the centuries they were used to creatures trying to take control or performing magical acts in front of them. As the smoke swirled it roamed around the room making its way around everyone encircling every single person in the room. Making their way further into the room closer to Katherine, she threw the pieces into the pool of water to finish her plans as the council came even closer. Behind them had been a pile of bodies with pools of blood from her recruits. The madam's followers hadn't mattered to her. She felt she could easily replace them now that she would have the power to control the very movements of the council as well as the presidium.

Now the guardians stood closer to Sophie as Katherine made her way in front of the council drinking down a portion of the water she had mixed everything in. Feeling invincible she raised her hand out expecting to throw the council along with the presidium to the ground. When nothing happened, she looked at Andrew angrily.

"What were those pieces you handed me? They looked exactly like the precious stones, the medallions." Her voice thundered around the cave.

Only momentarily had the council looked at Andrew.

"Did you think that I would hand it over to you? Those were basic stones from the local store. You never did ask what they were, you just assumed." Smiling rather proud of himself.

"What did you think you would do with the correct stones if you had them?" William had asked again even though he was already figuring out the situation.

"That is for me to know." Casting a spell quickly Katherine stepped backward expecting the guardians to remove her quickly from the cave.

Not one of them made their way towards her to help. While Katherine had spoken to the council, Sophie had taken out of her pocket the real stones that Lucian handed her feeling they were safest with her. Carefully dropping them into the pool the water had changed its dark black color to a clear clean ocean blue. Pouring another liquid into the mixture, it slowly made the water evaporate, leaving nothing behind for anyone to use. Sophie felt disappointed as she looked into the basin, it had only done partially what was expected. It hadn't solved her main purpose of doing this. Looking back, Katherine almost exploded in anger. The stones hadn't dissolved, as Sophie had Katherine's attention. Jessica moved Sophie out of the way when Katherine tried to react by attacking her. Anwen had taken the stones out of the basin before Katherine could look in, placing them into her pocket again.

"I searched you. How could you have had the stones." Stepping forward to look into the empty basin where the water once pooled.

"I didn't always have them on me; I handed them over to the guardians every time you checked me." Now had come the crucial moment.

"Do you seriously think you can wipe me from the earth? So many have tried before you and as long as there are elements surrounding this earth. I will always live, not even the council can kill me at this point. I might not be able to control their physical moves with the power, but they cannot kill me no matter how hard they try." As her voice echoed around the cave causing the walls to quake from the power in her voice.

The council launched an attack on her, trying to take an opportunity before she could stop them. Tearing her apart, shredding each of her limbs and tossing them apart from each other, setting each piece on fire to permanently destroy her as it would with any vampire. Except they had a main problem, they had yet to experience what she was capable of. Over the years Katherine learned to piece herself back together much quicker than in the past. Watching as the council was about to render judgment on the rest of us, they watched now in horror as each scrap of ash turned back into a piece of skin, and blood, now slowly rolled along the floor reforming her body instantly. The wind surrounding everyone now pulled the rest of her missing body parts rebuilding her from the very dust on the ground making up for the parts that could not be reformed. Fire would have put a natural fear into any vampire, yet as she assembled, she simply danced with the twirling flame as though it was her natural state, not experiencing the agony of fire but enveloping it.

"Nothing can stop me." Katherine laughed as she launched herself immediately toward one of the council members.

Lydia barely moved out of the way still receiving a large gash across the face. Langston had moved forward to block her from Katherine's second assault on her. Tearing into his shoulder, he blocked Lydia the best he could. Turning to attack whoever had been closest to her, Sophie was waiting for the moment she and the guardians had been waiting for. Not wanting to harm the council they had to be as patient as possible, not making a move too soon or they might not have a chance to save their own family from those who had survived. By this time not one of Katherine's recruits had survived. Feeling frustrated by the events things were lasting much longer than anyone had wanted especially since it increased the chances of the others getting hurt in all of this. Fighting Katherine. Had been like fighting a miniature army no matter how much damage they did to her she kept reforming her own body. With the gifts, the council had along with the presidium they could barely keep her down. When they had, she would simply reform herself, each time the winds surrounding her became much stronger as thunder could now be heard.

Katherine had been unlike any creature, especially any

vampire they had ever fought. With blood now, not just from Katherine's recruits, the council and the presidium had now been adding to it with their own from the damage Katherine had dealt with them. None of Charley's family ever understood why Katherine felt she had needed so much more power to take control when she clearly could have taken over just by proving what she was doing now. She always seemed to think there was something better or greater out there, something just as invincible as she was. She was power-hungry. Or she was worried someone would be more powerful than her. As Charley always secretly hoped and felt it made her not as evil, that perhaps secretly she even wished there might be something that could kill her making it so that she would not keep coming back.

Taking the first chance, Sophie and the guardians could as soon as there was enough space between Katherine and the others in the room, the guardians were ready. All had raised their hands when the council and presidium had blasted her with lightning bolts, fire, and ice.

Though the sacred pool had vanished after the initial surge, remnants of its power still lingered in the air, in the ground... in them. The guardians had called upon the echoes of that energy, drawn from what remained of the original stone's magic, and hurled it at Katherine. It wasn't enough to fully break her. Centuries of dark magic had made her nearly untouchable, but the force hit hard. She staggered, a flicker of uncertainty crossing her face for the first time.

Constantly hitting her with the power to be human while she was attacked allowed her to be vulnerable, even though the chemistry of her body kept trying to fight against it holding her together. The constant attack from all angles was wearing her down as she looked over at us from the stage she was once standing on herself. She had neither a look of fear or anger on her face.

Just like changing the chemistry of a tree or plant you might be able to cross it with another, or an animal breed might be able to be started by simply mixing breeds, it was still the original only now it had a slight change. Taking her athame from her dress pocket. Charlotte cut a chunk of her skin from herself, slicing it up into tiny pieces and launching it at Katherine. As she reformed herself pieces of it stuck to her, slowing down some of her reformations. Several members of the council and presidium began to follow doing the same act causing Katherine's reformation to slow down dramatically. As it had the guardians' put pieces of her in separate airtight bottles. The new pieces of flesh had confused the curse wanting to still piece all of it together, since it was not the original flesh of Katherine it prevented her from reforming. The only remaining air left in the bottles was quickly absorbed leaving no physical ties to the outside world and its elements. The only pieces left of Katherine were now surrounded by others unable to fix herself. Burning only a few pieces that had remained, the council took the remaining pieces of her deciding what they would do with it, until then they would keep it safe with them. The long fight with Katherine was over, even if it was a temporary fix.

Several of the council left the area knowing it would only take a few to render judgment and carry out the punishment. The council asked the guardians to leave the cave since they were not judging them; they were aware of what was about to happen in the cave once they were there. William filled them in once he found out himself as they were busting into the front of the cave. The guardians planned on keeping Katherine there for their judgment.

"We understand that you rule the world of vampires as well as many other creatures. We respect the fact you protect mortals from those who would wipe them out or use them as slaves, however, we owe so much to the McAllister's we can't exactly leave them. They are our family." As Jessica spoke the rest of the guardians stood near Charley, Sophie, Nichole, Anthony, Emma, Andrew, and Charlotte.

"You would attempt to stop us or remove them if you do not agree with our verdict?" William seemed more amused than insulted by the guardians.

"They have protected us the same as they would with the rest of their family, we choose to do the same, whatever that may be with whatever consequences. You experienced them protecting your members when they didn't need to." So far, the council only seemed to be interested in the family present, not that we knew if the missing members would be wanted also simply because they were related and would assume they would retaliate against the councils verdict.

Langston as always stood on the side watching everyone; the only difference had been Lydia standing by his side to the dismay of Gerard.

"Even though we would prefer to preserve you, then you will also be dealt the same punishment. For being part of Katherine's plans, for knowing all these years and not working with the council to eliminate her, your punishment is then death." Not bothering to hear them out, Emery was rather quick and harsh with his judgment.

"Is there any way we can make a deal in exchange for something you want, perhaps it's a matter of not wanting your reputation questioned if you were to let us go? Hand over one guaranteed death, the others can make it clear they were following your orders and showing respect. No one must know. So many of the council or presidium had to show up here. Only six are needed to render a verdict." Langston had spoken very calmly.

"Who do you propose we take as the victim? How are we to know they did not try to steal the power themselves by trying to take over our organization later?" William directed the question more at Charley than he had for Langston.

"We have tried living away from Katherine for many centuries except because of her prophecies has tried following us knowing we would eventually guard the pieces. We have had access to them for centuries and yet we have not used them ourselves, we have no need or desire for them, other than to keep others safe, especially from Katherine. We've already proven over the centuries that we can be trusted." There hadn't been much Charley could do to convince the council once they had decided.

"I could make this very easy for everyone. My reputation precedes me, even Charley here can attest to the fact. I was working with Katherine. I've worked for the council for many centuries showing nothing but loyalty. I helped create the disturbance the mortals were looking into. I even encouraged the disturbance here which I am sure mortals will be looking around here to see what all is connected and what started it. Except this time, they will find the blood stains. I will be the sacrifice if you let the others go." Langston was offering himself in exchange, not that he owed anyone the favor.

"We can't accept that exchange it's not worth it to us." Lydia had been rather quick with her response trying to protect Langston from handing himself over.

"It wouldn't be the first time we have had one of your family members working for us. What I don't understand is why would you be willing to give yourself for them?" Emery sounded as though he might go along with the suggestion.

"I have many reasons, far too many to list. Consider it a favor to an old friend of mine. I've had my hands covered in the blood of others for far too long, that I'm too warped to ever live among mortals. There is simply nothing left in this world that I want." Feeling disgusted by his comment Lydia walked away from Langston preferring to stand next to Gerard.

"I think we should hold onto the others to make sure there is no retaliation or problems. Who is to say because Katherine is gone the threat is also, that they may know something we don't? We are always under threat of others wanting to rule, that is nothing new. We gain nothing if we simply let them go. Perhaps make them work for us for a while to prove their worth, then we will consider letting them go?" Emery stated knowing not all of the members would agree with him.

Ruby was rather disappointed not being able to kill the rest of them.

"I think that might be a good idea.... for now. Take everyone back and we will make a final decision later. Besides, the rest of their family might be more useful to us." Ruby had walked out leaving the others.

Not wanting to travel the way the council would have brought them, we instead opted for the guardians to bring us. Even with that choice, we had brought the council members along with us so that we would not take off from them. We hadn't wanted the rest of the family to be brought in. Unfortunately, it was the original plan of the presidium to grab the rest of them. Right now, they were having a difficult time locating them. We had already been prepared and ready to hide, which was what they were doing. Charley couldn't help but smile when he found out the rest of the family was giving them such a problem being found. They might not have known what our circumstances had been, but they did know how important it was to stay hidden. Most had already been ready for our arrival since we wound up at the main building for the council. We had even seen a few we were not quite expecting. As the council took their seats to speak privately with each other, we had been moved out of the room into their holding cell until they came up with their verdicts as final. Not that many of us thought it would be any better than death. After all, what would they use us for?

In the other room, Valafar had shown up along with Goseck. Goseck had been with the rest of the family so to see him here was a surprise. Giving a nod towards Charley as we walked following the council's guard, we knew they would be safe still. We could only guess he had hidden them himself. Both Valafar and Goseck knew the council rather well having dealt with them before. Valafar himself had family members as part of the presidium. The one who had surprised us the most had been seeing Caoimhe standing next to Emery when he had taken his seat among the others. She sat right down beside him.

"The rest of their family is not a threat to us; they have lived this long without bothering us. We have already destroyed the creature who was responsible for all of this, they simply were in her way in the wrong place, at the wrong time." Valafar tried steering interest away hoping to lighten whatever might have been thought of for Charley and his family.

"For all the rumors I am amazed the guardians were willing to protect them so much. Being a guardian at one time, I never would have associated myself with vampires. If they trust them even to stand against us to protect them it shows, they are trustworthy." Caoimhe also tried to steer the conversation towards a result that would be favorable.

"That defiance against us could show they would be willing to go to war with us if they felt it was needed. I still say kill them all, why are we even considering this? When the presidium was the only power, we never waited this long let alone needed a second consideration for anyone." Ruby did not hide the fact she was disgusted with the outcome.

"We've also learned much more over the centuries, after all, we have had our best assassins by working with others we normally would have executed. Two of our best personal guards came from those who would have been eliminated by your view. Jerome has served us quite well and then so has Langston. Even though his latest attempt does surprise even me. Even Drezin worked out quite well until he mysteriously died." Emery seemed to be softening up a little since they came back onto his ground.

"We have his brother do we not? Charley is a sibling of his; perhaps the talents would run in his blood? We could use him and his wife Sophie; their kids might be more of interference to us than anything." William seemed to be thinking this over as the rest continued to discuss things.

"Angelita has located the rest of the family; do we wish for her to handle the situation or bring them here?" A fellow servant had walked in informing the council and a few presidium members who sat debating.

"Leave them for now. If we change our minds, we can always retrieve them later, for now, we will train Charley and Sophie here to work for us. As for Charlotte and Andrew, they will not have any outside interference, we can use them." William started thinking about what to do with the guardians.

"What will we do with the guardians, we don't know if they will listen to us or not? If we cannot control them, they are too much of a danger to us, especially if they try to free their friends." Hattie had always been logical when addressing others.

She wasn't as ruthless or excited over putting others to death the same way Ruby or Angelita had been.

"I am curious what they would decide if, given the choice, I would like to meet with them." Emery had asked for the guardians to be brought forward.

Waiting for all six guardians to be standing in front of them, with Valafar and Goseck sitting to the side listening. Even though they were not as active as the others, occasionally they still came for some meetings to keep in touch and find out what was going on.

"If we were to leave this decision up to you, that you would make sure we benefit, as well as your side so that no one retaliates against us, that you will not attempt to free your friends, what verdict would you give?" After Emery asked them this, everyone had been watching the guardians to see what their response would be.

Without having to say a word to each other they spoke silently so that no one else heard their conversation. They had already discussed this in the holding rooms with the others.

"As for the family, we would like to see the ones not here permanently left alone, they live by the rules and are extremely careful not to break them. They are not a threat at all. We would like to see Charley and Sophie released so they would be able to rejoin their families. Charlotte and Andrew have skills that would benefit you as well. I would stay behind while the rest of the guardians left for home." Aaron had spoken for the group.

It seemed rather unanimous for the guardians how they felt.

"Sounds rather well thought out. Instead, I think we will keep all four, we will let Charley and Sophie go after a year of working for us. We will also keep one of you as well. I believe it will be much easier to keep Jessica since Valafar has a personal interest in her; after all, you both are dating. You can hide it all you want except nothing escapes me." Emery seemed neither angered by this or betrayed by it.

"Perhaps we should be persecuting Valafar for not letting us know all of this had been going on let alone hiding such a thing from the rest of us?" Ruby was joined in this agreement by Lydia and Gerard.

"Yes... Perhaps we cannot trust one of our own anymore?" Gerard was ready to have them all still put to death.

Not because of trust issues, it would simply be fewer people getting in his way.

"There is no need to be so drastic, I have no intentions of going against my family, besides, I have not hidden or displayed my relationship, it is simply not involved with the business." Valafar had not flinched once while he made his statement directed at Ruby.

"I will also be more involved if Sophie and Charley are kept here. I will personally take responsibility for them." Goseck had spoken just as clearly to the point as Valafar had.

"Then it's settled, guardians you may choose to leave if you wish to now. I trust you will let the rest of your family know what our choice is." Not bothering to wait for the rest to agree or dispute what Emery had chosen, they had simply chosen to leave the room.

Even though the choices were made as a group. When Emery made up his mind, the others listened or found themselves destroyed. He by far seemed the most gentle and less threatening of the group until provoked and he made the entire group seem as though they were harmless compared to how dangerous his rage could be. Only Gerard, Lydia, and William remained in the room.

"Did we ever make a decision regarding Langston?" William seemed a bit surprised he had been left out of the group's choice.

"I don't think we have?" Even Lydia seemed surprised.

"We can make our final decision if you wish. I would prefer a chance to speak with him privately." Jerome had spoken up the second he came in not that he wasn't listening at the door to their conversation.

"Why do you want to speak with him?" Gerard looked at him rather accusingly.

"I've worked with him long enough and much closer than anyone to know what's going on in his head. Lydia might know him better than I do but she just enjoys messing with his head rather than studying it." Smiling at Lydia she refused to look at him.

"I'm sure I already know how he will answer that, he's told me before. He would rather die than wake up to another morning or see another night crawling with creatures. To him, it's just one more day." Lydia for once seemed a bit mournful almost as though she had the same feeling herself.

"We have a slight problem, no one bothered to put him in the holding cell. They must have thought he brought them in. He's gone." Shaking his head, Jerome knew he wouldn't run from the council but there were things he intended on finishing before he was ever caught or executed.

"You can count me out for searching for him; he knows my tactics far too well." Taking his leave Jerome wasn't interested in the rest.

Gerard turned towards his private guards, "search his home and see if he is there. The guards will find him, Lydia come with me." Gerard demanded as he started walking not watching to see if anyone else was around.

Gerard and Lydia left rather quickly with their guards leaving William to himself.

Chapter Fifteen

Another Bump

It wasn't very difficult to find the rest of the family, at least not for the guardians. Sensing where they had gone, they were in three separate locations due to size, it was easier for Goseck and Dinah to hide them in different areas and keep them safe.

Aaron and Lily were the first to locate and move to Lewis's family. They had hidden rather high up in the mountains, which would have been easier for their family to get around with their ability to shapeshift. Lewis had been the first out to greet them once he saw who was working their way to the little cabin. Trying not to let emotions show, both tried hard to hold back until they could at least speak with them. Evangeline didn't need an explanation, just one look at Lily's face, and she knew exactly what was going on. Thankfully her conclusion had been wrong.

"Did they execute them? Do the kids know yet?" Evangeline came right out assuming the worst, which was usually the safe bet when dealing with the council.

"No one was executed yet. The council wants them to

work for them for a year and then they said they would release Charley and Sophie. We just don't know what they will have them doing or while they are working for them if any of us will be able to see them." It was much harder not to show emotion since Aaron wanted to get the information out first.

He was thankful he didn't have to break the news to all the family feeling positive he wouldn't be capable of getting through it.

"Where are the rest of the guardians, did they keep all of them also?" Lewis had wanted to know right away.

"Delaney and Anwen have gone to speak with Nichole and Anthony. They chose to keep Jessica; I had volunteered to take her place, but they wanted her instead. Alexandra won't be coming back. We still don't understand what happened to her completely, but she had been made a member of the council. We haven't heard from her yet; Jessica keeps in constant contact letting us know they are safe." Lily finished speaking for Aaron; he was used to taking control or watching over their group even though Jessica had been the one to start them up.

He felt protective of the others the way a brother would look out for his sister.

"Where are Lucian and Teddy? They are the only ones we couldn't sense." Watching for their reaction they seemed just as sad.

"After we split to hide, we haven't heard from them, so we don't know if they died or if they are alive still, you're not being able to sense them isn't exactly reassuring." Lewis shook his head, not sure how to take it.

"Instead of staying separated I think we need to get everyone together, we might need each other for support. Besides, it's much safer right now for us to stay together, too much happens when we don't. We are stronger together than apart." Evangeline was already getting Amanda ready.

It might have been easier for Lewis's family to navigate the mountains except she knew her family would have a much harder time. That's when it hit her; this would be the safest and least likely of places for anyone to look for any of them. Searching for her phone, she was amazed she had a signal way out here, even with technology always changing she felt disappointed by it. Most vampires missed when the world went much slower, life was easier to blend in and enjoy rather than rushing to get nowhere. Calling on her phone she waited for Nichole to answer her phone. Only answering on the second ring her voice was rather shaky. Assuming they had been just told by the other guardians, we arranged for them to meet at the base of the mountain. That way we could help them if they needed it making it up to where our safe cabin was located.

It had taken about two days before they were able to join us, during that time we still hadn't heard from Lucian and neither had the guardians sensed him or Teddy yet. The move up the mountain had been a bit slow, only Nichole had taken a bit longer getting up; the rest had no problem. Larissa had grown quite a bit since the last time we had seen her. She blended in with the adults even though her and Amanda took off for her room to talk on their own.

"I just don't understand why Lucian hasn't contacted us. I don't want to think about the possibility the council had killed them; we knew Angelita was already watching us, but we hadn't heard from Lucian since we split back at Charley's summer cabin." Nichole was pacing as she spoke.

Anthony let her pace as much as she wanted since she became much more frustrated not moving around. Always having a special connection to Lucian, she felt sick not knowing what happened to him.

"What could they possibly want with Charley and Sophie? They couldn't possibly carry out the orders of the council, they might have been in physical fights before, but that was defending the lives of their family and themselves. Much of what would be demanded of them would be senseless killing, they won't survive that. They aren't heartless." Nichole was back thinking about her parents.

"They should be alright; they have been through a lot

and at least they have each other this time. Valafar and Goseck won't let anything happen to them. According to the guardians, they are closely keeping an eye on them both. Even though Charlotte and Andrew are protecting them as much as they can, if they stick together, they will survive through it. It's going to be a long year for us, but it will go fast for them." Anthony was still trying to reason or find a positive out of the situation.

"What we need to do is start searching for Lucian and Teddy, we need to find out one way or another just what condition they are in." Not that any of us wanted to find out the worst, we had to find out.

For the next few weeks, checking with old friends of Lucians or at least ones he had been in contact with at one time or another. None of them had heard or seen them. Checking all the places the family had known that he might go, not that they had very much success the other times when he had wanted to disappear, he was good at staying hidden when he wanted to. Even though this time we assumed he would want to know how the rest of the family was. Keeping in contact with Jessica had helped. So far, the council hadn't forced Sophie and Charley to do very much. For now, they were working inside the organization seeing to the needs of the council members and at times when the presidium found the need to use them. Eventually, Charley wound up working firsthand for Emery and his now-wife. Sophie became a firsthand to Taylor and Hattie. Two other high-end presidium members. It hadn't taken very long to prove their trustworthiness. We hadn't known too much of what Charlotte and Andrew had been up to even though Valafar was limited to the information. Angelita had sent them off on an order which could have been anything. Alexandra had been seen having private council with William being trained for her new role, which she seemed to take rather seriously as well as having no complaints. It appears this had been the life path she had chosen, sadly shutting herself off from the other guardians. Not sure why, not that she was ever rude. She still treated Jessica with respect however she no longer stayed in the mental network of the guardians.

Only three months passed when Lewis had been out shopping with his family when his sister had been given a note from a woman she had not recognized, not taking time to read the note leaving everyone in the store, she followed the woman who had given it to her. Slowing down no longer trying to outpace her she looked back at her.

"I can't talk; as soon as I hit the end of the town, I need to take off. I have my family matters to tend to." The woman had spoken in such a soft tone.

"Do you know us? I admit I haven't read this note yet, but I didn't want to risk you leaving without having the chance to ask you questions if I needed to." She couldn't mentally place who this woman was, Kara was thinking as quickly as she could.

"I understand your concern. Not to worry. Your family has many watching over all of you, we might not be able to prevent everything, but we can certainly help you along the way. We are more involved with your family than you will ever know. To your question. No, you don't know me. My name is Elizabeth. Just read the note and make sure the rest of the family is assured things will be just fine, all in due time, things have a way of working out even when we see no light at the end of the tunnel." Smiling at her, Elizabeth hadn't taken the time to stick around.

Just as she had stated that once she reached the end of town, and no one was looking she shot off faster than Kara could have kept her attention on her. Lewis had seen Kara leave the store rather quickly after the woman, feeling concerned he came out to watch from a distance just in case. Kara had looked over the note now making her way back. Waiting for the rest of the family to be together in the cabin everyone sat almost patiently waiting to see what had been on the note. Over the last several months the cabin had been expanded to fit the rest of the family. The only one who hadn't joined yet had been Larissa; she was still in high school. The family felt if anything needed to be told to her or if they needed to take off, they would wait at least for her school semester to be over. She had been through so many schools it was nice she was finally able to stay at the same one for a while. No one had paid attention to whether Amanda attended; being tired of repeating the same grades until the last year when she was able to fit in with the next grade up, Amanda had finally aged the slightest. Except for this year, she opted to skip school while Lewis had chosen to home school her this year. With the last family member at home, everyone sat down while Nichole read the note out loud with slightly trembling fingers. Anthony stood next to her lending his support. She finished the letter.

"To the guardians, McAllister, and Aubrey family.

We understand your feeling of distress and not having your entire family safely with you, however, rest assured they will be safe with the council, there are several very compassionate ones looking after them. We also understand this is the first time the guardians have not been able to detect someone which has for our selfish reasons helped us provide evidence that our experiment has indeed worked. Both Lucian and Teddy are safe and secure with us for now. My husband Arthur and I are taking care of them. However, it is not exactly safe to release them for reasons we cannot tell you in case you are ever questioned by the council or presidium. As soon as it is possible, your family will be reunited, keep hope and faith. Much love is sent to you."

At the end of the note in Lucian's handwriting which seemed neither stressed or forced, he also added.

"I have shut myself off for a while from you mom so that you won't be feeling what is going on, please don't worry. Both of us are fine and we will join you again when we can. We have already heard about grandpa and grandma; they are safe for now. We have also seen Charlotte and Andrew; they are fine as well. We will hopefully see you all very soon. Much love from Teddy Raynn and Daniel Lucian."